Linda Castillo's *New York Times* bestselling
Kate Burkholder novels are:

"GRIPPING." —*People*

"CHILLING." —*USA Today*

"EXCELLENT." —*Publishers Weekly*

"STUNNING." —*Lisa Scottoline*

"MASTERFUL." —*Booklist*

"FASCINATING." —*RT Book Reviews*

D0206819

THE DEAD
WILL TELL

Linda Castillo

St. Martin's Paperbacks

This is a work of fiction. All of the characters, organizations, and events portrayed in this novel are either products of the author's imagination or are used fictitiously.

THE DEAD WILL TELL

Copyright © 2014 by Linda Castillo.
Excerpt from *After the Storm* copyright © 2015 by Linda Castillo.

All rights reserved.

For information address St. Martin's Press, 175 Fifth Avenue, New York, NY 10010.

ISBN: 978-1-250-05985-7

Printed in the United States of America

St. Martin's Press hardcover edition / July 2014
St. Martin's Paperbacks edition / April 2015

St. Martin's Paperbacks are published by St. Martin's Press, 175 Fifth Avenue, New York, NY 10010.

10 9 8 7 6 5 4 3 2 1

*To all of my readers who have read
and loved the books. Thank you.*

ACKNOWLEDGMENTS

I'm incredibly lucky to make my living doing what I love. And while writing a book is a solitary endeavor, the publishing of a book takes the talent, the passion, and the hearts of many.

I wish to thank the team of publishing professionals at Minotaur Books for always going above and beyond to help me bring the Kate Burkholder series to life: Charles Spicer. Sally Richardson. Andrew Martin. Matthew Baldacci. Jennifer Enderlin. Jeanne-Marie Hudson. Sarah Melnyk. Hector DeJean. Kerry Nordling. April Osborn. David Rotstein. Courtney Sanks. Stephanie Davis. And of course I cannot close without mentioning the late and much-loved Matthew Shear, who is greatly missed by all. My heartfelt thanks to all of you at Team Minotaur!

I'd also like to thank Trisha Jackson, my wonderful editor at Pan Macmillan, for your always brilliant suggestions and editorial expertise. And of course for the lovely tea in Glasgow! It was a true pleasure to finally meet you.

I also owe many thanks to my dear friend and agent extraordinaire, Nancy Yost. You are the voice of reason and the architect of everything brilliant. Thank you for your keen guidance, your unwavering support, and for always leaving me with a smile.

I would be remiss if I didn't mention the group of women who are my inspiration and partners in crime. You are so much more than a critique group. You are my best friends, my writing sisters, my sounding boards and rabble-rousers, and instigators of all that is fun. I cherish each of you: Jennifer Archer, Anita Howard, Marcy McKay, Jennifer Miller, April Redmon, and Catherine Spangler.

As always, I'd like to thank my husband, Ernest, for being there from the beginning and through all the craziness that is sometimes a writer's life. I love you.

"Let the dead Past bury its dead."

—Henry Wadsworth Longfellow, "A Psalm of Life"

PROLOGUE

March 8, 1979

He dreamed of pneumatic sanders flying over the finest burled wood and full-blind dovetail joints chiseled with such precision that you couldn't see the interlocking pins and tails. He and his datt *were working on the dry sink his* mamm *had been pining for since spotting a similar one in the antique store in Painters Mill. He couldn't wait to see her face when they gave it to her—*

Fourteen-year-old Billy Hochstetler jolted awake with a start. He wasn't sure what had wakened him. A noise downstairs. Or maybe the rain hammering against the roof. He lay in the warm softness of his bed, trying to get back to the dream and failing because his heart was pounding and he didn't know why. He stared into the darkness, listening. But the only sound came from the growl of thunder and the intermittent rattle of the loose spouting outside his window. One of these days he and *datt* were going to get up there with the ladder and fix it.

"Billy?"

He'd just dozed off when his little brother's whispered voice brought him back. "Go back to sleep," he groaned.

"I heard something."

"You did not. Now, go back to sleep before you wake everyone."

"There are people downstairs. *Englischers.*"

Propping himself up on an elbow, Billy frowned at his younger brother. Little Joe had just turned eight and looked so cute in his too-big nightshirt that Billy had to grin, despite his annoyance at having been wakened. "You're just afraid of the storm. Scaredy-cat."

"Am not!"

"Shhh." Billy chuckled, not quite believing him. "Do you want to sleep in here?"

"Ja!" The little boy ran to the bed and jumped as if he were diving into the creek for a swim.

As his younger brother snuggled against him, Billy heard it, too. A noise from downstairs. A thud and then the scraping of wood against wood. He looked at Little Joe. "Did you hear that?"

"I told you."

Rolling, Billy grabbed his pocket watch off the night table and squinted at the glowing face. It was half past three in the morning. His *datt* didn't rise for another hour. So who was downstairs?

Billy got out of bed and crossed to the window. Parting the curtains, he looked out at the gravel driveway, but there was no one there. No buggy or vehicle. No lantern light in the barn. The workshop and showroom windows were dark.

He grabbed his trousers off the chair. He was stepping into them when the faint murmur of voices floated up through the heat vent at his feet. He and his family generally spoke *Pennsilfaanisch Deitsch* at home. Whoever was downstairs was speaking English. But who would be in their house in the middle of the night?

"Where you going?" Little Joe whispered.

Billy glanced at his brother, who'd pulled the covers up to his chin. "Go back to sleep."

"I wanna go with you."

"Shush." After slipping on a shirt, he opened the door and started down the stairs, already anticipating a big helping of *Mamm*'s scrapple. He hadn't yet reached the base of the stairs when the yellow slash of a flashlight beam played over the wall.

"Datt?" he called out. *"Mamm?"*

The shuffle of shoes against the wood plank floor was the only reply.

He reached the kitchen only to find himself blinded by the beam of a flashlight. He raised his hand to shield his eyes. "Who's there?"

"Shut up!" A male voice snarled the words.

Shock sent Billy stumbling back. In the periphery of the beam, he got the impression of a man wearing a denim jacket and a knit face mask. Then rough hands gripped his arm and hauled him into the kitchen. "Get over there! On your knees!"

A hammer blow of fear slammed into him when he saw his *mamm* and *datt* kneeling on the other side of the kitchen table, their hands clasped behind their heads. On shaking legs, Billy rounded the table. Who was this Englischer? Why was he here? And what did he want?

No one spoke as he knelt beside his *mamm*.

Leaning forward, he made eye contact with his father, hoping the older man could tell him what to do. Willis Hochstetler always knew what to do.

"God will take care of us." His father whispered the words in Pennsylvania Dutch.

"Shut your mouth!" The man drew a pistol from his waistband and jabbed it at them. "Get your hands up! Behind your head!"

Billy raised his hands, but they were trembling so violently, he could barely lace his fingers.

"Where are the lights?" the man demanded.

"There's a lantern," Datt said. "Next to the stove."

The man strode to the counter, snatched up the lantern, and thrust it at Billy. "Light it."

Billy jumped to his feet and crossed to the counter. Feeling the man's eyes on him, resolving to be brave, he pulled the matches from the drawer and lit the mantle. He thought about Little Joe upstairs and prayed to God the boy had fallen back to sleep.

"Give it to me."

Billy passed it to the man, who yanked it so forcefully, the kerosene sloshed.

"Get back over there and be quiet."

Billy took his place next to his *mamm,* praying they would just take what they wanted and leave.

A second man entered the kitchen, a flashlight in one hand, a pistol in the other. He was heavily built with blond hair and a bandanna over his nose and mouth. He glared at Billy's father. "Where's the cash?"

Billy had never seen his *datt* show fear. But he saw it now. In the way his eyes went wide at the sight of the second gunman. The way his mouth quivered. He knew the fear was not for his own safety or for the loss of the money he'd worked so hard to earn. But for the lives of his wife and children.

"There's a jar," his *datt* said. "In the cabinet above the stove."

Eyes alight with a hunger Billy didn't understand, the blond man walked to the stove and wrenched open the cabinet door. Pulling out the old peanut butter jar, he unscrewed the lid and dumped the cash on the counter.

Billy watched the money spill out—twenties and tens and fives. At least a month's worth of sales.

"If you were in need and asked, I would have offered you work and a fair wage," Willis Hochstetler said.

The blond man didn't have anything to say about that.

"Mamm?"

Billy jerked his gaze to the kitchen doorway, where Little Joe stood, his legs sticking out from his nightshirt like pale little bones. Something sank inside Billy when he noticed Hannah and Amos and Baby Edna behind him.

"Die kinner." Mamm got to her feet. *"Die zeit fer in bett is nau."* Go to bed right now.

"What are you doing?" the blond man turned and shifted the gun to her. "Get back over there!"

But *Mamm* started toward the children. She was so focused on them, she didn't even seem to notice that he'd spoken.

"Tell her to get down!" The man in the denim jacket shifted the gun to *Datt*. "I mean it! Tell her!"

"Wanetta," Datt said. "Obey him."

As if sensing the wrongness of the situation, Baby Edna began to cry. Hannah followed suit. Even Little Joe, who at eight years of age, considered himself a man and too old to cry.

Kneeling, *Mamm* gathered the children into her arms. "Shhh."

"We're not fucking around!" The blond man stomped to Billy's mother and tried to separate her from the children. "Get back over there!"

"They're babies." She twisted away from him, put her arms around the children. "They don't know anything."

"Mamm!" Billy hadn't intended to speak, but somehow the word squeezed from his throat.

"Wanetta." Datt lurched to his feet.

A gunshot split the air. The sound reverberated inside Billy's head like a shock wave. Like a bullet passing through water, the concussion spreading in all directions. His *datt* wobbled, an expression of disbelief on his face.

The house went silent, as if they were all trapped inside an airtight jar.

"Datt?"

Billy had barely choked out the word when his father went down on one knee and then fell forward and lay still. Billy held his breath, praying for him to get up. But his *datt* didn't stir.

The blond man swung around and gaped at the man in the denim jacket. "Why did you do that?" he roared.

The kitchen exploded into chaos. The two men began to scuffle, pushing and shoving. Angry shouts were punctuated by *Mamm's* keening and the high-pitched cries of the children. A terrible discord echoed through the house like a thousand screams.

Billy didn't remember crawling to his father. He didn't notice the warmth of blood on his hands as he grasped his shoulder and turned him over. *"Datt?"*

Willis Hochstetler's eyes were open, but there was no spark of life. Just pale gray skin and blue lips. "Wake up." Billy's hands hovered over the blood on his father's shirt. He didn't know what to do or how to help him. "Tell me what to do!" he cried.

But his *datt* was gone.

He looked at the man who'd shot him. "He gave you the money," he cried. "Why did you do that?"

"Shut up!" The man snarled the words, but the eyes within his mask were wild with fear.

"Let's get out of here!" the other man yelled.

"Put the money in a bag!"

Somewhere in the periphery of his consciousness, Billy was again aware of screaming. His *mamm* or the kids. Or maybe it was him.

A third man, wearing blue jeans and a sweatshirt, his face obscured with some type of sheer fabric, entered the kitchen. He pointed at Billy. "You and the kids! In the basement. Now!"

The children huddled around *Mamm*, whimpering, their faces red and wet with tears.

"Don't hurt them." *Mamm* looked at the man, her eyes pleading.

Billy made eye contact with her as he started toward the basement door, urging her to follow. But as she rose, the man in the denim jacket clamped his hand over her shoulder.

The three men exchanged looks, Billy got a sick feeling in the pit of his stomach. He was only fourteen years old, but he knew that as terrible as this moment was, the worst was yet to come.

The blond man raised his gun and pointed it at Billy's face. "Take the kids to the basement."

Billy's brain began to misfire. His body was numb

as he herded his siblings toward the basement door. He did his best to calm them as he opened it and ushered them onto the landing. Before stepping in himself, he turned to look at his *mamm*. The blond man had her by the arm and was forcing her toward the living room. A second man had his hand clamped around the back of her neck. At some point, her sleeping dress had torn, and Billy could see her underclothes.

He started to step back into the kitchen, but the man with the sheer fabric over his head slammed the door. The latch snicked into place. Darkness descended like earth over a casket. Billy tried the knob, but the door wouldn't budge. He could hear the children behind him, sniveling and whimpering again. He knew they were counting on him to keep them safe.

"Billy, I'm scared."

"I want M*amm*."

"Why wouldn't Datt wake up?" Hannah snuffled.

"Shush." Staving off panic, he turned to them. The meager light coming from beneath the door illuminated just enough for him to see the shine of tears on their faces. "Little Joe, there's a lantern on the workbench. Help me light it."

Without waiting for a response, Billy grabbed the banister and descended the stairs. Upon reaching the dirt floor, he went left and felt his way toward the workbench where *Mamm* made soap. He ran his hand along the surface, knocked something over; then his knuckles brushed the base of the lantern. He located the matches next to it and lit the mantle.

"Little Joe." Billy thrust the lantern at him. "I need you to be brave and keep an eye on your little brothers and sisters."

The boy took the lantern. "B-but where are you going?"

"I'm going to get *Mamm*." Billy hadn't even realized what he was going to do until the words left his mouth. He darted to the ground-level window. It was too high for him to reach without something to stand on. There was no ladder. He looked around. The wood shelves were jammed with tools and jars and clay pots. Then he spotted the old wringer washing machine in the corner.

"Help me roll the washer over here."

Choking back sobs, Little Joe handed the lantern off to Hannah and dashed to the washer. The old caster rollers dug grooves into the dirt floor as they shoved it to the window.

Billy heaved himself onto the rim of the washer tub, then stepped onto the wringer and used his elbow to break the glass. He glanced over his shoulder. In the flickering light from the lantern, he saw his siblings huddled a few feet away. A mass of wet, frightened faces and quivering lips.

"I'll be back with Mamm," he said. "I promise."

Grasping the window frame with both hands, he heaved himself up and wriggled through. Then he was outside. Drizzle on his face. Somewhere in the distance an engine rumbled. Turning, he spotted taillights and saw that the car was midway down the lane. Praying he could catch them before they reached the road, he sprinted toward the car. Gravel cut his bare feet, but he didn't feel the pain. Hot breaths tore from his throat. He didn't know how he was going to stop them. Didn't have a plan. All he knew was that he couldn't let them take his *mamm*.

The car was nearly to the road when Billy caught

them. He ran alongside the vehicle, slapped his palms against the window. "Stop! *Stop!*"

The tires made a wet concrete sound in the gravel as the car skidded to a halt. Billy stopped outside the driver's door. "I want my *mamm!*"

The door swung open. He saw movement inside. Mamm trying to claw her way out of the backseat. "Billy! No! Run! *Run!*"

The driver punched him in the face. Billy's feet left the ground. Pain zinged along the bridge of his nose. He landed on his back, head bouncing against gravel, his arms splayed above his head. Vaguely he was aware of mud soaking through his shirt. The sound of tires crunching over gravel. The smell of exhaust.

Groaning, he struggled to his hands and knees. Panic leapt inside him as the car turned onto the road. *"Mamm!"* he screamed.

He was thinking about pursuing the car when he noticed a strange orange glow against the treetops. Puzzled, he turned toward the house. Horror froze him in place when he saw the yellow flicker of a fire. Then he remembered the lantern.

A scream unfurled in his chest; then he was running full out toward the house. He tore around the side yard toward the basement window he'd crawled out of. Terror burst inside him when he saw smoke pouring out.

"Little Joe! Hannah!" Billy dived onto his belly, jammed his head through the window. Heat singed his face and burned his eyes. Ten feet away, a thousand yellow tongues licked at the ceiling. He could smell the acrid scent of burning plastic.

Billy looked around wildly. "Help!" he screamed.

Swiveling, he shoved both legs through the window, but the heat and smoke sent him back. He could smell his clothes singeing. Feel the terrible heat blistering the soles of his feet.

He called out again, but there was no response.

Only the hiss of smoke pouring through the window and the bellow of the flames as they devoured the house from the inside out.

CHAPTER 1

Present day

It had been a long time since he'd closed down a bar, especially a dive like the Brass Rail Saloon. The music was too loud, the liquor was bottom-shelf, and the crowd was too young and rowdy to do anything but give him a headache. It was the last kind of place you'd find a man like him. The last kind of place he wanted to be. Tonight, it suited his needs to a T. The place was dark and anonymous—and no one would remember him.

He'd received four notes so far, each becoming progressively more disturbing. He discovered the first in his mailbox last week. *I know what you did.* The second was taped to the windshield of his Lexus. *I know what all of you did.* He found the third note lying on the threshold inside the storm door off the kitchen. *Meet me or I go to the police.* Each note was written in blue ink on a sheet of lined notebook paper that had been torn in half. He'd found the fourth note earlier this evening, taped to the front door. *Hochstetler farm. 1 a.m. Come alone.*

At first he'd tried to convince himself he didn't understand the meaning of the messages. There were a lot of crazies out there. He was a successful man, after all. He had a nice home. Lived a comfortable lifestyle. Drove an expensive car. In the eyes of a few, that made him fair game. A target because someone else wanted what he had, and they were willing to do whatever it took to get it.

He'd crumpled the notes and tossed them in the trash. He'd done his best to forget about them. But he knew the problem wasn't going to go away.

I know what all of you did.

Someone knew things they shouldn't. About him. About the others. About that night. They knew things no one could possibly know.

Unless they'd been there, a little voice added.

He'd racked his brain, trying to figure out who. There was only one explanation: Someone was going to blackmail him. But who?

Then two nights ago, he saw her, walking alongside the road near his house. But when he'd stopped for a better look, she was gone, leaving him to wonder if he'd seen anything at all. Or maybe it was his conscience playing tricks on him.

It had been years since he spoke to the others. But after receiving the third note, he'd done his due diligence and made the calls. None of them admitted to having received any sort of suspicious correspondence, but promised to let him know if that changed. If any of them knew more than they were letting on, they didn't let it show.

After finding the latest note, he'd gone about his business as usual the rest of the evening. He'd ordered

Chinese takeout and watched a movie. Afterwards, he'd broken the seal on the bottle of Macallan Scotch whisky his daughter gave him for Christmas two years ago. At eleven thirty, restless and edgy, he'd opened the gun cabinet, loaded the Walther .380 and dropped it into the inside pocket of his jacket. Grabbing the keys to his Lexus, he drove to the only place he knew of that was still open: the Brass Rail Saloon.

Now, sitting at a back booth with chain saw rock echoing in his ears and two shots of watered-down Scotch burning a hole in his gut, he stared at the clock on the wall and waited.

I know what all of you did.

Watching two young girls who didn't look old enough to drink head toward the dance floor, he tugged his iPhone from his pocket and scrolled down to the number he wanted. It was too late to call, especially a man who was little more than a stranger to him these days, so he drafted a text instead.

Meet is on. Will call 2 let you know outcome.

He sat there for a moment before pressing Send, staring at the phone, assuring himself there was no way anyone could know what he'd done. It had been thirty-five years. A lifetime. He'd married, built a successful real estate firm, raised four children, and gone through a divorce. He was semi-retired now. A grandfather and respected member of the community. He'd put that night behind him. Forgotten it had ever happened. Or tried to.

Someone knows.

A knife-stab of dread sank deep into his gut. Sighing, he dropped the phone back into his pocket and glanced up at the clock again. Almost 1 A.M. Time to go. Finishing his drink, he grabbed his keys off the table and then made for the door.

Ten minutes later he was heading north on Old Germantown Road. Around him the rain was coming down so hard, he could barely see the dividing lines.

"Keep it between the beacons," he muttered, taking comfort in the sound of his own voice.

All these years, he'd believed the past no longer had a hold on him. Sometimes he almost convinced himself that night had never really happened. That it was a recurring nightmare and an overactive imagination run amok. But on nights like this, the truth had a way of sneaking up on you, like a garrote slipping over your head. And he knew—he'd always known—somewhere inside the beating, cancerous mass that was his conscience, that some sins could never be forgiven. He owed penance for what he'd done. And he'd always known that someday fate or God—or maybe Satan himself—would see to it that he paid his debt.

Gripping the steering wheel, he leaned forward so that his nose was just a few inches from the windshield. The rain drumming against the roof was as loud as a hail of bullets against tin siding. On the stereo Jim Morrison's haunting voice rose above the roar. There was something reassuring about music on nights like this. It was a sign of life and reminded him there were other people out there and made him feel less isolated and a little less alone. Tonight, he swore to God that was the same song that had been playing that night.

Glancing away from the road, he reached down and punched the button for another station. When he looked up, she was there, on the road, scant yards from his bumper. He stomped the brake hard. The Lexus skidded sideways. The headlights played crazily against the curtain of rain, the black trunks of the trees. The car spun 180 degrees before jolting to a halt, facing the wrong direction.

For the span of several heartbeats, he sat there, breathing heavily, gripping the wheel hard enough to make his knuckles ache. He'd never believed in ghosts, but he knew there was no way in hell he could have seen what his eyes were telling him. Wanetta Hochstetler had been dead for thirty-five years. It had to be the booze playing tricks on him.

Fearing a cop would happen by and find him sitting in his car in the dead of night with his hands shaking and the smell of rotgut whiskey on his breath, he turned the vehicle around. But he couldn't leave. Not without making sure. He squinted through the windshield, but his headlight beams revealed nothing on the road or shoulder. A quiver of uneasiness went through him when he spotted the old mailbox. The thing had been bashed in a dozen times over the decades—by teenagers with beer bottles or baseball bats—and even peppered with holes from shotgun pellets. But he could still make out the name: HOCHSTETLER.

He didn't have a slicker or flashlight, but there was no avoiding getting out of the vehicle. He was aware of the pistol in his pocket, but it didn't comfort him, didn't make him feel any safer. Leaving the engine running, he turned up the collar of his jacket and swung open the door. Rain lashed his face as he stepped into the night. Water poured down his collar, the cold clenching the back of his neck like cadaver fingers.

"Who's there?" he called out.

He went around to the front of the vehicle and checked the bumper and hood. No dents. No blood.

Just to be sure, he rounded the front end and ran his hands over the quarter panel on the passenger side, too. Not so much as a scratch. He hadn't hit anything, human or otherwise. Just his tired eyes playing tricks . . .

He was standing outside the passenger door when she stepped out of the darkness and fog. The sight of her paralyzed him with fear. With something worse than fear. The knowledge that he'd been wrong. That time never forgot, no matter how badly you wanted it to—and the reckoning had finally come.

Her dress clung to a body that was still slender and strong and supple. The pouring rain and darkness obscured the details of her face. But she still had that rose-petal mouth and full lips. Long hair that had yet to go gray. He knew it was impossible for her to be standing there, unchanged, after all these years. After what happened to her. After what they *did* to her.

"It can't be you." The voice that squeezed from his throat was the sound of an old man on his deathbed, gagging on his own sputum, begging for a miracle that wasn't going to come.

Her mouth pulled into a smile that turned his skin to ice. "You look surprised to see me."

"You're dead." He scraped unsteady fingers over his face, blinked water from his eyes. But when he opened them, she was still there, as alive and familiar as the woman who'd been visiting his nightmares for thirty-five years. "How—?"

Never taking her eyes from his, she opened the driver's-side door, and killed the engine. Keys in hand, she went to the rear of the vehicle and pressed the trunk release. The latch clicked and the trunk sprang open.

"Get in," she said.

When he didn't move she produced a revolver and leveled it at his chest. He thought of the Walther in his pocket, wondered if he could get to it before she shot him dead.

He raised his hands. "What do you want?"

Stepping closer, she jabbed the revolver at him so that the muzzle was just two feet from his forehead. Her arm was steady, her finger inside the guard, snug against the trigger. "Do it."

Shaking uncontrollably, he climbed into the trunk and looked up at her. "We didn't mean it. *I swear we didn't mean it.*"

He didn't hear the shot.

Belinda Harrington stood on the porch of her father's house and knocked on the door hard enough to rattle the frame. "Dad?" She waited a minute and then used the heel of her hand and gave the wood a dozen hard whacks. "*Dad?* You home?"

She'd been trying to reach him for two days now, but he hadn't returned her calls. That wasn't unusual; the man was independent to a fault. He'd been known to ignore calls when it suited him. Still, two days was a long time. Even for Dale Michaels.

Wishing she'd remembered to bring her umbrella, she scanned the driveway through the cascade of water coming off the roof. His Lexus was parked in its usual spot; he had to be here somewhere. She wondered if he'd found himself a lady friend and they were holed up at her place or a hotel up in Wooster. Belinda wouldn't put it past him. Mom hadn't come right out and said it, but she let Belinda know in no uncertain terms that fidelity had never been one of Dale Michaels's strong points.

Cupping her hands on either side of her mouth, she called for him. "Dad!"

Her eyes wandered to the barn twenty yards away, and for the first time, she noticed the sliding door standing open a couple of feet. Though he'd never been burglarized, her father was a stickler about security. He wouldn't leave the barn door open, especially if he wasn't home. The initial fingers of worry kneaded the back of her neck. Had he gone out to feed the chickens and fallen? Was he lying there, unable to get up and waiting for help? He wasn't accident prone, but she supposed something could've happened. What if he'd had a heart attack?

Tenting her jacket over her head, she jogged across the gravel. The rain was really coming down, and by the time she reached the barn, her shoes and the hem of her pants were soaked. Shoving open the barn door another foot, Belinda stepped inside and shook rain from her jacket. The interior was dark and smelled of chicken poop and moldy hay. A few feet away, three bantam hens scratched and pecked at the floor. Stupid things. She wondered why her father kept them. Half the time, they didn't lay eggs and spent their days tearing up the petunias she'd planted for him last spring. Pulling her jacket closed against the cold, she flipped the light switch, but the single bulb didn't help much.

"Dad? You out here?"

Belinda listened for a response, but it was difficult to hear anything above the incessant pound of rain against the tin shingles. There were a dozen or so places where water dripped down from the leaky roof to form puddles on the dirt floor. At least the chickens had plenty to drink.

The barn was a massive structure with falling-down horse stalls and high rafters laced with cobwebs. As kids, she and her brother had played out here; they'd even had a pony once. But neither she nor her brother had been interested in animals, and once her father had gotten his real estate company up and running, the place became a workshop where he tinkered with cars. The workbench with the Peg-Board back was still there, but the tools were covered with dust. A dozen or so boards were stacked haphazardly against the wall. The old rototiller stood in silhouette against the window where dingy light bled in. When her brother was twelve years old, he'd nearly taken his foot off with that thing.

The loose dirt from the floor stuck to her shoes as she crossed to the workbench. Belinda called out for him one final time and started for the door. She was midway there when something to her right, on the other side of a fat beam caught her attention. Cautiously, she moved closer and looked up, found herself staring at the leather soles of shoes and the hems of slacks. She stumbled back, her eyes taking in legs and then the torso of a man. One arm hanging down. Neck bent at an unnatural angle.

A sound she didn't recognize tore from her throat. Somewhere in the back of her mind, she knew that thing hanging from the rafters was her father. That he was dead and she was sad his life had ended this way, and without so much as a good-bye. But the shock of seeing his lifeless body, so grotesque in death, overrode any impending sense of grief or loss.

"Dad! Oh my God! Dad! What did you do?"

Screaming, Belinda Harrington turned and sprinted through the door and into the pouring rain.

CHAPTER 2

John Tomasetti is standing at the kitchen counter chopping green peppers when my cell erupts. I'm sitting at the table with my laptop open, pretending I'm not watching him, drafting an e-mail to Mayor Auggie Brock, and absently wishing diplomacy wasn't such a big part of my job.

"Saved by the bell," he says.

I toss him a sideways look as I rise and go to my cell, which is about to vibrate off the counter. I catch it on the third ring. "Burkholder."

"It's Glock."

Rupert "Glock" Maddox is one of four police officers that make up my small department. A former marine with two tours in Afghanistan under his belt, he's well trained, level-headed and laid back, traits I admire greatly, especially in law enforcement. He usually works first shift, but I vaguely recall he'd traded with another officer for a couple of nights this week.

"Hey." Out of the corner of my eye I see Tomasetti grab an onion off the cutting board and attack it with the knife. I can't help it—I smile. "What's up?"

"I got a DOA out here at the Michaels place. Guy hanging from the rafters in his barn."

"Suicide?"

"Looks like it."

"Any idea who it is?"

"I think it's Dale Michaels."

The name is vaguely familiar, but I don't believe I've ever met Michaels. I recall he had something to do with the development of the affluent Maple Crest subdivision. "Who found him?"

"Daughter."

"Doc Coblentz on the way?" I ask, referring to the coroner.

"Should be here shortly."

"I'll be there in ten minutes."

"Roger that."

I unplug the phone from where it had been charging and turn to see Tomasetti drying his hands on a dish towel. "Sounds like you've got a dead body on your hands," he says.

I nod. "Glock thinks it might be a suicide."

"You know who it is?"

"Guy by the name of Dale Michaels. I don't know him."

"Sheriff's office going to take it?"

"It's city, so I'm obliged." I glance at the bottle of Argentinean cabernet he'd opened on the counter to breathe, and a wave of disappointment moves through me. "I'm sorry, but I have to go."

"I guess that means I have to finish chopping all of these vegetables by myself."

"Not to mention drink all that wine." I smile. "One of the perils of cohabiting with the chief of police."

He crosses to me. His arms encircle my waist and I fall against him. He smells of aftershave and green peppers and his own distinct scent I've come to love. I close my eyes and press my face against his chest. I know it's a trifling thing in light of the discovery of a body, but I don't want to leave.

"Domestication looks good on you, Tomasetti."

"You're just using me for my culinary skills."

"That, too." I rise up on my tiptoes and brush my mouth across his. "I might be a while."

"I'll wait."

Pulling away from him I grab my jacket off the back of the chair. I look at him over my shoulder. He's already picked up the knife and resumed chopping the onion. "Don't drink that wine all by yourself," I say.

"Don't stay gone too long."

We're both smiling when I go through the door.

CHAPTER 3

It's the worst kind of night to be on the road—windy and stormy—and the drive from Wooster to the scene, which is just inside the township limits of Painters Mill, takes almost twenty minutes. Twice I have to slow down—once because the road is flooded, and the second time because the windshield wipers can't keep up with the deluge. The Michaels farm is located on a narrow road that runs parallel with the railroad tracks that cut through town. My headlights illuminate a gravel lane with a hump of weeds in the center when I make the turn, and for the second time tonight I'm glad I drive a high-clearance vehicle. Ahead, I see the flashing lights of Glock's cruiser.

I park behind a newish Lincoln Navigator and cut the engine. The windows of the large Tudor-style house to my right are dark. The immense barn hulks to my left. The sliding door is open and I can see the yellow cone of Glock's flashlight. I pick up my radio. "Ten twenty-three."

"Copy that, Chief," comes the voice of my second-shift dispatcher.

"Ten twenty-eight."

"Go ahead."

I squint through the rain streaming down the windshield and recite the plate number on the SUV. "David, Henry, Adam, three, seven, zero, niner."

Keys click on the other end as she enters the tag number into the BMV database. "Comes back clear to an oh-six Lincoln. Registered to Christopher Thomas Harrington here in Painters Mill."

"Ten four." Grabbing my slicker and Maglite from the backseat, I get out. My hair is half soaked by the time I get my hood up. I start toward the barn.

I enter to the din of rain against the tin roof. I get the impression of a cavernous space with a dirt floor and huge wood support beams. On the other side of one of those beams, I see the body hanging from the rafters. It's too dark for me to discern much in terms of detail, but in the light thrown off by a single bare bulb, I can see the contorted neck, and in silhouette, the protrusion of a tongue from the mouth. Well-worn wingtips dangle six feet from the floor, where Glock is in the process of setting up cones and taping off the immediate area. As always, his uniform is military crisp, the arch of his boots shined to a high sheen. He looks like he just came off the set of some police recruiting video.

A thirtysomething woman wearing a quilted jacket over yoga pants, her feet jammed into lavender-colored skimmers, is standing just inside the door to my left, crying softly into a well-used tissue. Daughter, I think. Probably the owner of the Navigator and the one who found him. Her hair is the color of a new copper penny and sticks to her scalp like wet corkscrews. Glock must have offered her his slicker, because she's got it draped over her shoulders. I can see her shivering beneath it.

I make eye contact with her, nodding to let her know I'll speak to her in a moment as I cross to Glock. "She found him?"

He nods. "Name's Belinda Harrington. Lives in Painters Mill."

"Have you talked to her yet?"

"Just to get an ID. Swinger's her dad. Evidently, she's been trying to reach him for a couple of days. He didn't return her calls, so she drove over to check on him. When he didn't answer the door, she got worried and came out here to the barn."

I look at the body and try not to shudder. The neck is bent at a severe angle with the rope biting into the larynx area of the throat. The fingers of his left hand are trapped between the rope and his flesh, as if he'd changed his mind after jumping, but the weight of his body made it impossible to escape. I'm no expert, but I've seen the result of a few hangings in the years I've been a cop. This one wasn't clean.

"Hell of a way to go," I say in a low voice.

Sighing, Glock glances up at the body. "What are people thinking when they do shit like this?"

I don't bother trying to answer. "Did you find a note?"

He shakes his head. "I'll do a more thorough search once we get some lights out here."

"We'll need to check the house, too." I motion toward the platter-size wet spot in the dirt beneath the body. "Any idea what that is?"

"Not sure. Some kind of biohazard."

It's not unusual for a hanging victim's bladder to release at the time of death, but something about it bothers me. I run my beam over the length of the body. That's when I notice the dark stain on his slacks near the waistband. Too dark to be urine. "That looks like blood," I say to Glock.

"Shit." He adds his beam to mine. "Looks like a stain on his shirt, too. Bloody nose? Maybe he bumped something on his way down?"

"I don't know, but we need to figure it out." The victim is wearing dark slacks. A white shirt and a sport coat. Looking up, keeping my beam poised, I circle. Sure enough, in the small space between the lapel hems of the jacket I see a dark stain on the shirt.

"Get some photos of the scene and the victim, will you? We'll take a closer look once the fire department gets him down." I motion toward the woman standing near the door. "I'm going to talk to the daughter."

"Sure."

I leave Glock to his work and make my way toward the woman. "Ms. Harrington?"

She's frantically blotting her nose with the tissue, which is now shredded, and tossing uneasy glances at her father's body. She watches me approach, her eyes huge and owlish. "My God. I can't believe he's dead."

"I'm sorry."

She closes her eyes and I notice a single fake eyelash stuck to her cheek. "I can't believe he would *do* something like this."

It's not the first time I've heard those words. The family members of most suicide victims are shocked initially. Only after they've had ample time to reflect on the things the victim said or did in the weeks and months preceding their death do they realize the clues were there. They just didn't see them until it was too late.

"I'm Chief of Police Kate Burkholder." I offer my hand and we shake. "Do you feel up to answering a few questions?"

"Sure." But her eyes keep flicking from me to her father's body. "Can you guys get him down from there? I can't stand seeing him like that. His neck . . . God."

"We will as soon as the fire department gets here with some equipment and lights." I motion toward the workbench twenty feet away, and we start toward it. "They're on the way."

I stop at the workbench and turn to face her so that her back is to the body. "When's the last time you saw your dad?"

"Oh gosh. A week ago Sunday, I think. We met for lunch up at LaDonna's Diner."

I pull out my notebook and make a note. "Were you close?"

She digs into her purse, pulls out another tissue, and dabs at her eyes. "I don't see him as much as I used to. But when I was younger, we were close. He was a good dad." She chokes out a sound that's part laugh, part sob. "He doted on the grandkids." Her face screws up and she begins to cry.

Comforting the bereaved is not one of my strong points, but I've done this enough times to muddle through. I set my hand on her arm and give it a reassuring squeeze. "Was he depressed?"

"That's what makes this such a shock. He wasn't. Not at all. I mean, he didn't get down in the dumps. He didn't have that kind of personality. He was strong. . . . I mean, not that depressed people are weak, but . . ."

"Did he have any health problems?"

"He'd slowed down in the last couple of years. Complained about his knees sometimes. Oh, and he had a little thing of skin cancer removed six months ago. But nothing since. He was healthy as a horse."

"Any issues with drugs or alcohol?"

"Never did drugs. Far as I know, he never drank too much."

"Has he been under any stress lately?"

"He never mentioned anything."

"Any deaths in the family recently? Or anyone he was close to?"

"No."

"Any financial problems?"

"No. He hit it big with the Maple Crest development back in the late '90s, so he was pretty much set for life."

"Did he have many friends, Belinda?"

"He used to hang out with some guys his age. They'd visit or play poker or go out to dinner."

"Do you know their names?"

She lowers her head, presses the heels of her hands to her eyes. "To tell you the truth, I don't know."

I suspect at least part of the display isn't grief, but guilt because they weren't as close as they'd once been.

"Did he have a girlfriend?" I ask.

"Not that I know of. But he was kind of secretive about . . . personal stuff."

Movement at the door snags my attention. Deputy Frank Maloney with the Holmes County Sheriff's Department lugs in a large fluorescent work light. An orange extension cord is looped around his shoulder like a rope. I reach into the pocket of my jacket, pull out one of my cards, and hand it to the woman. "Mrs. Harrington, if you think of anything else that might be important, will you give me a call?"

"Of course."

I nod toward her father's body. "You don't have to stay for this. And if you're not up to driving, I can call a family member for you or have an officer take you home."

"Thank you, but no." She shakes her head. "The least I can do is be here for him through this."

As I start to walk past her, I think of one more question. "Mrs. Harrington, do you have a key to his house?"

"Yes, I do. Why?"

"I thought he might've left a note."

"Oh." Her face crumples. "I didn't even think of that."

"Is it okay with you if we take a look inside?"

"Sure. Whatever you need."

Giving her a final nod, I turn my attention back to the scene. The Holmes County coroner, Dr. Ludwig Coblentz, has arrived. He's a rotund man and clad in his trademark extra-large scrubs, a slicker draped over his shoulders. There's a young technician with him. Judging from the tuft of peach fuzz on his chin, I guess him to be a trainee and new to fieldwork. I wonder how long he'll last.

While the doctor slips into biohazard gear, the technician, who's already suited up, kneels and unzips a body bag. Several yards away, two paramedics from Pomerene Hospital in Millersburg stand just inside the sliding door, watching. A volunteer fire fighter has set up an aluminum combination ladder beneath the body. A second volunteer stands on the platform section, trying to figure out the best way to lower the corpse to the ground.

I cross to Doc Coblentz and motion toward the biohazard on the ground beneath the body. "Do you guys have a field test for blood?" I ask.

"We do." The coroner nods at the technician. "Randy, grab one of those Hemastix strips, will you?"

The technician digs into his equipment bag, removes a bottle of Hemastix, and plucks out a single plastic strip.

"It'll test for the presence of hemoglobin, which indicates blood," the doc tells me. "If it's present, we'll get a color reaction."

We watch the technician press the colored end of the strip against the moist earth. Within seconds, the tip turns green.

"I got a positive," the technician says.

From his place near the workbench, Maloney plugs the work light into the extension cord, and the barn is abruptly flooded with severe fluorescent light. I get my first good look at the corpse—and the size of the reddish black stain on the shirt.

"Too much blood for a hanging," the doc says grimly.

"Let's get him down and take a closer look," I say.

We watch in silence as the firefighter standing on the platform uses a utility knife to cut the rope. Keeping it looped around the rafter for friction, he slowly hoists the body toward the ground. As the body descends, the technician and Doc Coblentz open the body bag on the ground. The victim's boots make contact first. The technician pulls the victim's feet toward the base of the bag and places him in a supine position. I can tell by the stiffness of the dead man's legs that he's been there awhile. Rigor mortis peaks at about twelve hours, then subsides after twenty-four to thirty-six hours. It would have been a much grislier scene had more time elapsed before he was discovered.

Beneath the glare of the work lights, Dale Michaels's face is swollen and purple. His tongue is twice its normal size and protrudes from his mouth like some overripe fruit. The flesh around his eyes is like crepe paper, fluid filled and nearly black in color. The eyeballs within are milky-looking and bloodred with petechiae. Though I've backed six feet away, I'm repelled by the odors of urine and feces.

Death is always an ugly sight to behold, whether it's homicide, suicide, accidental, or from natural causes. But from all indications, Dale Michaels's demise was particularly brutal. The doc has removed the rope from around the victim's neck. It left a two-inch-deep trench in the flesh and severely abraded the skin. The yellow nylon rope is about three-eighths of an inch in diameter, and there's about thirty feet of it. I watch as the technician coils it and then places it in an evidence bag. From where I'm standing, I see blood and abraded flesh embedded in the fibers.

Suicides don't require the same level of scrutiny from law enforcement as a homicide, but the scene must still be documented. In the state of Ohio, all unattended deaths require that an autopsy be conducted, and this case will be no different. Unless it is determined that foul play was involved, there will be little in terms of actual police investigation.

My mind drifts as the doctor goes about his work. I'm wondering if I can wrap this up in a couple of hours and get home in time to help Tomasetti with that bottle of cabernet when the coroner gives me a sharp look over his shoulder.

"Chief, I've got an irregularity here."

I walk over and kneel beside him. With gloved hands, he opens the jacket to reveal a partially tucked shirt. A hole in the fabric the size of my pinkie is surrounded by a wide bloodstain that spreads downward to soak into the waistband of his trousers and under-wear.

"There's the source of that blood," he tells me. "I'm pretty sure that's a gunshot wound."

"Self-inflicted?" I ask.

"Hard to tell." He looks at me over his bifocals. "The only thing I can tell you with relative certainty at this point is that he was alive when he was shot. There's not much blood, but enough so that I feel the heart was beating when he sustained that gunshot wound."

"So he was shot and then hanged?" I ask.

"Correct," the doc confirms.

I look at Glock and Maloney. "Anyone find a handgun on scene?"

"Nope," Glock mutters. "But I've only done a cursory search."

"Might've shot himself in the house and then walked out here and finished it," Maloney offers.

"Doubtful scenario," the doc tells him. "Judging by the location of the wound, I would venture to say it was debilitating."

"Have a look around," I tell Glock and Maloney. "Check for casings, too."

The men are already on their feet, their eyes seeking.

I stare at the blood, the pattern of the spread. "Looks like he was upright when he was shot."

"That's my thought, too," the doc says. "Blood traveled down with gravity."

I risk a look at the dead man's face and try not to shudder. That's when I notice something in his mouth. "Doc, is there something in his mouth?"

The coroner leans closer. "Tongue is pretty swollen, but it looks like there may be a foreign object in the back of his throat." He glances at the technician. "Hand me the large needle-nose pliers."

The tech removes a stainless steel instrument that looks like a combination pliers and tweezers. The doc sets his hand against the victim's face, turning the head slightly so that the mouth opens wider. After inserting the tip of the pliers, he gently tugs out an oblong object about three and a half inches in length.

I set the beam of my flashlight on it. "What is it?"

"Looks like some kind of . . . figurine," the doc murmurs.

Recognition sparks when he turns it over. "It's an Amish peg doll," I say.

The doc gives me a questioning look over the tops of his bifocals. "Come again?"

"A wooden doll." I move my flashlight closer for better illumination. "It's faceless, which tells me it's Amish."

With a turn of his wrist, he flips it upside down. I can just make out the faded and bloodied letters on the underside of the base: HOCHSTETLER.

"I know that name," I say.

The doc looks at me over his bifocals. "Used to be a business here in town. Amish family made furniture. Place closed when they were murdered back in the late 1970s."

I was only a year old at the time, but now that he's mentioned it, I remember the stories from when I was a kid, most of which were of the ghostly variety. "Interesting that this would show up at a murder scene thirty-five years later," I say.

The doc nods. "I'll say."

I look down at the bloody peg doll clamped within the pincers of the pliers, and I wonder why someone saw fit to shove it down Dale Michaels's throat. I start to reach for an evidence bag, but realize I'm not in uniform and look around for Glock. "Do you have an evidence bag?"

"Right here, Chief." He crosses back to us, working a bag from a compartment on his belt. He opens it, holds it out, and the doc drops the figurine inside.

"We're going to need to courier that to the BCI lab ASAP," I tell him.

"Sure thing."

The technician and coroner roll the victim slightly, and the doc checks the trouser pockets. "I've got a wallet here." He hands the beat-up leather wallet to Glock, who checks the driver's license and slides it into a second evidence bag. "Jacket is torn. No weapon on him."

I rise quickly, look around, aware that I'm seeing the scene in a completely different light. I address Maloney, who's standing a few yards away. "Frank, can you get everyone out?"

He's already motioning the two paramedics through the door.

"I want all vehicles except the coroner's van parked away from the house and barn, too." But I know the rain has more than likely eradicated any tire tread or footwear imprints.

I hit my lapel mike. "Jodie?"

"Go ahead, Chief."

"Call T.J. and get him out here."

"Ten four."

"And run Dale Michaels through LEADS." I spell the name. "And while you're at it, pull everything you can find on the Hochstetler case from 1979, will you?"

"Got it."

Watching the scene apprehensively, Belinda Harrington approaches me. "What's going on? Did someone *shoot* my dad?"

I give her a hard look, noticing the boat-size purse at her side, the bulky jacket, and I realize she has plenty of places in which to secrete a weapon. I don't think she shot her father or wrapped a rope around his neck and strung him up. But I learned a long time ago that taking things at face value is never a good idea when there's a dead body involved.

"We believe your father may have sustained a gunshot wound shortly before his death," I tell her.

"*What?* But . . . oh my God. He was *hanging.* Who would do such a thing?"

"Mrs. Harrington, does your father own a handgun?"

"I think so."

"Do you know what kind?"

"It's big and black." She shrugs. "I don't know anything about guns."

"Do you own a firearm, ma'am?"

"My husband does." Her eyes narrow. "Why are you asking me that?"

I step closer. "Do you mind if I take a quick look in your purse?"

"What? Why?" But she makes no move to stop me when I reach out and ease the purse from her shoulder.

"Just routine," I tell her, "since you were first on the scene." She starts to protest, but I keep her busy with questions while I open the bag and quickly determine there's no weapon inside and hand it back to her. "Did your father have any recent arguments with anyone, Mrs. Harrington? Did he have any enemies?"

"I don't know. I mean, not that he mentioned. Most everyone liked my dad." But her brows go together.

"Wait. I think he had some kind of problem with his neighbor. The couple that lives south of here. Their dogs were always loose and getting in my dad's trash."

"How long ago was that?"

"It's been kind of ongoing, I think."

Taking her arm, I guide her toward the door. "What's the neighbor's name?"

"Seymour."

"Is that a first or last name?"

"I don't know. He just goes by Seymour and my dad didn't like him much. That's all I know."

I nod. "Did your father have any kind of connection to anyone with the name Hochstetler?"

She looks at me blankly. "Not that I know of."

"Did he keep money or valuables here at the house?"

"I don't know. He probably kept some cash on hand. And there are plenty of nice things in the house. He remodeled the place after my mom divorced him."

"How long ago did they divorce?"

"Oh gosh, eight years maybe?"

"Any tension between them?"

She shakes her head. "Divorce is probably the best thing they ever did for each other."

"Did he have any work done on the house recently? Or hire any casual laborers? Anything like that?"

"Did that remodeling six or seven years ago." She shrugs. "He's handy and liked to tinker, so he did a lot of the work himself."

"Does your dad have a cell phone?" I ask, knowing that many times it's helpful to check incoming and outgoing calls.

"He just upgraded his iPhone."

"You've been a big help, Mrs. Harrington." I motion toward Glock. "Officer Maddox will walk you to your vehicle. This is a crime scene now, and we need to protect any evidence."

A round of fresh tears well in her eyes. "My poor dad. Shot like some old dog."

I give Glock a nod and he gently ushers her toward the door. "This way, ma'am."

I watch them disappear into the rain and then tug out my cell and hit the speed dial for Tomasetti, knowing he can get a crime scene unit out here faster than I can. Worry flickers inside me when he doesn't pick up, but I presume he's in the shower or on another line. I call my dispatcher instead. "Call BCI and request a CSU. Tell them we've got a possible homicide." I give her the address. "Check County records and get me the names and contact info of Michaels's neighbors. I'm particularly interested in a neighbor with the first or last name of Seymour. See if he's got a sheet."

"Okay, Chief."

I ring off in time to hear the coroner call my name. I walk back over to where he's kneeling next to the body, his gloved hand hovering near the bullet wound. "I'm guessing, Kate, but I'd venture to say the slug penetrated the stomach. If that's the case, there's no way he walked from the house to the barn after sustaining this wound."

I scan the interior of the barn, trying to get my mind around what might have transpired. "Is it possible Michaels was already hanging, perhaps by his own hand, and someone entered the barn and shot him?" I ask the doc.

"Possible, but doubtful," he replies. "There's only a small window of time that he was alive, after he was hanged. Once the carotid artery and jugular veins are blocked, unconsciousness would have occurred within minutes. Death may have taken another ten or fifteen minutes."

"Maybe someone shot him to disable him and then strung him up," Glock says as he comes through the door.

"Hell of a way to kill someone," Maloney adds.

I look down at Dale Michaels's body. "Unless maybe someone thought he deserved it."

CHAPTER 4

It's nearly 4 A.M. when I arrive home, exhausted and in need of a shower. Once the coroner's office transported the body to the morgue, Glock and I spent three hours searching both the barn and the house. As is always the case when murder is suspected, the question of motive is forefront in our minds. That question was addressed, at least in part, when we found eighty bucks and a gold class ring lying in plain sight on a night table. In the study, there was a sleek MacBook Pro, which I sealed in an evidence bag and sent to the lab. A flat-screen television in the living room. All those items are coveted by thieves: they're valuable, easy to transport, and quick to sell. And I was able to comfortably rule out robbery as the motive.

One item of interest that we didn't find at the scene was Dale Michaels's cell phone. I even dialed the number, hoping to hear the ring, but to no avail. Often, it's helpful to know with whom the victim spoke in the days and hours before death. According to his daughter, the cell phone should have been somewhere on the premises. Did he leave it somewhere? Lose it? Or did someone take it?

Another thing we couldn't explain was the locked house. If Michaels had been working or tinkering on some project in the barn, why would he lock the door? Crime is relatively low in Painters Mill and, for the most part, throughout Holmes County. Neither Glock nor I could think of a logical reason why Michaels would lock the house if he was going to the barn. In addition, there was no evidence that he'd been working on any kind of project in the barn. There were no tools out of place, nothing being repaired. We finally landed on the possibility that he may have been in the barn to feed and water the chickens. Still, why lock the house?

It was after 2 A.M. when the CSU arrived. I'd turned the scene over to them and was about to leave when I realized we hadn't yet looked at Michaels's Lexus. It was there that I found our first clue: blood in the trunk. Initially, we had surmised Michaels was accosted in the barn, shot, and while he was incapacitated, hanged from the rafters, all of which would have taken a good bit of time and effort. The discovery of blood in the trunk—which was later determined to be human—changed everything and raised a slew of new questions.

If the blood is determined to be Michaels's, how did he end up in the trunk of his own car? Did someone accost him on the highway, put a bullet in him, throw him in the trunk, then transport him back here and string him up in the barn?

We also discovered tire tracks in the barn. The crime scene unit took plaster copies of the tread, but they looked to be a match to Michaels's Lexus. Because the vehicle was part of the crime scene, I had it towed to the sheriff's department impound, where it will be processed by the CSU.

Because of the late hour, I'd considered spending the rest of the night at my house in Painters Mill, if only for a shower and a couple hours of sleep. I still own the place and most of my furniture is still there, including my bed and a few linens. But by the time I left the scene, all I could think about was getting home and spending a few hours with Tomasetti.

The house is dark except for the back porch light and the bulb above the stove, which he keeps on for me when he knows I'll be arriving home late. I let myself in, anticipating a shower, a warm bed, and the feel of him solid against me as I drift off to sleep. The aroma of homemade spaghetti—onions, green peppers, and garlic—still lingers when I enter the kitchen, and I smile because I like this new life I've stepped into. The domesticity. Having someone I can count on. Someone I look forward to seeing at the end of the day. Someone I love . . .

Leaving my boots next to the door, I set my keys on the counter and drape my holster and jacket over the back of a chair. I'm midway to the stairs where our bedroom is when a voice comes out of the darkness.

"Kate."

I startle and spin. I spot Tomasetti's silhouette against the living room window. He's standing ten feet away, something in his hand. I have a sort of sixth sense when it comes to his frame of mind, and I know immediately something has changed since I left a few hours ago. There's an edge in his voice that unsettles me. Something else in the way he's standing there, not moving.

I start toward him, suddenly needing to touch him. To make sure he's really there. That he's okay. That we're okay. "I thought you'd be sleeping."

"Couldn't sleep."

I stop a couple of feet from him, wishing I could see his face. That's when I notice the bottle in his hand. The careless way he's holding the neck. I smell cigarettes and whiskey on his breath and I know whatever it is that has changed, it's bad. "What's wrong?"

"Joey Ferguson walked today."

The words strike me with the force of a physical blow. Joey Ferguson is the last living person involved with the murders of Tomasetti's wife and children three years ago in Cleveland. According to the evidence and witness statements, he hadn't participated in the assaults on Nancy Tomasetti or the two pre-teen girls, Donna and Kelly. But he'd driven the getaway car and he'd helped set the house on fire afterward. The fire that ultimately killed them. The trial had been over a year ago. Tomasetti had taken the stand and painted a horrific picture for the jury, telling them what he found the night he came home to a burning house. That when he'd left that morning, he'd been a husband and father of two. When he arrived home that night, his family was dead, murdered by a career criminal intent on intimidating a cop who'd dared cross him. The media had capitalized on every minute of it, running photo after photo of Tomasetti's pretty wife and his curly-haired little girls, sensationalizing a brutal triple murder that had destroyed a family, shocked the country—and sent Tomasetti spiraling out of control.

But the evidence against Ferguson was sketchy. We'd been relieved and left with a sense of closure when he was convicted of conspiracy to commit murder and sentenced to thirty years in prison. But his high-profile, high-powered attorney immediately appealed. Tomasetti hadn't talked about it. Not once. We didn't discuss it or let it into this new life we've built for ourselves. But I know he followed the proceedings.

"What?" I blurt. "How?"

"He got off on a chain-of-command technicality."

For an interminable moment, I can't speak; I don't know what to say. I don't know how to reconcile this or help him deal with it, and I'm filled with a sense of injustice and impotence.

"I'm sorry." I reach for him, but he moves back slightly. "What can I do?" I ask.

"Thanks, Kate, but I don't think there's anything anyone can do. It's done."

For the span of a full minute, the only sound comes from the tap of rain on the roof. The water running through the spouting. The slap of it against the ground as it overflows gutters that are clogged with leaves. And for the first time in the four months that I've been living here with him, I feel something lonely and cold surround me.

I reach for the lamp on the end table.

"Don't," he says.

I motion toward the bottle at his side. "That's not going to help."

"Yes, it is." His laugh is a harsh sound. "I know that bucks conventional wisdom, but believe me, it's helping."

"I know you're hurting—"

"That's not quite the right word."

I don't agree with him. A man can't endure the kind of hell he did without pain becoming a constant in his life. But I don't argue. "Tell me what to do."

When he doesn't respond, I gesture in the direction of the door. "Let's sit on the porch and talk."

"I'm not in the mood to be psychoanalyzed."

"Then we can just sit."

"I'm not very good company right now. Why don't you go on upstairs and get some sleep?"

"I'm not leaving you alone."

He utters another laugh. "I don't think that's up to you." As if realizing the words were harsher than he intended, he softens. "Look, I'm all right. I just need some time alone to think. That's all. You've got an early morning. Go to bed. I'll join you in a while."

I stand there, debating, trying to figure out who needs whom, because at that moment my need for him is twisting my gut into a knot. "I'm worried about you."

"I'm okay. I can handle this. I've handled worse." He shrugs. "I don't want to bring this to what we have here. Just give me some space, all right?"

It's difficult, but in the end I opt to honor his request. "I'm going to take a shower."

When he leans close and presses his mouth against mine, his lips are cold.

I wake before daybreak to find Tomasetti gone. At some point during the early morning hours—without coming into the bedroom to say good-bye—he got into his Tahoe and left. Usually, if for whatever reason we don't connect during the day, he'll leave a note next to the coffeemaker. That's become our routine for touching base when we don't actually see each other. This morning there's no note. He didn't even make coffee. The house is cold and damp, and when I walk into the kitchen, I'm accosted by an unbearable sense of aloneness.

I make a pot of coffee, lingering longer than I should in the hope he'll return. When I dump yesterday's grounds in the trash, I find the empty bottle of Crown Royal along with a half a dozen cigarette butts. Neither are a good sign.

I tell myself not to worry and remind myself that Tomasetti is a strong man with a good head on his shoulders. Chances are, he went to his office at the Bureau of Criminal Identification and Investigation in Richfield because he couldn't sleep and wanted to get a jump on his day. But I am worried. I know Tomasetti. He's come a long way in the three years since his family was killed. But I'm ever aware that he has a dark side. An unpredictable side that, in the past, has been triggered by pain and injustice and all those gnarly emotions in between.

I'm the only person in the world who knows what he did in the months following the deaths of his wife and children. I know he turned to pills and alcohol—and spent some time at a mental health facility. I also know he took the law into his own hands and the killers paid hard for what they'd done. The knowledge isn't a burden; I'm glad he trusted me enough to share it, but this morning it's at the forefront of my mind. Right or wrong—moral or not—I've learned to live with what he did. Maybe because I understand his motives. Because I know he's a good man, and like him, I see the world in stark black-and-white.

The need to call him is powerful, but some inner voice advises me to wait. A call from me now would be seen by him as evidence of my lack of trust, an admission of my fear that he's going to fall off some emotional cliff. But the truth of the matter is that I don't fully trust him.

I arrive at the police station at 7 A.M. to find my third-shift dispatcher, Mona Kurtz, sitting cross-legged on the floor near her desk, several files spread out in front of her. She's wearing her headset and tapping her foot against the floor to Florence and the Machine's "Dog Days Are Over." She looks up when I enter and grins sheepishly. "Hey, Chief."

"Morning." I pull a stack of message slips from my slot.

"You're in early this morning."

"Murder makes for a busy day." I glance through my messages. "Anything else come back on Dale Michaels?"

"Guy didn't even have a speeding ticket." Rising, she reaches for a manila folder next to the switchboard and passes it to me. "I started a file, but there's not much there."

"What about the Hochstetler file?"

"Jodie couldn't find it. She thinks it's locked up in your office."

Tucking the file under my arm, I stop at the coffee station to fill my cup and then head to my office. I'm doing my utmost not to think about Tomasetti, but even with an unsolved homicide on my hands, I'm not doing a very good job of it.

At my desk, I open the file and find Glock's report along with a couple of dozen photos of the scene. I read the report twice and then take a few minutes to look at each photo. Of the body. The scene. And the mysterious Amish peg doll, including a shot of the name inscribed on the base. HOCHSTETLER. And I know this is one of those cases that won't give up its secrets easily.

I go to the file cabinet, kneel, and tug open the bottom drawer. At the rear, where several cold case files are collecting dust, I find the Hochstetler file and take it back to my desk. It's a thick folder containing dozens of reports from several law enforcement agencies. The Holmes County Sheriff's Department. The Ohio State Highway Patrol. The Bureau of Criminal Identification and Investigation. And, of course, the Painters Mill PD. Ronald Mackey had been chief back in 1979. Homicide investigative procedures have improved since, but he did a good job with documentation and included several dozen Polaroid photos of the victims—what was left of them—and the scene.

I read the reports first. Forty-two-year-old Willis Hochstetler owned Hochstetler Amish Furniture, which he ran out of the home he shared with his wife, Wanetta, and five children. In the early morning hours of March 8, one or more individuals went into the home, probably looking for cash. In the course of the robbery, Willis Hochstetler sustained a fatal gunshot wound. At some point thereafter, the house caught fire—possibly from a lantern. Four of the children perished in the fire. According to the sole survivor, fourteen-year-old William, there were at least three men in the house, possibly more. They were armed with handguns and covered their faces so he was unable to identify them. When they left, they took his mother, thirty-four-year-old Wanetta, with them. The Amish woman was never seen or heard from again.

According to the coroner's report, the four children died of smoke inhalation. It was also determined that Willis Hochstetler died of the gunshot wound, which he sustained before the fire. I pick up the photos. They're faded, but I can see enough to know there wasn't much left of the house—or the victims. In the back of the file, Chief Mackey made a notation that

William Hochstetler was taken in by an Amish couple and later adopted by Jonas and Martha Yoder, taking their name.

Now, William and his wife, Hannah, own Yoder's Pick-Your-Own Apple Farm. I've stopped by there a dozen times since I moved back to Painters Mill, to buy apples or cider or apple butter, all of which are delectable. It's a good way for me, as chief, to keep a finger on the happenings within the Amish community.

I close the Hochstetler file, and pull out the photos of the Amish peg doll. Why was the figurine left inside the mouth of the victim? Is there some connection between the two cases?

I call out to Mona. "Did you get anything back on Michaels's neighbors?"

"Did I ever." She enters my office with another file in hand and passes it to me. "I guess you never know who you're living next door to."

"Until you run him through LEADS, anyway." I open the file and look down at the printout. Sure enough, Kerry Seymour had amassed an extensive record as a younger man. An assault charge in 1985. Burglary conviction two years later. Drunk and disorderly. Two DUIs. He did eight months in Mansfield for a felony assault in 1999.

"Busy man in his youth," I say dryly.

She motions to the folder. "I put contact info and Glock's old incident report in there, too."

"Thanks." I look at the report. True to Belinda Harrington's assertion, Dale Michaels had filed a complaint, claiming Seymour's dogs were loose and digging in his trash. Seymour was issued a citation and that had been the end of it. Or was it?

* * *

I blow most of an hour returning e-mails and phone calls. At 8 A.M., I'm back in my Explorer and heading toward the home of Dale Michaels's neighbors. Kerry Seymour and his wife live on a small tract of land just south of the Michaels property. I pull into the asphalt driveway and park next to a maroon Ford F-150. The house is a redbrick ranch that looks professionally landscaped or else someone has a green thumb. Ahead is a good-sized metal building with an overhead door. A chain-link dog kennel with a concrete run is located on the south side of the building, but there are no dogs in sight.

Drizzle floats down from a cast-iron sky as I leave my vehicle and take the sidewalk to the house. I open the storm door and use the brass knocker, which is, not surprisingly, in the shape of a dog's head. The door opens a few inches and I find myself looking at a middle-aged woman wearing a pink robe over flannel pajamas. Lower, two Labrador noses sniff at me through the opening.

"Mrs. Seymour?" I ask, showing her my badge and identifying myself. "Is Kerry Seymour home, ma'am?"

"He's here." She looks past me as if expecting to see the SWAT team preparing to swoop in. "He do something wrong?"

"Not that I know of," I say. "But I'd like to ask both of you some questions."

The door opens the rest of the way. Mary Ellen Seymour is holding a coffee mug in one hand, a magazine tucked beneath her arm. At her feet, the two dogs stare at me, panting.

"What happened?" she asks.

"Your neighbor, Mr. Michaels, was killed last night."

"Killed? Oh my God. How?"

"That's what I'm trying to figure out."

"Mary Ellen?" A man wearing striped pajamas and a ratty-looking robe enters the foyer. He's tall and thin, with a narrow face framed by a horseshoe mustache. He comes up behind his wife, sets his hand possessively on her shoulder. "What can I do for you?"

The woman doesn't give me a chance to answer. "Kerry, Mr. Michaels next door is dead! Can you believe it?"

"Dale? Dead?" Brows knitting, he rubs his hand across his chin. "Damn."

I purposely didn't reveal *how* Michaels was killed. It doesn't elude me that he didn't ask.

"His daughter found him last night," I tell them, watching them carefully for any outward signs of previous knowledge or nervousness. "I'd like to ask you some questions," I tell them. "May I come inside?"

"Oh. Sure." Glancing down at the dogs, the woman sets down the magazine and points. "Greta! Dagmar! Go!"

Canine toenails click against the tile floor of the entryway as the animals trot off. When the dogs are gone, the woman motions me in. I step into a small entryway jammed with a console table that's too big for the space. To my left is a living room crowded with plaid furniture, a gurgling aquarium full of iridescent orange fish, and walls painted 1980s blue.

The couple doesn't invite me to sit, so I go to my first question. "Did either of you notice anything unusual over at Mr. Michaels's place in the last few days?" I ask. "Did you hear or see anything? Any visitors or strange vehicles in the area?"

"We can't really see his house from ours." Kerry

Seymour points through the storm door at the row of blue spruce trees that obscures the view of the Michaels house. "I planted them four years ago. For privacy."

He adds the final word in a way that tells me the trees have more to do with complete separation than simple privacy, and it makes me wonder just how serious the issues between them had been. "I understand there have been some problems between you and Mr. Michaels," I say.

"We've had a few skirmishes over the years."

"What kind of skirmishes?"

"Our dogs got out a couple of times. He called the law on me."

"They're good dogs," Mary Ellen adds quickly.

"I know about the citation," I tell them. "Any other problems? Arguments?"

"I called the County on him once for burning trash during a burn ban." He rubs his thumb and forefinger over his mustache. "That guy never liked me."

"Any particular reason?" I ask.

He stares at me, and I notice red blotches at the base of his throat.

"I know about your record," I tell him.

As if unable to bear the tension, Mary Ellen pipes up. "Mr. Michaels threw some trash on our side of the fence once. Pop cans. Kerry went over and asked him about it and he denied it. Said our dogs had gotten into his trash and the wind blew it over."

"How long ago was that?" I ask.

"Two weeks ago," she says.

Kerry glowers at his wife and she swallows hard. I raise my brows and wait.

"I had a few words with him a couple of weeks ago," he admits.

"About what?"

"In addition to his bogus trash complaint, he said our dogs were barking and keeping him awake at night."

"They sleep inside with us," Mary Ellen says quickly.

I ignore her. "Did any of these confrontations ever get physical?"

His wife laughs. "Of course not."

I don't take my eyes off Kerry.

He tosses me an I-know-where-you're-going-with-this smile that isn't friendly. I've met plenty of cop-haters in my time. People who, for whatever reason, detest anyone in law enforcement, and Kerry Seymour fits the mold to a T. "You got something to say, just say it," he says.

"I'd appreciate it if you just answered my question."

"I never laid a hand on the guy."

I nod. "When's the last time either of you saw Mr. Michaels?"

"Last week," Mary Ellen blurts. "Wednesday morning. I was on my way into town to see the eye doctor in Painters Mill—Dr. Driver—and Dale was getting his mail at the end of his lane."

I turn my attention to her husband. "And you?"

"I don't recall. Couple of weeks, probably."

"Can both of you account for your whereabouts for the last two days?"

"Kerry was at work." Mary Ellen fingers her coffee cup nervously. "He works for the railroad. Eight to four thirty."

"Do you work, ma'am?"

"I'm the gardener, maid, and cook."

"What about the last couple of evenings?" I ask.

"We were here. Both nights."

"Can anyone else vouch for that?" I ask.

"Well, no," she admits. "But he was here."

The dogs have inched their way over to us. Feeling a cold, wet nose against my hand, I reach down and stroke the head of the nearest Labrador, which is sitting at my feet. "Pretty dogs."

"Thank you." She beams, and I'm instantly forgiven for asking such impolite questions.

Her husband isn't quite so magnanimous. "So am I a suspect?"

"I'm still in the information-gathering stage of the case, Mr. Seymour." I pet the other dog to give the couple a moment to consider everything that's been said, everything they've learned about their now-deceased neighbor. "Is there anything else you can add that might help us figure out who might've done this?"

Kerry sighs. "Look, I barely spoke to the man. Didn't know him."

"Did either of you ever see or hear him arguing with anyone?" I ask. "Or do you know of any arguments or disputes?"

Mary Ellen shakes her head. "As far as I know, the only people he yelled at was us. Cussed me out once because Greta pooped in his yard. Shook me up something awful."

CHAPTER 5

Yoder's Pick-Your-Own Apple Farm is located on a pretty tract of land that includes a thirty-acre orchard where hundreds of McIntosh apple trees flourish. When I was a girl, my *datt* brought my siblings and me here, where we were given bushel baskets and spent entire afternoons picking apples for pies, apple butter, and of course, cider. It was hot, buggy work but we always found a way to make it fun. Not only did I get to eat my fill—which I usually regretted later—but it was a prime opportunity for unsupervised playtime. Jacob and I would duck into the rows of trees and play hide-and-seek. He'd climb the tallest trees and then laugh when I couldn't reach him. He was older and stronger, but I was a determined child and once took him out with a well-placed rock. Jacob never ratted on me for that; I think he was secretly proud of me, and Datt was never the wiser.

Four years ago, after moving back to Painters Mill and spending several weekends scouring the local tourist shops for the perfect Amish quilt, I was told

that Hannah Yoder was one of the best quilters in the
county. I stopped by their fruit stand and spotted a
lovely gray geometric with the requisite seven stitches
per inch and black detailing. I ended up paying too
much, but I walked away with the knowledge that it
was money well spent.

I've always been aware that William was the lone
survivor of a violent crime. I knew his father and four
siblings had been killed, that his mother had disappeared, and the perpetrators were never apprehended.
I didn't, however, know the details until I read the file.
Those details haunt me as I turn into the gravel lane
bordered on either side by razor-straight rows of Mc-
Intosh apple trees.

A colorful sign welcomes me to Yoder's Pick-Your-
Own Apple Farm, where the BEST CIDER IN OHIO is
one dollar a glass. I park adjacent the large produce
stand. The small frame building is nestled between
two maple trees that offer welcome shade in summer.
Through the open window that runs the length of the
structure's facade, I see shelves filled with jars of
apple butter, applesauce, and spiced apples. A dozen
or more jugs of cider take up an entire lower shelf.
Beyond, more shelves are dedicated to embroidered
doilies, canvas tote bags, and bird feeders designed
to look like Amish buggies. At the rear, handmade
quilts hang on wooden arms set into the wall, the bold
colors and geometric designs beckoning one to
stop and browse.

I'm midway to the produce stand when a female
voice calls out. "Here for another quilt, are you?"

I glance up to see Hannah Yoder standing just
inside, her elbows on the counter, looking at me
through the front window. She's in her mid-thirties
with a fresh, pretty face and an infectious smile. She's

wearing a dark blue dress, black apron, and a black winter head covering.

"I wouldn't rule that out." I return her smile. *"Wie geth's alleweil?" How's it going?*

"Ich bin zimmlich gut." I'm pretty good. She arches a brow at my Pennsylvania Dutch. *" 'Sis kald heit." It's cold today.*

I look up at the sky. "More rain on the way, too."

"The apples will be sweet and plentiful this year."

I enter through the side door and extend my hand. "You remember me."

She nods, giving my fingers a firm squeeze. "Of course. I sold you my favorite quilt."

I look around and my eyes are drawn to the quilts. Winter colors. Maroon and cream and brown. My fingers itch with the urge to touch, but I resist. They're not cheap, and on the salary of a police chief, I can't afford another.

"Is your husband home?" I ask.

A male voice calls out. "That depends."

I glance to my left to see William "Hoch" Yoder emerge from a small storeroom. He's a tall, thin man clad in typical Amish garb—black trousers, blue work shirt with suspenders and a flat-brimmed hat. This morning, he's wearing a black barn coat.

"Hi." I approach him and offer my hand. "Mr. Yoder."

"Call me Hoch."

The story behind the nickname is well known among the Amish. After William's family was murdered, an Amish couple with the last name of Yoder adopted him. Rumor has it that fourteen-year-old William resisted changing his name from Hochstetler to Yoder, and in the months that followed, the Amish fell to calling him Hoch, honoring his wish to keep at least part of his name.

"Hoch," I begin, "if you have a few minutes, I'd like to talk to you about what happened to you and your family back in 1979."

His eyes widen. "Did you find them?" he asks. "The men responsible?"

"No." I let my eyes slide to his wife. "Is there a place where we can talk?"

"Let's go inside," he tells me. "Hannah will make us some hot cider."

A few minutes later, Hoch and I are seated at opposite sides of a large kitchen table. Behind us, his wife is at the stove, heating cider in a kettle. I detect a hint of kerosene in the air from a space heater, and cinnamon from something recently baked. To my right, a fire blazes in the hearth, chasing the chill from the room. The place smells very much like my childhood home, and fingertips of nostalgia press into me.

"How much do you remember about what happened that night?" I begin.

He blinks rapidly an instant before looking away, telling me that even after all these years, the horror of it haunts him.

"I remember too much. For too many years." He shakes his head. "It was a terrible thing."

"I'm sorry to put you through this again, but I need to know what happened."

His gaze meets mine. "Why now? After all this time?"

"I think it might be related to another case I'm working on."

"You mean the man who was murdered?"

"I can't get into the details with you yet, but yes."

Hannah crosses to the table and sets a wicker tray with three mugs of cider and a plate heaped with oatmeal cookies on the table between us. "Cookies will go nicely with that cider," she says. "They're not too sweet."

Hoch helps himself to a cookie. "She's determined to make me fat."

"The only thing making you fat is your lack of willpower," she replies in a teasing voice.

"Danki." I pick up one of the mugs and sip. The cider is steaming hot and spiced with cinnamon and nutmeg and dances happily on my tongue.

"Hoch," I say, "I know it's difficult, but I need you to take me through what happened."

Hannah starts to leave, but he stops her. "Stay."

She takes the chair next to him and looks down at the dish towel in her hands. Then her eyes find mine. "Chief Burkholder, it's taken him a long time to come to terms."

He sends her a grateful half smile. "You helped."

I sip the cider, giving them a moment, then turn my attention back to Hoch. "You were fourteen years old?"

Taking a deep breath, he nods, and begins to speak. His words are practiced, telling me he's relived this story many times over the years. His voice is monotone, as if eradicating the emotion will somehow protect him from the impact of the words and the pain they conjure. He paints a brutal picture. An Amish boy wakened by a younger sibling in the middle of the night. Downstairs, he finds his parents held hostage in the kitchen by armed gunmen. In the ensuing scuffle, his father is shot and killed. Hoch and his siblings are locked in the basement. Hoch escapes, but the children never make it out of the house. . . .

"I tried to reach them," Hoch says, "but the flames were too hot. There was too much smoke. . . ." His voice trails.

"You were a *kinner.*" *A child.* Hannah lays a comforting hand on his shoulder, then turns her gaze to me. "He was terribly burned."

I don't ask him to elaborate. I read the fire marshal's report. I know that kerosene from the lantern caught fire, and all four of his siblings perished. Their little bodies were recovered the next day, all burned beyond recognition.

The detective with the Holmes County Sheriff's Department believed the perpetrators were local. There were rumors that Willis Hochstetler didn't use a bank and kept a lot of cash at the house. The detective surmised the culprits had heard about it and decided an Amish family would be easy prey. But despite an exhaustive investigation, no arrests were ever made and Wanetta Hochstetler was never found.

Word around town is that Hoch Yoder has suffered with depression and nightmares for years. The shrinks have all sorts of official names for it: survivor's guilt; post-traumatic stress disorder. But the bottom line was that Hoch Yoder blamed himself, and the guilt affected every facet of his life. While most Amish men are married with children by the age of twenty-five, Hoch didn't marry Hannah until just a few years ago, when he was already into his forties.

I look across the table at Hoch. "I understand your *datt* was an excellent furniture maker."

Pleasure flashes in his features, and I know that while the past holds plenty of bad memories, some were good, too. "He made everything we sold in our store."

"Hoch's a furniture maker, too." Hannah motions toward a cabinet set against the wall. "He made that for me a few years ago." She nods with pride. "He won't admit it, but he's as good as his *datt*."

Hoch looks down at the table, where his hands are folded. "He taught me everything I know."

"Did your *datt* make peg dolls?" I ask.

He nods. "When he had time. The small ones. Sometimes he gave them away to the children of customers." He gives me a quizzical look. "I haven't thought of those dolls in years. Why do you ask?"

"Just curious." I hold his gaze. "Did you know Dale Michaels?"

"The man who was murdered?"

I nod. "Have you ever met or spoken to him?"

"No. I mean, I don't think so."

"I don't want you to read anything into what I'm going to ask you next, Hoch, but I need to know where you were the last two nights."

Hannah sets down her mug with a little too much force. "Chief Burkholder, surely you don't think Hoch had anything to do with that awful murder?"

I ignore her, keeping my gaze locked on her husband.

"I was here," he tells me.

"Both nights?"

"That's right."

"All evening?"

"Yes."

"Do you own any firearms?" I ask.

"I have a muzzle-loader that was passed down from *Grossdaddi* Yoder. For hunting." He cocks his head. "Would you like to see it?"

"What about a handgun?"

"No."

I reach into my jacket, tug out my card, and hand it to him. "If you think of anything else, will you get in touch with me?"

He nods. "The men responsible for what happened to my family will be judged not by you or me or even by some *Englischer* court," he tells me. "They will be judged by God and God alone."

"Not if I have anything to say about it." Pushing away from the table, I rise and start toward the door.

CHAPTER 6

They met at The Oak, an out-of-the-way wine bar a few miles out of Dover. The place was windowless and dark with a generous amount of antique brick and rough-hewn barrels for an ambience not quite achieved. It was the kind of place where no one would notice a group of middle-aged, financially comfortable friends getting together for a liquid lunch and some chitchat about old times. But the conversation they were about to have wouldn't be about children or grandchildren, their looming retirement or even the good times they'd once shared. In fact, the man they called Brick was pretty sure if they weren't frightened when they walked in, they would be when they left.

They'd been known as the Goldens back in high school. Thirty-five years ago, they'd been a tight-knit group of hotshots with the world at their feet and a future as bright as the sun. Brick had been the leader of sorts. The bad boy with a reputation he'd done his utmost to live up to. He'd dabbled in drugs and alcohol and gotten into a few fights, but nothing too serious—until college, anyway. When he was seventeen, he took his aunt's car for a joyride and ended up wrecking it. His parents managed to talk her out of pressing charges, but he'd spent an entire summer working a shit job to pay for the damage.

Pudge had been his best friend. The little guy with skinny legs who made up for his lack of stature with a mind that kept him on the honor roll the entirety of high school and earned him a full scholarship to the University of Michigan. Studious and diligent, Pudge had always been the serious one. The one who, back in high school, had been voted most likely to succeed. The one most likely to become President of the United States. Brick always thought he would, too.

Snipe had been the football star, the charmer, the quarterback with the Hollywood good looks who could throw a fifty-yard pass and outrun any cornerback who tried to stop him. He was the athlete who could run a four-minute mile and barely break a sweat. The girls had thrown themselves at him. Rumor had it Snipe took the virginity of more girls than he'd made touchdowns, and that was a lot. But Brick and the rest of them knew about the darker side of the football star's personality. The binge drinking. The marijuana deals and rumors of harder drugs. The girls who'd said no—and whose voices he hadn't heard. He'd gone to Kent State on a football scholarship. Rumor had it, he'd got into a scrape with the law up there. A girl told him no and Snipe hadn't listened. When Brick had asked him about it, Snipe was vague about the details. Somehow, the whole incident had been swept under the rug and the football team went on to win the season.

Jules was the perfect one. She was Farrah Fawcett

and Bo Derek rolled into a perfect ten with a capital *T*. The blond-haired, blue-eyed beauty queen with the face of an angel and a body designed by Satan himself. She'd been a cheerleader, class valedictorian, president of the Girls Athletic Association—and a purported virgin throughout high school. She was the one you fantasized about fucking not only because she was beautiful, but because you knew it would be a wild ride. Back in high school, all the boys had wanted Jules. The girls had wanted to be her. If you were lucky enough to be her friend, everything you did was for Jules, even though she didn't reciprocate in any way. Jules always said no, but every male who met her secretly clung to the desperate hope that sooner or later, she would change her mind.

Brick had known all of them since he was he was thirteen years old and broke Snipe's front tooth in a game of stickball. They'd been best friends ever since. Baseball games. Campouts. Long days at the public pool. He'd laughed with them. Fought with them. Cried with them. He'd had more fun with them than at any other time in his life. He'd been closer to them than to his own brothers and sisters, a closeness he never found again. He'd shared the best days of his life with this group. But not all of those memories were good.

They were older now—strangers, in fact, having gone their separate ways years ago. They rarely saw each other. Rarely spoke. But there was one thing that would always bind them. An inescapable link that would connect them until they died.

He was on his second cognac when Snipe and Jules walked into the bar. At fifty-three, Jules was still a stunner. She was wearing a pale blue suit with pearls at her throat and high-heeled shoes. Her hair was still the same shade of blond. The kind that made your fingers itch to run through it. Beneath that skirt and jacket, he could see her body was still slender and athletic. She still had it and people still noticed, including him.

Snipe, on the other hand, at the age of fifty-four looked as bent and grizzled as the old man they'd once beat down for leering at Jules. He'd heard Snipe had a problem with booze. From the looks of him, the gossip wasn't too far off the mark.

Raising his hand, Brick motioned them over to the table. It was still early, but he was pretty sure he was going to need another drink, so he caught the bartender's eye. Phony smiles and overly cheery greetings were exchanged as his onetime friends settled into the booth, polite strangers bringing with them the redolence of the past—and the knowledge that this was no happy reunion, no matter how hard they tried to pretend.

Across from him, Jules offered a nervous smile. Her lips were still pouty and full and painted an appealing shade of red. Brick knew he'd never rated with her; he'd always been her least favorite, but in those early days, that didn't keep him from fantasizing about her.

Returning her stare, he smiled. "How's it going, Jules?"

"I've been better." She pressed her lips together and looked at Snipe. "Pudge called you, too?"

He nodded. "Talking crazy."

"I can't believe he's dead," she said. "Pudge. Murdered. My God."

Snipe sat in the booth next to Jules, his elbows on the table. He wore a JCPenney shirt with a pair of khakis that were too long and baggy for his frame. "Have either of you been receiving notes?" he asked.

Brick nodded. "First one came two days ago."

Jules looked from man to man. "Me, too. Two of them. Frankly, all of this is scaring the hell out of me."

"Especially since Pudge turned up dead," Snipe put in.

"Maybe we ought to go to the police," Jules suggested.

Brick glared at her. "And tell them what, exactly?"

She looked away and didn't mention it again.

The barkeep came over to their booth and took their orders. Snipe ordered whiskey. No brand. Jules asked for the house cabernet. Brick got a refill of cognac.

When the bartender was out of earshot, Snipe said, "Maybe Pudge wasn't talking so crazy after all."

Brick looked at him. "What's that supposed to mean?"

Snipe stared back, his eyes bloodshot and full of fear. "I saw her, too."

Checking to make sure no one could hear them, Jules leaned forward and addressed Snipe. "What do you mean you saw her?" she whispered. "That's impossible."

"I saw her," Snipe said. "I swear to God. She was at my place. Three days ago."

Jules's pretty blue eyes went from Snipe to Brick as if wishing he'd intervene with some logic. When he didn't, she said, "You couldn't have seen her, Snipe. For God's sake."

"I saw her," he maintained. "Standing in my driveway like she lived there. By the time I got the shotgun, she was gone."

"You never could hold your booze," Brick muttered.

Snipe looked from Brick to Jules, his expression telling them he'd known they wouldn't believe him—but he didn't give a good damn. "I know what I saw. She was there. Left tracks, too. I saw them the next morning when it was light."

"So it was dark," Jules said hopefully.

"Someone might've been there, but it wasn't her," Brick cut in. "Unless you believe in ghosts."

Snipe glared at him. "So if it wasn't her, who's sending the notes? Who murdered Pudge?"

"Not her," Brick snapped.

They fell silent when the bartender returned with their drinks. Snipe reached for his and downed it in two gulps. "I saw her out at the old Hochstetler place, too."

The three of them exchanged meaningful looks.

Jules fingered the stem of her glass nervously. "God, I wish none of that had happened."

"We all wish that," Brick said. "Can't go back. Can't change it."

Snipe leaned forward, his expression intense. "Look, is there some way she survived? That we're wrong about what happened? That she's alive and she's come back for a little payback?"

"Is it?" Jules asked.

Brick sighed. "You didn't see her," he said. "No one did."

Crossing his arms over his chest, Snipe leaned back in the booth. "I know what I saw. And let me tell you something: She saw me, too."

"What are you saying?" Jules asked, looking alarmed.

Snipe tossed her a nasty look. "Connect the dots."

"Stop scaring her," Brick growled.

"Better scared than dead." Glancing over his shoulder, Snipe lowered his head and spoke urgently. "I'm not the only one who saw her. I was down at Ladonna's Diner last Saturday, and I heard Tyler McKay say he saw her, too."

"Tyler McKay is a drunk," Brick said.

"Maybe we're wrong about what happened. Maybe she survived." Jules drank some of the wine, leaving a red imprint of her lower lip. "Maybe she's come back."

"Come back to do what?" Brick asked.

"To get revenge on us for what we did," Snipe said.

"For what *you* did," Brick snapped.

"We were all there." Jules looked down at her glass of wine. "We're all guilty."

Snipe grimaced. "I heard Pudge was gut-shot and strung up in his barn like a side of beef."

"Do the cops have any idea who did it?" Jules asked.

"No one knows anything," Brick said. "We need to make sure it stays that way."

"They'll know about the calls he made to us," Jules pointed out.

"There's no law against old acquaintances calling to catch up on old times." Brick looked from Jules to Snipe, wanting to make sure they understood what he was telling them. Snipe had never been smart, and evidently the years hadn't changed that.

Jules nodded. "Okay."

"All right." Snipe leaned forward. "How do we keep her from coming after us, too?"

"Keep your imagination in check," Brick said dismissively.

The words hung in the air, and for the span of several minutes, they drank in silence. "I know it sounds crazy," Snipe said, "and I'm not saying I believe in ghosts, but I do know what I saw. I think she killed Pudge. And I got a feeling she isn't finished."

Jules pressed her hand against her chest. "Snipe . . . please."

"Lots of people have seen her up to the Hochstetler place," he maintained.

"Those are just . . . silly ghost stories," Jules said.

"Silly until she sinks a knife in your back," Snipe returned evenly.

Brick slapped both palms down on the tabletop so suddenly, Jules jumped. "Ghosts? Really? For God's sake, Snipe, are you hearing yourself?" he asked in exasperation. "No one saw her. She's not alive. And she's sure as hell not back from the dead. You got that?" He divided his attention between Jules and Snipe. "She's dead. She's been dead for thirty-five years. People don't come back from that."

Jules stared down at her wineglass.

Snipe glared at Brick, but he didn't speak.

After a moment, Brick sighed. "Anyone heard from Fat Boy?"

"I called him." Snipe glanced at his watch. "He should have been here."

"Figured he wouldn't show," Jules added.

"Never liked that two-faced, do-gooder punk," Snipe muttered.

Brick picked up his glass and drank, enjoying the heat of the cognac on the back of his throat. "Do either of you know if the cops have any leads?"

Snipe shrugged. "Haven't heard."

"I'll ask around at the gallery," Jules offered.

Brick nodded. "Look, what happened to Pudge

could have been a random thing. A robbery or something. He made all that real estate money back in the '90s."

He could tell by their expressions, neither of them believed it. He wasn't even sure *he* believed it. Still, it was better than the alternative.

Across from him, Snipe finished his whiskey, set the glass down with a little too much force. "It was her." He said the words without looking up. "Or someone else is a dead ringer and knows what went down that night."

"Nobody knows what happened," Jules whispered. "Except us."

"The Amish kid," Brick offered.

"He didn't see our faces." Snipe rubbed the back of his neck.

"What do we do?" Jules's eyes searched theirs. "About the notes?"

"Lock your doors." Having had his fill of ghost stories and nonsense, Brick scooted from the booth. "And hope she can't walk through walls."

He left without finishing his cognac.

CHAPTER 7

John Tomasetti left his office in Richfield at just before 3 P.M. and took Interstate 77 north toward Cleveland. He assured himself he wasn't going to do anything ill-advised. Just a little recon. He liked to know what he was dealing with, after all. A cop could never have too much information, even if he didn't use it.

Regardless of his intentions—or lack thereof—he had to be careful. Three years ago, there had been rumors about John Tomasetti. Ugly rumors that after his wife and children were murdered, he'd gone rogue and taken the law into his own hands. Nothing had ever been proved. Cops made the best criminals, after all. Besides, everyone knew that certain kinds of people tended to have a short shelf life. Just because you had a reason to want someone dead didn't mean you'd done the deed.

But Tomasetti knew that if anything happened to Joey Ferguson in the coming days or weeks or months, he would be scrutinized. He might as well have the word "motive" tattooed on his forehead. He hadn't missed the way people looked at him this morning when he'd walked into the office. Some of his coworkers had gone out of their way to say hello and ask him how he was doing. Others had steered clear, as if maybe they were worried he might prove all those rumors true and snap. None of them had had the guts to ask him how he felt about Ferguson's release.

Tomasetti wasn't too worried about it. He had a better handle on the situation this time around. A more solid grip on himself. He'd had three years to deal with his losses, to climb out of that black abyss of grief, and to extinguish the wildfire of rage that had burned him from the inside out. He'd come to terms with the past and learned to accept the unacceptable. He was fine with a capital *F,* and everyone who mattered knew it. That's what he told himself as he headed north to a city he'd avoided for the better part of three years.

He hit traffic on I-90, and by the time he arrived in Bay Village, an upscale suburb west of Cleveland, a lowering sky spit rain against the windshield. He exited at Clague Street, passed the tennis courts and baseball diamond in Reese Park, and headed west on Lake Road. Flanked on both sides by mature trees, the narrow, two-lane street cut through a fashionable residential area with Lake Erie just a few hundred yards to the north. There were older, well-kept bungalows and ranch homes to his left and pretty side streets lined with blue spruce and maples and Bradford pear trees that would be budding in a few weeks. The lakefront lots to his right were long and narrow, as if the developer had tried to squeeze in as many waterfront properties as possible. Many of the older homes on the lake—even those of historical significance—had been torn down and replaced by extravagant mansions with tennis courts and swimming pools and stunning views of the water.

He'd memorized the street number and slowed upon reaching the two-acre lakefront estate Joey Ferguson had inherited from his parents. Trees obscured the house from full view, but Tomasetti could see that the place was lit up like a football stadium. It looked like Ferguson was celebrating his newfound freedom.

He drove slowly past. Ten yards from the driveway entrance, a heavy wrought-iron security gate and post-mounted card reader warned off interlopers. He continued west on Lake for a hundred yards and then made a left into the parking lot of the Presbyterian Church, turned around, and idled past the estate a second time. From this vantage point, he could see the tennis court through the trees and a dozen or so cars parked in the circular driveway. He knew there were a pool and gazebo at the rear of the estate and a boathouse where Ferguson parked his parents' thirty-four-foot Sea Ray. It was amazing what you could see from the sky without ever leaving the ground.

He had to hand it to the guy; Joey Ferguson knew how to live. He had a reputation for throwing world-class parties, hiring local chefs and bartenders, and shelling out plenty of cash for musicians or comedians. He lived in one of the most exclusive areas of the city, with a wine cellar filled with booze that cost more than Tomasetti earned in a year. Yes, Joey Ferguson lived his life to the fullest. He'd amassed most of his fortune back when he worked for the late Con Vespian. Before his untimely demise, Vespian had had his fingers in all the nasty pies. Extortion. Money laundering. Heroin. He'd been riding high—until the night they hit Tomasetti's family.

He could barely remember the days and weeks that followed, but he knew something terrible had been unleashed inside him. In the end, Vespian paid dearly for his sins. For Tomasetti, the victory had been bittersweet, heavy on the bitter.

The Cuyahoga County prosecutor hadn't taken it sitting down. John Tomasetti might have been one of their own, but that thin blue line went only so far when it came to murder. He'd been put before a grand jury. But the evidence was sketchy and the citizens of Cuyahoga County were sick of the bad guys getting away with murder. They'd handed down a no bill and Tomasetti walked away without so much as a scratch on his record. Chalk up one for the good guys.

Once the media coverage dropped off, Tomasetti quietly resigned his position with the Cleveland Division of Police and, with the help of one of the few friends he had left, landed a job with BCI. In the following months, he worked hard to put that dark chapter of his past behind. But he didn't forget. A man never forgot something like that. The only question that remained now was if he was going to do something about it.

The blare of a horn jerked him back to the present. Not giving himself time to debate, Tomasetti turned into the sleek blacktop driveway, pulled up to the call box, and pressed the button.

"Name?" came a youngish male voice.

"John Tomasetti," he said.

"I don't see you on the invitation list."

"Ferguson will see me."

They made him wait nearly ten minutes. Two

cars crowded against his bumper—a vintage Jaguar and a Viper—the drivers looking put out and anxious to get at all the swag awaiting them inside. Tomasetti was considering turning around and leaving when the gate slid open.

The asphalt curved right, snaking through a forest of tall, winter-dead trees. The Viper swept past, the passenger sticking her hand out the window and flipping him off. Tomasetti caught a glimpse of long blond hair an instant before the sports car skidded around a rococo fountain, swept through a brick archway, and disappeared from view.

He parked behind a black Escalade with darkly tinted glass and got out. He barely noticed the rain as he started toward the tall double doors. He could smell the cold, wet air of the lake now. The earthy scent of rotting foliage and the bark nuggets surrounding the boxwoods and blue point junipers growing on either side of the front door. He'd just stepped onto the Italian tile of the porch when the door opened.

"I've got to hand it to you, Tomasetti. You've got balls showing up unannounced."

"I like to keep things spontaneous."

Joey Ferguson was thinner than he remembered. Tomasetti knew he was forty-six years old, but Ferguson looked closer to fifty.

"What do you want?" Ferguson asked.

"Just a quick chat."

After a too-long hesitation, he opened the door wider and ushered Tomasetti inside. "Is this an official visit?"

"Personal." Tomasetti stepped into a foyer with twenty-foot-high ceilings, a crystal chandelier, and fieldstone floor. A curved mahogany staircase, its far wall adorned with oil paintings framed in gold leaf, beckoned the eyes to a railed balcony. Through a wide doorway, he could see into a living room, where a dozen or so people milled about, martini glasses held in elegant hands, curious eyes cast his way. Beyond, a wall of glass looked out over a brooding Lake Erie.

"Hell of a view," Tomasetti said.

"My lawyer owns it now."

"I guess he earned it." He pretended to enjoy the vista. "I bet Vince Kinnamon is wishing he had as good a lawyer as you did."

Ferguson stiffened at the mention of Kinnamon's name. Word on the street was the men had once been partners. Tomasetti didn't know that to be fact, but judging from the other man's reaction, it was damn close. Ferguson motioned toward the hall. "We can talk in my study."

Tomasetti didn't turn his back to him. Ferguson got the message and started down the hall first. They passed framed photographs of women and children in a sick parody of the all-American family. He was aware of the din of voices behind him. Ferguson walked a few feet ahead, and Tomasetti wondered if he could pull his weapon and shoot Ferguson in the back of the head before someone pulled out their piece and cut him down.

At the end of the hall, Ferguson opened a set of double doors that took them into a paneled study. The scent of woodsmoke and pipe tobacco met Tomasetti when he stepped inside. Mahogany hardwood shelves filled with thousands of books comprised three walls. The fourth offered another stunning view of the lake. A corner hearth crackled merrily, giving the room a warm glow. Despite his hatred for the man, Tomasetti was impressed.

Ferguson seemed completely at ease as he crossed

to a bar, where crystal decanters sat atop gleaming mahogany. "Can I get you anything? Scotch? Or maybe you're a bourbon man?"

Instead of taking one of the two visitor chairs, Tomasetti strode to the window and looked out at the lake, placing himself between Ferguson and the desk. "I don't need anything from you."

Ferguson tossed ice into a tumbler and poured amber liquid from a decanter. "You're not going to do something you'll regret later, are you?"

"I haven't decided."

Ferguson must have seen something in Tomasetti's eyes because suddenly, he didn't look quite so sure of himself. "A hasty decision at this point would be unfortunate for you."

"It would be unfortunate for one of us."

Making a sound of annoyance, Ferguson picked up the tumbler and threw back the alcohol in a single gulp. "So talk. I don't have all night."

"So, how is it that you get the six-thousand-square-foot mansion on the lake," Tomasetti said breezily, "and Vince Kinnamon gets a trial with the possibility of life in prison?"

Ferguson smirked. "Don't you love the criminal justice system?"

Tomasetti was across the room before the other man could set the glass down. Vaguely, he was aware of Ferguson's eyes going wide. He took a step back, opened his mouth as if he couldn't believe Tomasetti was actually going to cross the invisible line that had been drawn. Tomasetti slapped the glass from his hand. The tumbler thudded dully on the floor. He clamped his other hand around Ferguson's throat, digging his fingers into the flesh, and shoved him against the bar.

"You cut a deal, Joey?" Tomasetti ground out. "Is that what you did?"

Ferguson clawed at Tomasetti's hand. "Can't . . . do . . . this," he choked out. "You're . . . cop."

Crushing the other man's throat with his fingers, Tomasetti leaned so close, he could smell the whiskey on his breath, the stink of fear coming off his skin. He could feel Ferguson's pulse raging beneath his fingertips and he marveled at how easy it would be to kill him. He squeezed harder, long-buried rage driving him toward a precipice and inevitable drop.

Tomasetti put his mouth an inch from the other man's ear. "I haven't forgotten what you did."

Ferguson made a strangled sound, his mouth gaping, tongue protruding. His face turned purple. Veins throbbed at his temples. He slapped at Tomasetti, but his blows were ineffective.

All Tomasetti could think was that he wanted him dead. Gone. In hell, where he belonged. It would be so easy to cross that line.

But this wasn't like before. Far from it, because for the first time since the deaths of his wife and children, Tomasetti had something to lose. Thoughts of Kate and the life they'd built flashed in his mind. He knew if he took this any further, he would lose her and destroy everything he'd worked so hard to build.

Ferguson went slack. Tomasetti released him. The other man went to his knees, leaned forward, sucking in great gulps of air. "You son of a bitch," he croaked.

Giving himself a hard mental shake, Tomasetti stepped back. He watched impassively as the other man got to his feet. He saw the imprint of his fingers on his throat, but there was no satisfaction. No sense of justice.

"You fuck." Ferguson's hands fluttered at his throat.

His face was red. He was breathing hard, glaring at Tomasetti, murder in his eyes. "You're a cop. You can't come in here and assault me."

"You're right." Tomasetti let his mouth twist into a smile. "I can't." He started toward the door.

"What's that supposed to mean?" Ferguson snarled.

Tomasetti twisted the knob, let the door roll open. "Enjoy the rest of your party."

CHAPTER 8

By the time I reach the station, the rain is pouring down so hard, I drive past my designated parking spot and have to back up to turn into it. Flipping up the hood of my jacket, I hightail it to the door. The interior is dry and smells of heated air and paper dust laced with nail polish. It's after 5 P.M.; Despite my fatigue, I'd been entertaining thoughts of heading back to the farm, if only for a shower and to check on Tomasetti, but there are a few more things I need to tie up before I can call it a day.

"Hey, Chief." Jodie Metzger, my second-shift dispatcher, is sitting at the phone station, a magazine spread out on the desk in front of her.

"Hi." I stop at her desk and glance down to see her quickly stash the nail polish in a drawer. "I like the blue."

She grins sheepishly as she hands me a stack of messages.

My conversations with Hoch Yoder and the Seymours dog me as I walk to my office and unlock the door. While I have no concrete proof that any of them were involved in the murder of Dale Michaels, I can't discount the connections.

I've barely made it to my desk when my cell phone vibrates. I glance down and see BCI LAB on the display and snatch it up quickly. "Burkholder."

"Hi, Chief. This is Chris Coleman with the lab. I have some preliminary info for you."

"Anything on the blood in the car?"

"We're still processing the car, but we do know the type is O positive. There was quite a bit, actually, so he may have sustained the gunshot wound right before being put into the trunk or maybe even while he was *in* the trunk. DNA is going to take a few days. Sorry for the delay, but things are stacked up here."

"Prints?"

"All over the place. We were able to match Michaels's. We should have the rest tomorrow sometime."

"What about the tire marks?"

"We picked up a successful tread. I scanned them into the computer, and we were able to match it to Michaels's Toyota."

I'd been hoping the tread would implicate an as-of-yet unidentified vehicle, and I try not to be disappointed. "Did you guys look at the wooden doll yet?"

"We did. There's not much there. No prints we could pick up. Blood is the same type as the victim's."

I think about that a moment. "Is there any way to tell if the doll is old or new?"

"I can have one of the other lab guys take a look at the paint. Might be able to give you a ballpark."

"That'd be great."

"Back to the car," she says. "We found yellow nylon fibers on the rear bumper."

"From the rope?"

"We've still got to do the matching, but I'm betting they're one and the same."

"Any idea how the fibers got there?" But my imagination is already running with possibilities, none of them good.

"We inspected the rope and found that it had some recent damage, as if it had been abraded. A few of the nylon strands were sort of scraped off; some were broken. Could have been from the bumper or even the wooden beam in the barn."

Disturbing images flood my mind. "As if someone tied one end of the rope around the victim's neck, looped it around the beam, and tied the other end to the bumper of the vehicle and strung him up."

"I'd say that's a possible scenario." She pauses. "But get this: Remember the tear in the victim's jacket?"

"I do."

"We found fibers from that jacket on the trunk latch."

"So maybe he caught his jacket on the latch?" I ask.

"Jacket is canvas, which is a pretty sturdy fabric," she tells me. "I'd say the jacket caught on that latch while he was being forcefully pulled from the trunk."

"You mean with his own vehicle?"

"I can't say for certain, of course, but that's a possibility."

I think about that a moment and try not to shudder. "Anything else?"

"Saved the best for last, Chief. We found an iPhone registered to Michaels."

My interest surges. Michaels's daughter had told us her father owned a cell phone. Glock and I did a cursory search of the vehicle, but once we discovered the blood in the trunk, I decided it would be best not to risk contaminating possible evidence, so we stopped and turned everything over to BCI.

"Where did you find it?" I ask.

"Trunk. Under the mat. Looks like while he was inside the trunk, he dropped it or was incapacitated and couldn't get back to it."

"Did you get any phone numbers off of it?" I ask.

Paper crackles on the other end. "I put all the names and numbers into a spreadsheet. You want me to e-mail it to you?"

"That'd be great." I give her my e-mail address and disconnect. In the outer office, I hear Jodie talking to someone on the phone, laughing. She's got her radio turned up too loud, but I don't mind. My exhaustion from earlier is gone. I'm energized by the prospect of new information. I launch my e-mail software and a flurry of messages pours into my inbox, the last of which is from the BCI lab with a PDF attachment. I open the document. It's a spreadsheet with names, phone numbers, dates, and a slew of unrelated numbers that are meaningful only to the technician who entered the data. I hit the Print key as I skim the document on my monitor.

There aren't many calls, incoming or outgoing. Apparently, Dale Michaels wasn't much of a talker. In the month leading up to his murder, he received thirty-two calls, most from his daughter, Belinda Harrington, and lasting a few minutes. I skim over several names and numbers I don't recognize, then go to the second page. There are twenty-six outgoing calls, several to his daughter. Local businesses. A car dealership. The farm store. Some of the names I don't recognize.

I go to the final calls Michaels made. One to

Belinda Harrington on the morning of March 6. At 11 P.M. on March 7—which was probably the last day of his life—he made a call to The Raspberry Leaf, which is a local art gallery. A few minutes later, he made a call to Jerrold McCullough, whom I don't know. Shortly thereafter, he made his final call to a name I do recognize. Artie "Blue" Branson is a well-known pastor of a local multidenominational church—and the last man in the county I'd have paired with Dale Michaels.

In his early fifties, Blue spends every Sunday preaching the gospel from his pulpit at the little frame church he built with his own hands. The rest of his time is dedicated to counseling troubled souls—drug addicts, prostitutes, and ex-cons—and providing for people who can't provide for themselves. Known for his trademark black suits and sporting a goatee, Blue looks like a modern-day version of Johnny Cash, but he and his church have done more good for the impoverished than anyone else in the area.

I look at the list, but there's only that one call to Blue. It lasted fourteen minutes. Did the two men know each other? Were they friends? Was Dale part of Blue's congregation? There could be a dozen or more reasons for the call, but the timing of it bothers me, and I'm compelled to take a closer look.

I forward the PDF to Jodie with instructions to run all the names through LEADS to see if any of the callers or recipients have a criminal record or warrants.

On the third page, incoming and outgoing texts are listed in order by date. The BCI technician transferred the actual text into a separate cell, so I'm able to read them. Again, there are several to his daughter. *Dinner @ 7:00 PM Sun. Damn good game! Thanks for all the help. Will call U when I get home. Meet for lunch noonish?* At the bottom of the page, the final text Dale Michaels sent snags my attention. *Meet is on. Will call 2 let you know outcome.* I look at the date column and see that it was sent on March 8 at 12:45 A.M. to Blue Branson.

Who did Dale Michaels meet with that night and why? What does Blue Branson know about it? And why, if he'd received news of Dale's murder, didn't he come forward?

"Only one way to find out," I mutter.

Grabbing my keys off the desk, I start toward the door.

The Crossroads Church is located on an acre or so of what had once been farmland, four miles outside of Painters Mill. Bounded on three sides by plowed fields, the clapboard structure reminds me of the Amish school where I received my early education. I've heard that Blue Branson built the place with his own hands and paid for the materials out of his own pocket. Rumor has it, he worked like a man possessed—going without sleep for days at a time—until the church was complete. Word around town is he's a good public speaker and gives a rousing sermon twice on Sunday and once every Wednesday evening.

I've met Blue a handful of times over the years, mostly at LaDonna's Diner, where I stop in for coffee some mornings or dinner if I'm working nights. Usually we exchange a nod or smile, or maybe we comment on the weather as we pass. Until now, that's been the extent of my contact with the self-made preacher. I have a feeling I'm about to get to know him a lot better.

I park in a gravel lot that's demarked with railroad

ties. There are two other vehicles in the lot: a pickup truck that looks as if it won't be running much longer and a vintage Mustang, which I recognize as Blue's. I get out and start toward the front door. A huge cross constructed of railroad ties stands sentinel in the front yard. In the flower bed at the base, I see the pointy green tips of irises peeking out through a layer of mulch.

Double wooden doors open to a large room with a cathedral ceiling and exposed beams that have been painted white. Mullioned windows usher in a meager amount of natural light. Pews line either side of a wide aisle. Ahead is a raised stage with a podium at its center bearing an inscription: WE DON'T CARE WHERE YOU'VE BEEN; WE JUST CARE ABOUT WHERE YOU'RE GOING. There's no mike, but then I've heard Blue doesn't need one. To the right of the stage, a door stands open. I hear voices from inside and head that way.

I find Blue and another man seated at a rectangular table. Blue's looking down at some type of register that's open in front of him. Dozens of corrugated boxes line the wall to my left, and I see that each is packed with foodstuffs: canned goods, cereal, sugar, flour, packaged pasta, Sam's Club–size jars of peanut butter and coffee.

I tap on the jamb. "Looks like you two are conspiring to feed everyone in the county."

The men look up. I see surprise on their faces when they notice my uniform.

"A lot of hungry families out there, Chief Burkholder." Taking his time, Blue hefts his substantial frame from the chair. He's got a commanding presence and seems to fill up all the space in a room. He stands somewhere around six-four and probably weighs in at about 250. His thick gray hair is combed straight back from an interesting face with a broad forehead and high cheekbones. Deep grooves on either side of his mouth add yet another layer of character to an already compelling persona. His goatee is black and trimmed with razor precision. He's wearing his trademark clothes: Black sport jacket. Crisp white shirt that's open at the collar to reveal a large silver cross on a chain. Dark slacks and oxfords polished to a high sheen.

"It's our aim to feed them until they can feed themselves." He extends his hand to me and we shake. "Welcome to Crossroads."

His grip is firm, but not excessively so, and his eyes are level on mine. "I hear you do good work here at the church," I tell him.

"We do our best."

I nod at the man sitting at the table and then address Blue. "Can I speak with you in private?"

"There are a dozen or so pews out there could use some more breaking in." He looks at the man he's with. "Box up the rest of the canned goods, and I'll help you load them."

Blue ushers me through the door, and we walk into the main room of the church, our shoes echoing against the high ceilings and unadorned walls.

"I understand you built this place yourself," I tell him.

"Never picked up a hammer until I got the calling. Once I did, I couldn't put it down. Didn't have much capital, but we made do. A few volunteers lent a hand. . . ." He shrugs, as if the feat is inconsequential. "Spreading the word of God doesn't require anything fancy. With your being Amish, I'm sure you probably already know that."

"I do."

He motions toward the first pew, and I slide onto the hard surface. "I need to talk to you about Dale Michaels."

His gaze sharpens on mine as he lowers himself to the bench next to me. His eyes are steel gray beneath heavy brows. He's got a kindly, grandfather's face, one that's full of adventure stories and love for his grandchildren. But there's something darker behind those eyes, too. Scars, I think, left by a harsh past.

"I heard." He hangs his head, and his body seems to sag for a moment. "He was a good man. Any idea who did it?"

"Not yet," I tell him. "How well did you know him?"

"He came to services on occasion." He chuckles. "Not often enough to suit me, but that's the way it is sometimes."

"How long have you known him?"

"We went to high school together. Never knew him well, but I do remember him."

I purposefully delay asking him about the call and the text, giving him the chance to bring it up first. "When's the last time you spoke to him?"

"At church probably. A few weeks ago. Just to say hello. See how he was doing. That sort of thing."

"How did he seem? Did he mention any problems he was having?" I ask. "Or any people he was having problems with?"

"He seemed fine. Upbeat. Warm, as always."

I nod. "Do you know who his friends were?"

"He usually came to church alone. I'm not sure about his friends."

"Is there anything else you'd like to tell me, Blue?"

His eyes meet mine. I see something I can't quite read in their depths, and I suspect he's just realized I know about the call. "He called me a couple of days ago. Late. I thought that was a little odd."

"What was the purpose of his call?"

His facial expression doesn't change. He doesn't look upset by the fact that he got caught withholding information from me. "Just to talk. I think maybe he was a little lonely. He's divorced, you know. Children are grown. Not every parent adjusts to those things well."

"Were you surprised to hear from him?"

He nods. "My first thought was that he was sick. Found out he had cancer or something. I asked him about it, but he assured me his health was fine."

"Is there some reason why you didn't bring this to my attention when you found out he'd been murdered?" I ask. "Or maybe when I first arrived?"

"Look, Chief Burkholder, I don't have anything to hide. There wasn't anything unusual or suspicious about the call. Dale just wanted someone to talk to." He sighs again. "We welcome everyone at Crossroads. As you probably know, some members of my congregation have troubled pasts. Honestly, I didn't want my church involved in this murder investigation."

"Who was he meeting with that night?"

He stares at me a moment and then shrugs. "I have no idea what you're talking about."

I pull out my notes and read the text message to him. " 'Meet is on. Will call 2 let you know outcome.' " I make eye contact with Blue. "Dale Michaels sent you that text shortly before he was murdered. In fact, you're probably the last person he communicated with before he was killed. I need to know who he was meeting with and I need to know right now."

"I wish I could help you, Chief. But I don't even recall receiving that text." He pulls out a sleek little smartphone and begins to scroll with his index finger. "To tell you the truth, I'm still learning how to use this thing."

"Mr. Branson, I feel the need to remind you that it's against the law to withhold information from the police in the course of a murder investigation."

"I haven't lied to anyone." He turns the phone so I can see the screen. Sure enough, there's a small icon for unread messages with a small *2* next to it. I watch as he thumbs a button and the text from Dale Michaels appears, along with the date and time.

Blue stares at it, grimacing. "As a pastor, it's disturbing to know he needed me and I wasn't there for him."

"The content of that text makes it seem as if you had previous knowledge of the meeting," I say.

"I can assure you, I didn't."

I wait, saying nothing, reestablishing eye contact, looking for a chink in his righteous armor.

"Look, I'm sorry I didn't mention the call," he says, "but as you must know by now, I've got a past, too, and I'm not exactly proud of it. I didn't want it dredged up and I didn't want to involve the church. You know how folks are around here. They like their gossip, and they've got long memories when it comes to that sort of thing. Some people in this town still look at me like I'm a criminal."

He's right about the gossip. Having been the subject of many a malicious conversation when I was an Amish teen and left the fold, I know how painful it can be. But I'm not sure I believe the slew of explanations he's so diligently thrown out for me, and I don't cut him any slack.

"Are you?" I ask. "A criminal?"

"I did my time. Paid my due to society. And by the grace of God, I turned my life around."

It doesn't elude me that he didn't answer my question. Rising, I extend my hand. "Thanks for your time."

He gets to his feet and we shake. "I'm a firm believer in that everyone gets their due, Chief Burkholder, even if they don't get their day in court."

"It's my job to make sure they get that day in court."

I feel his eyes burning into my back as I make my exit.

CHAPTER 9

Julia "Jules" Rutledge locked the gallery doors at 7 P.M. Usually at the end of the day, she liked to wind down with a glass of chardonnay in her small office at the rear. She should be feeling celebratory this evening, especially since she'd sold the most expensive painting of her career earlier in the day. It was an oil she'd aptly titled *Nochmiddawks,* the *Pennsilfaanisch Deitsch* word for "in the afternoon." She'd completed it last summer and priced it well above market value. It was an Impressionistic style and depicted an Amish girl walking alongside a tree-shrouded dirt road, her feet bare, the strings of her *kapp* dangling down her back. It was one of the few paintings she'd done that she actually loved. One of the few in which she thought she'd captured the magical light of dusk. The softness of the summer air. The thin rise of dust in golden sunlight. And the heart of a girl whose life was straightforward and simple—two elements people seemed to long for these days. Jules certainly did.

The sale was a surprise since business was usually slow this time of year. Things didn't pick up until summer, when tourists from all over the world flocked to Holmes County to ogle the buggies, savor the home-cooked food and locally made cheeses, and take in the beautiful countryside.

Ten years in the making, The Raspberry Leaf Gallery was a dream come true. A dream for which she'd made sacrifices and worked like a madwoman to achieve. It was the place where she was the woman she'd always wanted to be. An artist and lover of beautiful things. The gallery had always been a safe place the past could never sully.

But the past had found her, like a monster capable of gaining entry by seeping under doors and through the cracks of the windowsills, like a vicious winter wind. She'd found the most recent note upon her return from lunch. It was taped on the alley door. A single word scrawled on a sheet of lined notebook paper in blue ink. *Murderer.*

The sight of it had shaken her so thoroughly, she'd nearly closed early and gone home. But Jules knew there was no running from this. No escape. Someone knew she'd been there that night; someone knew what they'd done. And she hadn't the slightest idea what to do about it.

How do you stop a ghost?

For the dozenth time, she thought about Dale, what had happened to him, the atrocity that was his death. And she knew that even locked away in a place where she'd always felt safe, she wasn't. None of them were. She didn't know what to do. Didn't know who to turn to or who to trust. She thought about calling the police, but knew that would raise too many questions. Questions she had absolutely no desire to answer.

On impulse, she picked up the landline and called the only person she could think of. "It's Jules," she said. "I received another note this afternoon. Here, at the gallery. I'm scared."

A too-long silence on the other end. "You're calling from the gallery?"

"Yes."

"The police know about Dale's phone calls to us."

"I know. I'm sorry. I know that's . . . dangerous at this point. I just . . . This is serious. For God's sake, someone *murdered* him. I'm fucking scared."

He sighed. "Do you want to meet? Same place?"

"I thought maybe we could talk. See if we can come up with . . . a plan or something." She looked at the clock on the wall. "I don't know what to do."

"All right. Meet me there in twenty minutes."

"Thanks. See you then." Grabbing her bag off the credenza behind her desk, she took a final look at her gallery and left through the back door.

After leaving the Crossroads Church, I grab a large coffee and a BLT at LaDonna's Diner and head to the station. It's fully dark by the time I arrive, and the drizzle from earlier has turned into a steady downpour. I walk in to find my second-shift dispatcher, Jodie Metzger, standing at the reception station with her hair mussed and my second-shift officer, Chuck "Skid" Skidmore, standing a scant foot away from her, his hands shoved deep in the pockets of his uniform trousers. I can tell by the way they're looking at me that I'm the last person they expected to walk in on them, and I think, *Uh-oh.*

"You two look busy," I say by way of greeting.

Surprisingly, it's Skid—who doesn't have a sensitive bone in his body—who blushes. Not because I walked in on them during a compromising moment, but because I'm his direct supervisor and I'm pretty sure I just caught them locking lips on the job.

"Hey, Chief." Jodie tugs down her tunic and taps on the keyboard of her computer with a freshly painted nail, pretending to be embroiled in the screen in front of her. "You put in a long day."

"Probably going to get longer," I tell her. "Anything come back on those names?"

"Nothing on Julia Rutledge or Jerrold Mc-Cullough," she tells me. "Running Blue Branson now."

"Thanks." I look at Skid, who glances away guiltily. "Call Pickles and tell him I need to see him ASAP, will you?"

"Happy to, Chief."

I unlock my office and head directly to my desk. Despite the fact that I haven't eaten all day, it's not the BLT—or even the case—I'm thinking about as I unwrap the sandwich and pop the lid off the coffee. Usually Tomasetti and I touch base at least once during the day, no matter how busy we are, but he hasn't called. Somehow I made it through the day without calling him, and as much as I don't want to admit it, I'm starting to worry.

I don't let myself think about any of that as I pick up the phone and dial.

He answers on the second ring. "I was wondering when you were going to call," he begins.

"I was hoping you'd check in."

"I was going to."

Since I'm not sure I believe that, I don't respond. "Are you home?"

"Not yet." He doesn't elaborate.

Because we've arrived at an impasse of sorts, I

mentally shift gears and spend a few minutes giving him the rundown on the Michaels case. But I sense neither of us is fully focused on the business at hand. There's another presence on the line with us, and it has nothing to do with my unsolved homicide.

"I'm probably going to be late," I tell him.

"That's okay," he says easily. "I'm running behind here, too."

"You're still at the office?"

I wait a beat, but he doesn't respond. I sigh, not sure if I'm annoyed with him because he's being evasive—or myself for pressing him when I know he doesn't want to be pressed. "Tomasetti, I'm trying to give you space."

"You know I appreciate that, Kate. But no need to worry. I'm fine."

"You'd tell me if you weren't?"

"Look, I don't like it that Ferguson got off. I don't like it that he's out. That he got away with what he did. But I'm dealing with it. I'm not going to do anything stupid."

"You're not trying to tell me to stop worrying about you, are you?"

"Something like that." But there's a smile in his voice.

I pause, trying to get my words right, fumbling a bit. "Just so you know . . . Tomasetti, I've got your back. You can count on me. You don't have to go through this alone."

"I know. And I know you're worried about me. But you're going to have to trust me."

The words echo for a beat too long before I say, "I'll see you tonight."

He hangs up without responding.

* * *

I've just booted up my computer when my most senior officer, Roland "Pickles" Shumaker, peeks his head into my office. "You wanted to see me?" he asks.

At the age of seventy-six, Pickles has been a member of the Painters Mill PD for over fifty years. He's my only auxiliary officer and puts in about ten hours a week, usually at the school crosswalk. During the 1980s he worked undercover narcotics and took down one of the largest drug rings in the state. His glory days ended a few years ago when, during a call for a domestic dispute, he was attacked by an aggressive rooster. Pickles shot and killed the chicken, which happened to be a prized animal owned by a woman who dabbled in local politics. The town council got involved and Pickles nearly lost his job. I'm well aware that a police chief must choose his or her battles wisely. But I couldn't see throwing away fifty years of service over a dead chicken, so I went to bat for him and, by a narrow margin, saved his job. The move cost me politically, and I fell out of favor with some of the town council members, a few of whom are still pressuring me to retire Pickles. So far, I've been successful in holding them off and will continue to do so as long as I'm chief or until Pickles voluntarily decides he's ready to throw in the towel.

He's slowed down the last couple of years, but he never misses a day of work, he's never late, and more important, he's still an effective cop. He's a fixture in this town—a favorite of many citizens, including me—and stands in testament that age doesn't define the person or what they can accomplish.

"You were around when the Hochstetler crime happened, weren't you?" I begin.

He shuffles into my office and lowers himself into the chair adjacent my desk, bringing a wave of

English Leather aftershave with him. "First major crime of my career, and let me tell you something, it gave me nightmares."

I tell him about the Amish peg doll found in Dale Michaels's mouth. "We're not making that bit of information pubic, but the doll was inscribed with the Hochstetler name. I'm wondering if you remember any kind of connection between Dale Michaels and the Hochstetlers."

"Well, my memory isn't what it used to be, but I sure don't recall Michaels's name coming up in the course of the Hochstetler case. Michaels was probably just a kid back then."

I recap everything I know about the case so far, including the final calls Michaels made before his murder. And the text to Blue Branson. "Do you know Blue?" I ask.

"Thirty-five years ago, I had more run-ins with Branson than my own wife." Pickles's brows knit. "He was quite a troublemaker in his youth."

I tell him about my earlier conversation with Blue. "Blue told me Dale Michaels attended services at his church sometimes. Evidently, he hadn't yet read the text about Dale Michaels's mysterious meeting."

"That's interesting," Pickles says. "Because now that you mention it, I remember Blue Branson and Dale Michaels running around together as teenagers. Michaels was a good kid. Kept his nose clean. Blue, not so much."

"That *is* interesting." I wonder why Blue would lie about something so seemingly benign. "What kind of trouble did Blue get into?"

"I arrested him for felony assault back in the early '80s. He was out of high school by then. Got a conviction for it, too."

"So our righteous pastor has a checkered past."

"I'll say. Night I busted him . . . it was a bar fight. Saturday-night crowd. Rowdy place called Suzy's Lounge that burned down a few years back. I was off duty, having a drink, and I saw Blue coldcock a guy with a set of brass knuckles." Setting his elbows on his knees, Pickles leans closer to my desk, his eyes level on mine. "One punch, and that guy was in a coma for a week, lost his front teeth, and let me tell you, he wasn't the same when he woke up. All over a ten-dollar game of pool."

"Sounds like Blue has a temper."

"Or a mean streak that runs right up his self-righteous back." His eyes hold mine. "You think he had something to do with Michaels's death?"

"I don't know," I tell him.

"Well, once upon a time, they ran in the same circles. If they'd had some kind of falling out"—he shrugs—"might be worth looking into."

We fall silent and for a moment the only sound comes from the rain smacking against the window and the ringing of the switchboard in the reception area.

I turn to my computer and pull up the spreadsheet from the BCI technician. "I'm working through Michaels's phone records. Right before calling Blue Branson, he made a call to Jerrold McCullough. Another one to The Raspberry Leaf, a gallery owned by Julia Rutledge."

Pickles sits up straighter. "I think McCullough ran with them, too. He was a big-shot high school football star. I remember him because he got aggressive with a girl once and she called the law. No one pressed charges and everything sort of got swept under the rug. But I always had my doubts about that guy."

"Chief?" Skid taps on the doorjamb and enters my office. Nodding at Pickles, he passes a sheet of paper to me. "This just came in on Blue Branson."

Taking the paper, I scan the list and read it aloud. "Arrested in 1978 for possession of a controlled substance. No conviction. Two years later, he was convicted of felony assault and did four months in Mansfield. Nothing after that."

"He's kept his nose clean since he found God and turned his life around," Pickles says dryly. "But thirty-five years ago, he was a scary fuckin' guy."

I consider everything I know about Blue Branson and the stark contrasts between the man he is now and the man who chalked up an arrest record—and I can't quite reconcile the two. "Do you think Blue's church is some kind of cover for something else?"

"Oh, no." Pickles gives a short laugh. "I think that son of a bitch got saved, all right. But all the praying in the world can't change who you are, and it doesn't erase the things you did in your past. I think Old Blue's trying hard to save his own soul. And I think he's probably got a ways to go before he gets the job done."

Fifteen minutes later, Skid and I are in my Explorer heading south on a gravel track that runs parallel with Painters Creek. The ditches on both sides of the road are filled to the brim with runoff from the rain. The gravel beneath the tires feels spongy and I can hear the mud and stones pinging against the wheel wells. We cross a small bridge and even in the darkness, I can see that the creek is swollen to twice its normal size. If the rain doesn't let up soon, we're going to be dealing with serious flooding issues.

I park next to a brown Riviera, circa 1975, and shut

down the engine. Through the trees, I see the yellow glow of lights and the silhouette of a modest frame house.

"So Michaels called McCullough a few hours before he was murdered?" Skid asks.

I'd briefed him on the case on the drive over. "Pickles says they knew each other when they were young. I thought it was worth a visit."

We get out of the Explorer. The woods around us are extremely dark, so I grab my Maglite and aim it toward the house. The cone of light illuminates a crude path through the trees. Gravel, clumps of concrete, and pieces of plywood are tossed about haphazardly, forming just enough of a walkway to keep our shoes from being swallowed by mud.

The drizzle is cold against my face and hands as I start down the path. It winds through mature trees and eventually takes us to the front porch, which is lighted with a bare yellow bulb. I open a storm door and knock. While we wait, I discern the roar of rushing water from Painters Creek behind the house. I wonder how far the house is from the water.

The door swings open and I find myself looking at a short gray-haired man with a snarlish mouth and wire-rimmed glasses, the lenses of which are smeared with fingerprints.

"Jerrold McCullough?" I ask.

"You're looking at him." I hear a hint of the Kentucky hills in his voice. He looks past me at Skid, but he doesn't smile and makes no move to let us in. "If you're here to evacuate me, I'm not leaving, so you might as well just turn around and go." He jabs his thumb in the general direction of the road. "That creek back there hasn't flooded in thirty years, and it's not going to flood now."

"We're not here about the flooding, Mr. McCullough," I assure him. "We'd like to come in and ask you a few questions about Dale Michaels."

"Dale, huh?" He grimaces. "I heard about the murder. Hell of a thing." But he makes no move to invite us inside and I find myself hoping it doesn't start raining harder. Talking to McCullough is going to be unpleasant enough without doing it with wet hair and cold rain pouring down my neck.

"Do you mind if we come inside, sir?" I ask.

He's staring at me as if he's afraid we're going to force our way in and cart him off against his will. But after a moment he steps back and opens the door. "Might as well. Come on."

We enter a living room that's lit by a single lamp and the glowing screen of an old-fashioned tube television set. I get the sense of a cramped, claustrophobic room. It doesn't take me long to realize McCullough is a hoarder. The room is jam-packed with every type of household item you can think of. Piles of clothing, shoes, and newspapers are scattered everywhere. A small plastic doghouse is shoved against the wall. Magazines spill from cardboard boxes with busted sides. The smell is worse than the mess, an unpleasant combination of a recently microwaved TV dinner, moldy towels, and a bathroom that hasn't been cleaned in a very long time.

I glance over at Skid. He's not exactly a neatnik, but he's looking around the place as if he's afraid of picking up some contagion. We're standing in the entryway and there's barely enough room for the three of us to face each other and speak from a comfortable distance. McCullough doesn't seem to notice.

"You get the person who did it?" he asks.

"Not yet," I tell him. "But we are following up on some pretty solid leads."

He licks his lips, his eyes flicking to Skid and then back to me. "What kind of leads?"

I give him a pointed look. "Were you and Dale friends?"

"I knew him. A long time ago. You know, high school." He gestures with the final word and I notice his right hand is missing at the wrist. The flesh is puckered with layers of scar tissue. He doesn't appear to be self-conscious about it and makes no effort to conceal it.

"When's the last time you talked to him?" I ask.

Same as Blue Branson, McCullough walks right into the trap. "It's been a while." He shrugs. "Seen him around town a few times."

"Are you sure?"

"Well, I saw him at the grocery store. Gas station a couple weeks ago."

"Mr. McCullough, Dale Michaels's cell phone records show that the two of you had a conversation the day before he was murdered."

His eyes widen behind the lenses of his glasses. For a moment he looks flustered. "Oh. That." His laugh is forced. "Nearly forgot."

"Why did he call you?" I ask.

He blinks at me, his eyes darting, and it strikes me that Jerrold McCullough isn't nearly as good a liar as Blue Branson. But why would he lie about his relationship with Dale Michaels? "Mr. McCullough, if you could just answer the question, I'd appreciate it."

"He called me just to see how I was doing. That's all. Just to say hello. You know."

"Is that all?"

"Yep. That's it."

"Did he happen to mention a meeting or say he was meeting someone later?"

"No, he didn't say anything about a meeting."

I spend fifteen minutes going through the same questions I posed to Blue Branson. McCullough seems to have settled into the idea of the police showing up at his door. He keeps his cool and his answers are consistent. Still, in those first few minutes, he'd seemed shaken and uncertain.

"Did Dale have any enemies that you know of?" I ask. "Anyone who didn't like him or might've been holding a grudge?"

"I don't know. He was a nice guy. I can't imagine anyone hating him enough to do him harm." He shrugs. "Everyone liked Dale. He was a family man. A dad and a grandpa. Worked hard his whole life." His eyes meet mine, and for the first time, I get the sense his answer isn't rehearsed. "He shouldn't have met that kind of end. He didn't deserve what happened to him."

"How well do you know Blue Branson?"

"Pastor Branson?" His hesitation is so subtle, I might have missed it if I hadn't been anticipating it. He shakes his head and I notice him rubbing the stump of his right wrist. I wonder if it's a nervous habit. I wonder what he has to be nervous about. "I know who he is, what with the church and all."

"Are you friends?"

"No, but I knew him back in high school."

"Were Dale and Blue friends?"

"I'm not sure. I haven't seen either of them in years."

"Is there anything else you can tell me that might help us find the person who did this?" I ask.

For an instant, his eyes search mine. Then he looks away. "That's all I know."

I hand him my card. "If you think of anything else, call me." I catch his gaze again and hold it. "Day or night."

"All right."

Midway to the Explorer, Skid says, "That son of a bitch is a terrible liar."

"I got the same impression." I reach the vehicle and look at him across the hood, pleased I'm not the only one who noticed. "The question is, what is he lying about and why?"

"Gotta be hiding something."

"Or he's guilty of something."

"You think he's involved in the murder? Hired it out, maybe?"

"If he did, we don't have a motive. And it sure doesn't explain the Amish peg doll." I think about that a moment. "But he's hiding something." I unlock the door and slide inside.

Skid does the same and I look at him across the seat. "You have time for one more stop?"

"Sure."

I put the Explorer in gear. "Maybe Julia Rutledge can shed some light."

CHAPTER 10

Julia Rutledge lives in a stately home surrounded by mature trees in an established neighborhood of Painters Mill. I pull into the driveway and park behind a green Jaguar XJ6.

"Nice wheels," Skid says as I shut down the engine.

"A little above your pay grade," I say. "So is she."

"A guy can hope."

"Are you referring to the car or the woman?"

At his grin, I get out and slam the door. We walk in silence to the well-lit front porch, where baskets of pansies and asparagus ferns hang from freshly painted eaves. It's raining again, but I can hear the television inside. I knock and a moment later a female voice comes at me through the door. "Can I help you?"

"I'm Chief of Police Kate Burkholder," I say loud enough to be heard through the door. "I'd like to talk to you for a few minutes, Ms. Rutledge."

"Would you mind showing me your ID?"

"No problem." Surprised by her vigilance, I glance at Skid as I reach for my badge. He looks back at me and shrugs. I hold my ID a foot or so from the peephole. A moment later the bolt lock snaps open. I hear the security chain disengage. The door swings open and I find myself looking at a striking woman with wavy blond hair that falls well past her shoulders and perfectly arched brows that frame eyes the color of lake ice. At fifty-three years of age, Julia Rutledge is attractive with a slender, athletic build and cheekbones any runway model would pay a year's salary to possess. She's wearing a pale blue linen blouse with black slacks. Bloodred toenails peek out of embroidered espadrilles.

"Julia Rutledge?" I show her my badge again.

Taking her time, she gives it another once-over. "Sorry about that. A single woman can't be too careful these days." She has the deep and melodic voice of Lauren Bacall, but with a touch of the South. Her gaze sweeps to Skid and her mouth curves. "Hello."

Skid touches his hat. "Ma'am."

"This is Officer Skidmore," I tell her. "May we come inside? We'd like to ask you some questions."

"Please do. It's awful out there." She steps back and opens the door wider. "Weatherman says there's more on the way."

Skid and I step into a large, neat living room with gleaming hardwood floors covered with an Amishmade braided rug. An oil painting depicting an Amish woman standing in the middle of a wheat field, a woven basket in hand and a dog at her side is displayed on the wall next to the fireplace. The air smells of cigarette smoke that's not quite masked by the otherwise-pleasant scent of vanilla.

"You have a beautiful home," I tell her.

"Thank you."

I motion at the painting. "Are you the artist?"

She smiles at the painting as if it's a cherished old friend. "A doctor up in Wooster asked me to paint that one for him." She chuckles. "When I finished, I couldn't part with it."

"I hope he understood."

"He didn't." But she waves it off. "Such is the life of an artist."

"Mrs. Rutledge—"

"Call me Jules, please."

"Jules," I repeat. "I don't know if you're aware, but a Painters Mill man by the name of Dale Michaels was murdered a couple of days ago."

"I heard about it at the gallery today. Just . . . awful."

Though she doesn't actually move, she seems to curl in on herself. Then without a word, she crosses to the nearest end table and snags a pack of cigarettes. I watch as she taps one from the pack and lights up. That's when I notice the Beretta on the lower shelf of the end table, within easy reach from the sofa. . . .

I wait, wondering if she'll mention the call he made to her the night he was killed.

"I'd been talking to him about a painting he wanted to buy," she tells me. "He told me he'd walked by my gallery one evening after hours and saw it in the window."

"When was that?"

"I think it was the day before he was killed," she tells me.

"Were you and Dale friends?"

She shakes her head. "I knew him in high school, but then everyone knew everyone in high school back then. Until that night, I hadn't spoken to him in years."

"Do you always take late-night calls from people you don't know?"

Her eyes sharpen on mine. "That particular call came in on the gallery number. I had forwarded calls to my cell and just happened to pick up."

I nod. "Did you talk about anything besides the painting?"

"I don't think so. He mainly wanted to know if it was for sale and how much I wanted for it."

"Do you know Blue Branson?" I ask.

"I see him around town on occasion." She considers me a moment. "We went to high school together."

"What about Jerrold McCullough?"

"What about him?"

"You went to school with all three of those men, didn't you?"

"Painters Mill is a small town, Chief Burkholder. If you have a point, I'd appreciate it if you'd make it."

"Did you keep in touch with any of them after high school?"

"No."

I nod. "Is there anything else you can tell me that might help us figure out who killed Dale Michaels?"

"If I think of something, I promise I'll let you know."

I hold her gaze for a moment. She doesn't look away. She's got pretty eyes, I think. But there's something in their depths I can't quite put my finger on. Secrets? Fear?

I motion toward the pistol on the lower shelf of the coffee table. "Any particular reason you keep that so handy?"

"I'm not breaking the law, am I?"

"No," I tell her. "I'm just curious."

"With news of this murder . . . I was feeling uneasy, I guess."

I nod. "Thank you for your time, Ms. Rutledge."

I reach for the knob and open the door. Skid and I step onto the front porch. Jules Rutledge follows as far as the doorway. "I hope you find the killer."

"I'll do my best," I assure her.

She closes the door. I hear the bolt lock and the security chain being engaged and look at Skid. "She seem kind of nervous about something to you?"

He nods. "Definitely uptight about security."

"She doesn't look like the type to keep a pistol handy while she's watching TV." I start down the steps.

"You think she's afraid because of the murder?" he asks.

"Or else she's expecting trouble."

It's past nine thirty, and I'm in the process of packing the file and my computer into my laptop case when a knock sounds at my door. I glance up to see Town Councilman Norm Johnston standing in the doorway, looking like he'd been physically dragged into my lair and I'm about to jab my spider fangs into his heart and suck out all his blood.

He's not one of my favorite people, and the sentiment runs both ways, I'm sure. Shortly after I became chief, I busted him for a DUI, dashing his mayoral aspirations and setting the tone for an adversarial relationship that's lasted almost four years now. The rift deepened during the Slaughterhouse Killer investigation when his daughter was murdered. I was the primary investigator, and like so many family members of victims, he blamed me.

"Hi, Norm." I set down my laptop case. "Come in. What can I do for you?"

Norm is never comfortable around me. I know it's because he doesn't like me, but his job requires him to set his personal feelings aside. Tonight, I get the sense there's another reason for his discomfort.

"I need to talk to you." He enters my office and closes the door behind him. "Confidentially."

I wonder if he's going to cut my budget again despite the fact that it's barely enough to keep my small department afloat. I mentally shore myself up, formulating my arguments as he settles into the visitor chair across from my desk.

"I think someone's stalking me," he begins.

It was the last thing I expected him to say. I try not to show my surprise. "Who?"

He glances over his shoulder at the door, as if expecting someone to come through it and catch him in here with me, and I realize he's not merely upset; he's frightened. "I'm not sure, but in light of this recent murder, I thought I should let you know."

I may not like Norm, but I've never known him to be an alarmist. I know he wouldn't be here talking to me about this if it wasn't serious. As a cop, I've learned to take any threat seriously.

I pull out a yellow legal pad. "Tell me what's going on. From the beginning."

He reaches into an inside pocket of his jacket and retrieves several folded sheets of what looks like lined notebook paper. "I found the first one taped to my car window. Three days ago."

I open my drawer and pull out a single latex glove, then work my right hand into it. I take the papers, lay them on my desktop, and unfold them. I see cursive scrawl in blue ink. *You knew.* Nothing else. Puzzled, I go to the second page.

You looked the other way. I go to the final page. *You're next.*

"Kind of cryptic," I say.

"Not to mention threatening," he says.

"Do you have any idea why someone would send them to you? Or what the notes refer to?"

"Some nutcase." He shrugs. "Maybe some council business I was involved with? A decision I made someone didn't agree with. Believe me, it happens."

I nod, but sense I'm not getting the whole story. "You said this was taped on your windshield and yet it doesn't look as if it's been wet."

"My car was parked in the garage."

"So whoever left this entered your home without permission?"

"That's correct."

"That's trespassing." I think about that a moment. "Any idea how they got in?"

"There's a dog door that goes into the backyard. Probably came in at night."

Turning, I pull an evidence bag from a drawer in my credenza. I slide the notes into it and then seal it. "I'll send these to the lab to see if they can pick up some latents."

"I appreciate that."

"You know, Norm, most stalking victims know their stalkers or they've had some contact with them at some point." I make the statement without looking at him.

"Well, I have no idea who this is."

"Are you sure?"

"Of course I'm sure."

"Do you think it's from a male or female?"

He hesitates. "I don't know."

I tap the evidence bag with my finger. "Are these the only notes you've received?"

"Yes."

"Has anything else unusual happened? At home? At your office? Or when you've been out and about?"

"No."

"What about social media? Facebook or Twitter? Or e-mail? Any strange messages? Or phone calls?"

"No. Nothing like that."

"Anything taken from your garage?"

"I checked. No." Pulling a kerchief from the pocket of his jacket, he blots at the sheen of sweat on his forehead. "This person came into my home, Chief Burkholder. In light of this recent and as-of-yet-unsolved murder, I felt as if I was being threatened."

I pick up the evidence bag and recite the notes aloud from memory. " 'You knew.' 'You looked the other way.' 'You're next.' " I furrow my brow. "They seem to be referring to a specific incident," I say. "You're sure you don't have any idea what this stalker is referring to? Maybe he or she feels you've somehow wronged them? Maybe you had an argument or altercation that you didn't think was important or significant at the time?"

"I have no idea what they could be referring to."

"Norm, I know it's frightening when something like this happens, and I know it can be disruptive to your life, but we don't know that it's related in any way to the murder."

"I didn't say it was," he says defensively. "I said in light of the unsolved murder, I felt I should let you know." He lowers his voice. "I'd appreciate some protection, Chief Burkholder. I want a police car at my house. At least at night."

I pause to choose my words with care, because I know he's not going to respond well to what I'm about to tell him. "Norm, I'm not discounting the threat posed to you by these notes. I think we should take this very seriously. But as town councilman, you know I don't have the manpower to assign an officer to you, especially with this homicide on my hands."

"I'm part of the governing body of this town. It's your responsibility as chief to keep me and the rest of the citizens of Painters Mill safe from harm."

"I can step up patrols—"

"I'll go over your head. I'll—"

I cut him off. "Norm, all you can do at this point is be vigilant about your personal safety. Keep your doors and windows locked. Keep your alarm system engaged. Be aware of your surroundings—"

"I don't have an alarm system," he snaps.

"Well, then get one installed," I say firmly. "If you're frightened, I suggest you hire private security."

"Private security? Are you kidding?" He rises so abruptly, the chair back strikes the wall and chips the paint. "I knew better than to come in here and ask for anything from you."

I rise as well. "Norm, calm down."

"Don't tell me to calm down!"

"I'm doing the best I can."

"Not good enough. As usual." He jabs his finger at me. He's so angry, his hand is shaking. "If anything happens to me, Burkholder, it's on your fucking back." He jabs again. "*Yours!*"

"Norm—"

"Go to hell."

He turns away, stalks to the door, and pushes it open with both hands. It swings wide and bangs against the wall hard enough to rattle the framed map of Holmes County.

CHAPTER 11

I'm usually pretty good at letting things roll off my back, especially when it comes to my job. A police chief invariably encounters a high level of conflict in the course of his or her duties—and a fair share of criticism. I learned a long time ago that you can't please everyone. When you're chief and you have an entire town counting on you to protect and serve, it's foolish to try.

Still, my conversation with Norm Johnston troubles me as I head toward the farm. It's not until I reach the county road that I realize it has more to do with his overreaction to the situation than his actual overt hostility. Worse, I can't shake the feeling that he's not telling me something. But what?

It's after ten when I arrive at the farm. I'm preoccupied with the case, the conversations and suppositions of the day. Thoughts of work evaporate when I spot Tomasetti's Tahoe parked in its usual spot. Anticipation swells in my chest. It seems like days since I last saw him. In reality it's been less than twenty-four hours, but suddenly I can't wait to see him. I park beside his vehicle, shut down the engine, and get out. It's raining again, so I grab my umbrella from the backseat and hightail it to the house.

I open the door and step into the brightly lit kitchen. Tomasetti is sitting at the table, his laptop open in front of him. The room smells of spaghetti and the bowl of potpourri I keep on the console table in the hall.

He looks up from his computer as I shake the rain from my coat. "Hey," he says, rising.

"Hi." I hang my coat on the hook, but not before I notice the tumbler of whiskey on the table beside his laptop.

He goes to the cupboard and pulls out the bottle of cabernet we opened the day before. He pours a generous amount into a glass and hands it to me. "You look tired," he says.

I take the drink. "You're a sight for sore eyes, Tomasetti."

"In that case, first things first." Taking the glass from me, he sets it on the counter, then raises his hands to either side of my face and kisses me.

Even after living with him for almost six months, this kind of intimacy still feels foreign and new. It moves me and I lean into him, my legs seeming to melt beneath me.

After a moment, he pulls back and hands me the wine. "Hungry?"

"Starved."

He turns to the stove and removes the lid from a small saucepan. "Leftovers okay?"

"You're not trying to make up for leaving without a word this morning and avoiding me all day, are you?" I ask.

He looks at me over his shoulder and grins. "I thought I'd try."

"It's working." I walk to the stove and look into the saucepan to see that he kept spaghetti warm for me. "Smells great."

"Have a seat."

I take my glass to the table and sit across from where he was sitting and sip the wine. It's dark and rich and leaves my tongue with a happy aftertaste.

Tomasetti places a plate of spaghetti, French bread, and a small salad in front of me. "So how's the case going?" he asks as he takes the chair across from me.

I give him the highlights, ending with a recap of my conversation with Blue Branson.

"You think he's involved with the murder?" he asks.

"I don't think so, but he's hiding something."

"Protecting someone?"

"Maybe," I tell him.

He turns his attention to his laptop. I take the opportunity to wolf down the food. "You wouldn't think less of me if I licked my plate, would you?" I ask.

"No." He doesn't look up from the laptop, but his mouth twitches. "But I might get turned on."

Smiling, I rise and take my plate to the sink. "What did you do today?"

"I went to Joey Ferguson's house up in Bay Village."

I nearly drop the dish in the sink, and I turn to face him. "Are you kidding me?"

He types something on the keypad. "Nope."

"Tomasetti, I don't have to tell you that was a bad idea, do I?"

He says nothing.

But I'm not ready to let it go. "You can't have any contact with Ferguson."

His sigh holds a hint of annoyance that doesn't come through in his voice. "I'm aware."

"But you did it anyway?" My temper begins to spiral, an uncomfortable pressure in my chest that climbs up my throat like some clawed animal. I know at least part of what I'm feeling is because I'm sleep deprived and frustrated with my case. But the bigger part of me is angry because this man I love doesn't seem to grasp the fact that his actions no longer affect just him.

Taking a deep breath, I reel myself in, focus on keeping my voice level. "Tomasetti, I know this thing with Ferguson is difficult. And I know you've suffered. I get that. But you have to let this go."

"In a perfect world—" He cuts off the rest of the statement, but the words hover between us, so tangible I could reach out and snatch them from the air with my fist.

In a perfect world, my wife and children would still be alive.

While I hate it that he was hurt so horribly, that three people he loved were stolen from him by violence, another part of me wants to remind him that he has me now. *My* heart. *My* love. And that if his family were here now, he and I would never have met.

After setting the plate in the sink, I go back to the table and sit across from him. "Tomasetti, if something happens to Ferguson—"

"If anything happens to Ferguson, it'll be his own doing."

"What's that supposed to mean?" I stare at him, refusing to acknowledge the pinpricks of unease on the back of my neck.

"It doesn't mean anything." He picks up the tumbler of whiskey sitting beside his laptop and sips. "I'm not going to do anything, so you can stop worrying. All right?"

"You're going to his house. You're talking to him. What do you call that?"

He doesn't look up from his laptop. I see his eyes moving and I realize he's reading, and that only pisses me off more. "I mean it, Tomasetti. This isn't just about you anymore. The things you do affect me, too. It's incredibly selfish of you not to consider that."

He closes the laptop and looks at me. "Joey Ferguson is a piece of shit. He's a murderer and a rapist and he's going to continue fucking up people's lives until someone stops him."

"It doesn't have to be you."

"Who else is there, Kate? The Cleveland PD? BCI? A jury of his peers? Here's a newsflash for you: They didn't get the job done. The law failed me. It failed my family. *My children.*" Up until this point, he hasn't raised his voice, but that final word is fraught with emotion, and I know that's the heart of the matter here. That he lost his children. That they'd suffered before they died, and he hadn't been there to protect them. . . .

"Your kids loved you," I tell him. "They wouldn't want you to sacrifice yourself in the name of revenge."

"You don't know anything about them."

"For God's sake, Tomasetti, you know better than anyone that sometimes terrible things happen to good people. The people we love get hurt. Sometimes we lose them."

"Not like that!" His shout is so abrupt, so loud and filled with emotion that I jump. "They didn't deserve what he did to them. He didn't just murder them, Kate. He tortured them. He raped and terrorized them. And then he burned them alive. I couldn't even bury them, because there was nothing left."

"I know what they did!" I shout back. "And yes, it was the most horrible thing imaginable. But you survived—"

"Did I, Kate? Did I really?"

"Yes! Damn it, you're just getting your life back on track. Tomasetti, you've got a lot to lose. *We've* got a lot to lose if you do something stupid."

"Should I just let it go, Kate? Let that son of a bitch go on with his perfectly happy life while those caskets full of bone and ash rot in the ground?"

"Don't go there. Don't do this to yourself."

He rises and approaches me. His nostrils are flared, teeth clenched. When he speaks, his voice is deadly and soft. "Do you know what he was doing earlier this evening?"

"It doesn't matter. *He* doesn't—"

"It matters, damn it. It matters to *me*." His hand shakes when he scrubs it over his jaw. "Ferguson threw a party at his mansion on the lake. To celebrate his freedom, evidently. He hired a band and caterers and invited all of his sleazy friends." I see him pulling himself back, but he's having a difficult time of it because some vital part of him has already gone over the brink. "There were kids there," he grinds out. "I saw them. Playing in the yard. Oblivious to the fact that their host is a monster."

"I know. And I'm sorry, but—"

"All of us are sorry. But you know what, Kate? Sorry doesn't cut it. It doesn't help. Being *sorry* doesn't erase the fact that my kids suffered. I can't get that out of my head. You know what makes all of this even worse? They died because of me. Because of what I do. Because of who I am. The same laws I devoted my life to enforcing failed me, Kate. Failed them. How the fuck am I supposed to live with that?"

"I don't know," I say, stepping toward him. "I don't have the answers. But you can't let Ferguson destroy you, too."

"He already has."

"No!" I shout. "I don't accept that."

For the span of a full minute, we stand silent, listening to the water pouring off the roof and the wind whistling around the eaves outside the window above the sink. I can feel my nerves zinging just beneath my skin. My breaths coming short and fast. My thoughts ricocheting inside my head so that I can't focus on a single one.

After a moment, he says, "Living in a fantasy world won't keep your nightmares from coming true."

"What are you planning to do?"

"I'm not going to do anything."

I stare at him, my heart pounding. "I don't believe you."

"I don't think there's anything I can do about that."

A little voice of reason tells me to go upstairs, take a shower, and go to bed. *Let it go.* But I'm angry with him. Worse, I'm scared. I'm terrified he's going to do something that will jeopardize this precious thing we've built.

"I can't compete with them." In the periphery of my consciousness, I hear myself say the words, hating them the instant they're out because they sound jealous and shallow and petty, three things I've never been.

The air around me feels fragile, like if I move, something will shatter and I'll never be able to pick

up the pieces. For an instant, I'm frozen in place, un-
decided, unable to breathe.

But I can't stay. Not like this. Rising, I snag my
coat and keys and then head for the door.

"Kate."

I open the door. His voice follows me into the night,
but he doesn't come after me.

CHAPTER 12

She dreamed of that night. Even after all this time, and so many years spent trying to forget, it was as vivid as if it had happened yesterday. The absolute dark of an Amish farm. A drug-fueled plot that had gone horribly wrong. The spill of innocent blood. It was a night in which a series of bad decisions had led to more bad decisions and culminated in a nightmare. People she thought she'd known turned into strangers she wished she'd never met.

Six people had died because of them. An Amish mother and father. Four innocent children. A teenaged boy had been left alone, to fend for himself. But those weren't the only tragedies that night. Four other lives had been irrevocably changed. Promising young lives wrecked by unfathomable guilt and secrets they would have to live with forever.

Those secrets had destroyed her life, stolen her innocence, and any semblance of happiness or hope for the future. In the weeks that followed, she'd even found herself questioning whether she wanted to re-

main on this earth. But somehow she'd gotten through
those dark days. She'd graduated from high school.
Gone to college. Gotten married and had children.
After the divorce and with the kids grown, she'd
thrown herself into her art and opened the gallery.
Through it all, Jules had never found happiness. She
knew something about herself she couldn't live with.
It was like living with a person you hated—someone
you could never trust nor leave.

Murderer.

Jules woke with a start, the word a whisper in her
ear, her heart pounding, her body slicked with sweat.
Sitting up, she threw her legs over the side of the bed
and put her face in her hands. "Damn you," she muttered, not exactly sure whom she was cursing. Herself. Or maybe the others.

She grabbed her robe off the foot of the bed and
worked it over her shoulders as she padded to the
kitchen. Like so many nights before, she went to the
refrigerator for the bottle of chardonnay she kept in
the door for such occasions. Mild annoyance rippled
through her when the fridge light didn't come on, but
she knew by heart where to find the bottle. The wine
didn't kill the pain; nothing could do that. But it would
get her through the night.

In the murky light coming through the window
above the sink, she uncorked the wine, snagged a
stemmed glass from the cupboard, and poured. She
stood at the counter and drank it down without stopping. She poured a second glass and recorked the
bottle. A glance at the wall clock told her the elec-
tricity had gone out at 3 A.M. Vaguely, she wondered
if any of the others were awake. If they were as
frightened and tortured as she was. If they ever considered doing anything about it.

Goddamn them.

Back at the refrigerator, she tugged open the door and replaced the bottle. Quickly, she drained her glass, then turned to take it to the sink. Ice slinked through her body when she noticed that the window was open. She stood there, frozen in place, trying to make sense of it even as she realized the screen had been removed. It was the only window she ever opened. It faced the pretty backyard and sometimes in the morning, she'd stand at the sink drinking coffee and watch the squirrels and the birds and think about all the things that might have been.

A faint sound—a shoe against tile—spun her around. Adrenaline burst in her midsection when she saw the woman standing in the kitchen doorway. She discerned the silhouette of an Amish dress. A winter head covering shadowed her face. Still, Jules thought she recognized her. That image of her had been burned into her memory for thirty-five years.

"But . . . how can it be you?" she whispered in a voice that was bizarrely calm, considering the circumstances. "I saw you die."

Even in the meager light she could see that the woman's expression was devoid of emotion. Eyes as dead and blank as a mannequin's. *Dead like me,* she thought vaguely.

Her eyes never left Jules as she entered the kitchen. "You remember me."

"Every day of my life." Jules knew it was crazy, but she wanted to throw herself at the woman and beg her for forgiveness. "If I could change what happened, I would."

The woman stared at her.

Jules told herself this couldn't be happening.

Prolonged stress could do strange things to one's mental health, after all. But as impossible as it was, she knew this was no hallucination.

"I'm sorry for what they did," she said.

"For what *they* did?" There was something cruel in the twist of her mouth. "Or for what you *didn't* do?"

"I'm so sorry." Jules didn't realize she was crying until her voice revealed it. She'd never believed in ghosts, but knew she was seeing one now. Deep inside, she knew she wouldn't survive the encounter. "What do you want? Why are you here?"

"You know why I'm here. Dale Michaels knew."

A landslide of fear tumbled through Jules at the mention of Dale. Then she spotted the knife the Amish woman held at her side—the butcher knife from Jules's own kitchen—and her heart went wild in her chest. She thought of her ex-husband's pistol on the night table beside her bed, but she knew she wouldn't reach it before that blade found its mark in her back.

"I'm sorry!" she cried. "All of us are sorry. Please don't hurt me!"

"Too late for sorry."

Jules dashed to the counter, where her cell phone was charging. The woman blocked her way, raised the knife. Screaming, Jules darted left, leaving the kitchen. Through the dining room. Toppling a chair. If she could reach her bedroom and the gun—

"Help me!" Her bare feet pounded through the living room, down the hall. Her hand brushed a framed photo, sent it crashing to the floor. Breaths rushing between clenched teeth. Heart exploding with terror. The knowledge that she was going to die. That she deserved this. That hell was waiting for her with open arms.

She heard the woman scant feet behind her. Shoes hard against the floor. "You killed them! *Die kinner!*" The children. *"Die kinner!"*

At the end of the hall, Jules started to go right toward the bedroom. The blade slashed down. The searing heat of a cut flashed on her right forearm. She felt the warm spurt of blood. Panic leaping in her chest. Crying out for help, she ran toward the bathroom.

A dozen feet away. The door standing half open. Jules hit the door with both hands. It slammed wide, hit the wall like a gunshot. Then she was inside. Spinning to close the door. Lock it. Lock out the past. Lock out death.

The door burst open, striking her in the face. She reeled backward, dazed. The knife arced to her left. The blade glinted, pierced her shoulder. She danced back. Slapped at the knife with both hands. "No!"

Pain streaked across her left palm. Blood warm on her arm. She turned, looked around wildly. The bathroom window. If she could break it, get through before she was mortally wounded . . .

She was midway there when the blade slammed into her back with the force of a baseball bat. She felt the blade hit bone. Another scream ripped from her lungs. Electric pain streaking down her spine. And then she was falling.

On the floor. Cold tile against her bare legs. She twisted, sat up. The woman hovered over her. Dead calm expression. Knife raised. Murder in her eyes.

"Murderer," she said.

Jules scrambled away, made it to her hands and knees. She floundered, bare feet sliding on tile slick with blood. She grabbed the shower curtain, pulled herself to her feet, partially ripping it from the rod. She faced her attacker, raised her hands to protect herself. "Don't." The word came out in a pant of panic. "Please."

Mouth contorted in rage, the woman slashed. Violently, putting her body weight into it. Fire flashed across Jules's throat. The knowledge that it was a death blow. Terror ripping through every nerve ending.

Jules tried to scream, gargled blood. She saw blood on the blade. On the tile. Red against her bare arms. Her right calf hit the side of the tub. The knife came down again, a hammer blow to her sternum. No air in her lungs. No way to breathe. She fell backwards into the tub. Darkness closing in. The familiar face looking down at her, now as impassive and cold as a predator on prey.

I didn't mean for you to die, she thought.

And then the knife came down again.

Tomasetti calls my cell twice during the drive from the farm to my house in Painters Mill. As much as I want to speak to him and work this out, I don't answer. There's no simple fix for the issues we're dealing with. And I've got too many emotions pinging around inside me to partake in a meaningful conversation. An uncomfortable mix of fear and anger and, as much as I don't want to admit it—even to myself— jealousy. Probably better for both of us to cool off before we talk.

I park in the driveway and sprint through the pouring rain to the front door and let myself inside. The house is dark, and even though I've gone to great lengths to maintain it as I try to decide whether to sell or rent, it has the feel of a place that's been closed up without fresh air for a long time.

A pang of melancholy moves through me. This was my first house, and I've loved it since the first time I saw it four years ago. I painted every room myself and chose the colors with such care. I spent a week's salary on the Amish rug in the living room. This place is so much more than a house. It symbolized a fresh start for me, a new phase of my life when I moved back to Painters Mill and became chief.

Tonight, standing in the living room, looking down at the layer of dust on the coffee table that had once been polished to a high sheen, it no longer feels like home.

I don't let myself think about Tomasetti or the harsh words between us as I pull linens from the hall closet and put them on the bed. A quick shower, and I climb between the sheets. Despite my exhaustion, sleep doesn't come easily and I end up tossing and turning for an hour before I can turn off my mind. When slumber finally descends, it's restless and fraught with dreams.

I'm wakened by the chirp of my cell phone. For several seconds I'm disoriented and unsure where I'm at. I reach for Tomasetti, only to remember the argument we had earlier. I curse him as I grapple for the phone. "Burkholder."

"Chief, sorry to wake you, but I thought you should know about a call I just took."

"Hey, Mona." I push myself to a sitting position. A glance at the alarm clock tells me it's just past 5 A.M. "What is it?"

"Kid tossing newspapers says Julia Rutledge's front door is standing open. He got a little freaked out and called his dad. Dad called us a few minutes ago. T.J.'s working an injury accident out on Delisle Road and said you were just out there tonight and I should let you know."

Wide awake now, recalling my recent meeting with Rutledge, I set my feet on the floor and snatch my uniform trousers off the back of a chair. "I'm on my way."

CHAPTER 13

Ten minutes later, I pull into Rutledge's driveway to find the house dark and quiet. No movement inside. No cars in the driveway or on the street. I hit my lapel mike. "Ten twenty-three."

"Ten four."

I grab my Maglite from the seat pocket and get out. Sure enough, from where I'm standing, I can see that the front door is open a couple of feet. A newspaper still in its clear plastic sleeve lies on the threshold. "Shit." I walk toward the house and take the steps to the porch. Pushing open the door the rest of the way, I peer inside. "Hello? Ms. Rutledge? It's Kate Burkholder with the Painters Mill PD. Is everything all right?"

Before I'm even fully through the door, I sweep the beam around the living room. Nothing appears out of place. I flip the switch on the wall, but it doesn't produce any light. I stand there a moment, listening, but the house is so quiet, I can hear the heat rushing through the vents.

"Ms. Rutledge?" I call out her name and identify myself a second time. The last thing any cop wants to happen when entering a premises is to be mistaken for a robber and get shot.

I go to the lamp on the end table and turn the switch. Again, no light. I'm midway across the living room when my beam illuminates a muddy shoe print on the hardwood floor. I can't tell if it's male or female, but someone has recently come in from outside.

I reach the far end of the living room. "Ms. Rutledge? Are you there?"

The lack of a response makes the nerves at the back of my neck crawl. I know it's possible she's sleeping and didn't hear me. Some people are sound sleepers; they take sleeping pills or wear earplugs. But ever present in my mind is that she was one of the last people to speak with Dale Michaels before his death and the situation has a high probability of going downhill quick.

I point my beam down the hallway, where I presume the bedrooms are located. I get the impression of a narrow space with hardwood floors and three doors, all of which stand partially open. Framed photographs on the walls. Ahead, a picture frame lies on the floor, the glass broken. I shine the beam on the wall and see a smear of something dark against the light paint. I can't be sure, but it looks like blood.

"Shit," I whisper. I transfer the Maglite to my left hand and draw my service revolver. "Mrs. Rutledge?"

The first door I come to is on my right. The hinges squeak as I push it open. Quickly, I sweep the beam around the room. It's a small, tidy bedroom with a queen-size bed covered with an Amish quilt. Curtains drawn. A small desk and chair. Guest room, I think. The closet door stands open. I see summer clothes hung on plastic hangers—shirts and jeans and an Ohio State hoodie lying on the floor next to a pair of sneakers. There's no one in the closet, so I continue down the hall.

A narrow door to my left opens to a good-size bathroom. At the end of the hall is the master bedroom. I see the outline of a window. Sheer curtains. A bed with a frilly skirt and a comforter that's turned down. Night table with a lamp and e-reader. It looks as if someone had been sleeping in the bed, but threw the covers aside and rose. I step into the room and try the light switch, but it doesn't work. The closet door is closed, so I stride to it and pull it open. The beam of my flashlight reveals blouses and jeans and a couple of dresses, all neatly hung. Boots and low-heeled pumps lined up on the floor. But there's no one there.

I back out of the room, shift my light to the bathroom. The sink and medicine cabinet are to my right. Tub to the left. Window ahead. "Julia Rutledge," I call out. "Police."

The bathroom is small. No closet. No place for anyone to hide. I step inside. My beam reveals blood. On the floor. On the sink. The wall ahead. I'm reaching for my mike when a sound spins me around. The burn of adrenaline in my gut. Then I notice movement in the bathtub. Stumbling back, I thrust my light toward it. The shower curtain has been torn from the rod. I see the shocking red of blood. Blond hair against porcelain. Staring eyes within the pale oval of a face.

"Ms. Rutledge!" I hit my lapel mike. "Ten seven eight!" I hear fear in my voice, make an effort to crank it down. "Ten thirty-one C."

"You want me to send County?"

"I need an ambulance!" I rush to the tub and drop to my knees.

"Stand by." A quick scratch of static and then. "What's your twenty?"

I relay the address from memory. Quickly, I set my flashlight on the floor with the beam pointing toward the tub. Jules Rutledge is lying on her back with one hand pressed against her chest, blood flowing between her fingers. The other hand is slung over the side of the tub, fingers twitching. She's wearing a white night-gown, the front of which is blood soaked. Her eyes are open and on me, blinking. In their depths I see terror and I hate it that she's afraid, because I don't think she's going to survive this.

"There's an ambulance on the way," I tell her. "Who did this to you?"

A clawlike hand reaches for me. Fingers grasping air. Eyes beseeching me to help. Panic on a face that already knows it's too late. Her bloody mouth opens and whispers, "We didn't . . . mean for it to . . . happen."

I try to pull away, but she clenches my jacket lapel with surprising strength. "Didn't mean for what to happen?" I ask.

Her lips move. A bubble of red-tinged saliva between them. "Kill . . . her."

I stare at her, not sure if I heard correctly, not sure if she's cognizant of what she just said. I hear gurgling in her chest and throat. Part of me wants to tell her not to speak, to save her strength. But the part of me that is a cop wants her to name the son of a bitch responsible.

"Tell me who did this," I press.

". . . ghost . . ."

The hand at my lapel falls away. Her body sinks more deeply into the tub. Her head lolls.

"Julia," I say. "*Julia*. Stay with me." But I know it's too late.

"Goddammit." I tug a latex glove from a compartment on my belt, slip my right hand into it, and reach over to check her carotid artery for a pulse, but she's gone. "Shit. *Shit.*"

"Chief?" Mona's voice scratches over the radio.

Uneasy with my back to the door, I snatch up my Maglite and get to my feet. "Ten seven nine," I say, requesting the coroner.

"Ten four." Another short hiss of static. "You okay?"

I don't know how to respond to that, so I go with, "Suspect at large."

"Description?"

"No." I peel off the glove and tuck it into my pocket. "Call BCI and get a CSU out here to the scene. Tell T.J. to set up a perimeter."

"Copy."

"Get Glock out here, too."

"Will do."

Keeping an eye on the door and the hall beyond, I shift the beam back to the tub. The shower wall is splattered with arterial spray. Julia Rutledge seems to stare at me from within that deathbed. I can't meet her gaze. The wet-iron stench of blood is stifling in the small space, and my stomach jitters. The urge to leave the room is strong, but I don't concede to it.

I shift my light to the faucets at her feet and see signs of a struggle. Several long smears of blood mar the tile, as if she'd lashed out with her feet.

"Sheriff's Department! Sheriff's Department!"

I startle at the shout, swing my beam to the door. "Back here!"

Another flashlight beam joins mine, and then a Holmes County deputy steps into the bathroom. "Chief?"

I recognize him as Deputy Frank Maloney, and I holster my .38. "I'm okay."

He averts his beam to avoid blinding me, but there's enough light for me to see his eyes widen at the sight of the blood before he pulls his cop's mask into place. "Holy shit." He takes a step back.

"Coroner's on the way." I let out a breath, surprised when it shudders slightly. "Frank, she was alive when I arrived."

"She ID anyone?"

"I tried, but . . . I think she was out of it. Said something about a ghost."

His gaze meets mine, but there's no hint of a cop's black humor in them. The hairs on my arms prickle, and for the first time in the course of my career, I feel threatened. Not by some crazy guy with a knife, but by something intangible and dark.

"Aw, hell." He glances at the body. "You see anyone?"

"No."

Head bent to his lapel mike, he sends out the code for homicide. "Unknown perpetrator at large." He motions toward the body. "You know her?"

I nod. "Julia Rutledge."

He edges closer to the bathtub, sets his beam on the body. "Damn."

A macabre scene dances in the beams of our flashlights. I can't help but think that just a few hours ago, Jules Rutledge was a lovely, vibrant woman who seemed to be enjoying her life. Now her mouth sags open, her lower jaw jutting slightly. Her head is cocked to one side, and from where I'm standing, I see a horrific wound high on her chest.

"What's that?" Maloney points at the wound. "Knife handle?"

Leaning closer, I set my beam on her chest. The fabric of her gown is blood soaked. There's a slit in the material, evidently from the blade. Something protrudes about half an inch from the wound.

"I don't think it's a knife," I say.

"Coroner's going to have to dig it out."

But I can't stop looking at the small foreign object. Deep inside, I already know what it is, and the knowledge is so disturbing, I have to withhold a gasp. "I think it's a wooden figurine," I whisper.

He gives me a sharp look. "Come again?"

"An Amish peg doll." Quickly, I fill him in on the Michaels homicide. "We didn't release that information to the public."

A siren wails in the distance, but neither of us acknowledges it.

"BCI on the way?" he asks.

"Yeah."

He whistles. "Two major crime scenes in a single week. They're going to start a running tab for you."

Despite the grimness of the scene, I smile, and I'm glad there are no civilians around to notice. Cop humor is one of those things that can easily be misinterpreted and blown out of proportion, usually by someone who doesn't understand that sometimes the only way to combat despair is through humor, even when it's dark.

Concerned now with contaminating the scene, we carefully exit the bathroom and walk into the living room. The flash of emergency lights through the window draws my attention. I look over to see an ambulance pull into the driveway, followed by a fire truck that parks curbside. I see Glock on the front porch and motion him in.

"Anyone find a point of entry?" Maloney asks.

"Kitchen window is open," Glock tells him. "Screen was cut and removed."

"What about the lights?" Maloney asks.

"We'll need to check the breaker box," I say.

I brief both men on everything I know about the scene. "I'm pretty sure the foreign object in the wound is similar to the peg doll we found in Michaels's mouth."

"So this isn't random," Glock says.

I nod. "When Skid and I talked to her, she said Michaels had been in touch with her about a painting he wanted to buy." I think about that a moment. "Skid and I both noticed she seemed nervous about her security. Bolt lock on the door. Security chain." I shine my beam at the end table where I'd seen the Beretta earlier, but it's gone. "She had a nine mil on the bottom shelf of that end table."

"Guess she couldn't get to it in time," Glock says.

"We need to find it," I add.

"Do you think Blue Branson or Jerrold Mc-Cullough are involved?" Maloney asks.

"I don't know." I shake my head. "But I think they know more than they're letting on." I consider that a moment and repeat Rutledge's dying words. "I think she said something like: 'We didn't mean to kill her.'"

Maloney cuts me a sharp look. "What the hell is that supposed to mean?"

I shrug. "When I asked her who did that to her, I'm pretty sure she said 'ghost.'"

The words hang suspended, as if no one knows how to respond.

I break the silence with, "The peg doll we found in Dale Michaels's mouth was made by Willis Hochstetler."

"That doesn't make any sense," Glock says. "Willis Hochstetler has been dead for over thirty years."

"But it's a link," Maloney says.

"*Something* had Julie Rutledge running scared," I tell them.

Maloney laughs. "Fucking ghosts."

I look from man to man. "Did either of you happen to run across any keys here at the scene?"

"There's a ring of keys on the kitchen counter," Glock tells me.

I go to the kitchen, pick up the keys, and go back to the living room, where Glock is standing. "Will you keep the scene secure until the CSU arrives?"

"No problem."

"Get photos of everything. A sketch if you can manage. And see if you can pick up some prints or footwear tread. Plenty of blood in that bathroom."

"Sure thing, Chief," he says. "Where are you going?"

"I'm going to take a look around Rutledge's gallery."

CHAPTER 14

The horizon is awash with Easter egg hues of lavender and orange when I park in front of the small boutique art gallery Jules Rutledge had owned and operated. It's not yet 8 A.M., and around me, Painters Mill is opening for business. The lights are on in the bakery across the street, and the aroma of fresh-baked apple fritters rides the breeze. At the end of the block, I see Steve Ressler, the publisher of the *Weekly Advocate* newspaper, hightail it toward the front doors of his offices, a newspaper tented over his head in an attempt to stay dry.

I look at the darkened storefront of The Raspberry Leaf Gallery and I can't help but think Julia Rutledge should be here instead of me, making coffee and preparing for another day. Instead, her body is on its way to the morgue and I'm here looking for clues that might tell me who hated her enough to murder her.

Grabbing my umbrella and my canvas equipment bag off the seat, I get out and jog to the sidewalk, where the striped overhead canopy shields me from the rain. I set down the bag, open it, and pull out shoe covers, gloves, and a disposable gown. Before going inside, I put on the protective gear, then pull the key chain from my pocket. The second key I try fits the door and I let myself in.

I find myself standing in a narrow space with gleaming hardwood floors and walls painted designer gray. Crisp white woodwork and wainscoting that looks original to the building. A good-size areca palm in a teal-colored pot sits near the window. The air smells the way an upscale art gallery should, with the faint aromas of bergamot and coffee and a hint of dark chocolate. In the far corner, a couple of sleek chairs with a retro '60s-style fabric are grouped with a coffee table sporting an antique lamp. The long walls to my left and right are covered with paintings: There are a dozen or more oils on stretched canvas, a few photographs, and lots of acrylics in simple black frames. Each work of art has its own light. This morning, the lights are dark, as if in reverence to the absence of Julia Rutledge.

My shoe covers crackle as I venture deeper into the gallery. In the corner to my left, several canvases are set up on easels, and I remember reading in the local paper that Julia gave art classes here at the gallery one evening per week. A divider upon which an artist has painted a mural of an Amish horse and buggy trotting past a cemetery separates the showroom from the rear of the gallery. I walk past the divider. While the front section of the gallery is sleek and stylish, the rear is dedicated to the business side of running things. Ahead and to my right is a sink with a fat roll of paper towels mounted above it. There's a shelf jammed with painting supplies and a glass-front cabinet filled with brushes and jars. The faint scent of turpentine laces the air. An espresso maker and a dozen or so colorful demitasse cups sit on the coffee station to my right. A door that's been painted glossy red bears a sign that proclaims OFFICE.

I cross to the door and try the knob, but it's locked. I dig for the keys and try several before locating the one that fits. The door opens to a small, cramped office. The lighting isn't as good as it is up front. A high-end vacuum cleaner for hardwood floors sits in the corner. A pair of sneakers peeks out from under a battered wood desk set against the wall. A Tiffany lamp adorns the corner of the desk. Two lavender-colored folders are stacked neatly in the in-box. I pick up the top file and find credit card bills, gas bills, and an invoice from a local hardware store. The second file contains receipts from recent sales and photos of artwork.

I'm not sure exactly what I'm looking for. Chances are I won't find a damn thing that will be helpful in terms of the case. But if I've learned anything in the years I've been a cop, it never hurts to look.

I decide to search the desk first, only to discover it's locked, too. I go back to the key chain and try the smallest key, which fits. I tug open the pencil drawer. It contains a phone message pad. Yellow sticky notes. A roll of postage stamps. A tube of lip gloss. Letter opener in the shape of a Toledo sword. Finding nothing of interest, I go to the second drawer. I see a box of fine-point Sharpies. A tin of handmade thank-you cards. A small dictionary. Box of tissues. Hand cream. I'm about to go on to the file drawer when, tucked beneath a roll of utility tape, several pieces of lined notebook paper catch my attention.

I pull out the papers; there are four, each of them folded twice. Though I'm wearing latex gloves, I touch only the corners and unfold the first one. Scrawled in blue ink are the words: *Dale sends his regards from hell.*

Surprise rattles through me. Quickly, I go to the second note, unfold it, and read. *I know you were there.* I page to the next sheet. *You could have stopped them.* The final note contains a single word: *Murderer.*

The notes are cryptic, threatening, and frightening. Someone had been terrorizing Julia Rutledge. But who? And why?

I turn on the Tiffany lamp. Light rains down on the four letters lying side by side on the desktop. That's when it strikes me that they're similar to the ones Norm Johnston gave me earlier. They're written on the same type of paper, the same color of ink, and I'm pretty sure that if that handwriting isn't the same, it's damn close.

"What the hell is going on?" I whisper.

The only answer is the pound of rain against the roof and the echo of anxiety in my voice.

I try to reach Norm on his cell phone twice on my way to the Painters Mill City Building, where the town council meeting room and offices are located. When I call his office line directly, I'm informed by the administrative assistant that he called in sick this morning.

"Shit," I mutter, and make a quick turn into the Dairy Dream, which is closed for the season, turn around, and head in the opposite direction. Worry nips at my heels as I head toward the Maple Crest subdivision where he lives, and I crank the speedometer up to sixty. The lighted waterfall cascading from atop a stone wall greets me as I make the turn into the subdivision. The homes are spacious and new here, the oversize lots professionally landscaped. My tires hiss against the wet blacktop as I look for Walnut Hill Lane. Another left, and I spot the stucco-and-stone ranch three houses down.

I park in the driveway, where rain beads on a Lexus with the dealership sticker still in the window, letting everyone know he'd laid down sixty thousand dollars for it. Or maybe that's just my less-than-affectionate feelings for Norm shining through. Rain patters against my head and shoulders as I get out and start toward the door. I use the brass knocker, aware that my pulse is up and that I'm suddenly terrified I'll find something inside besides an unpleasant conversation. I'm keenly aware of my hair getting wet. Damp soaking through my jacket to chill my shoulders and arms.

Relief slips through me when I hear the security chain and bolt lock disengage; then the door swings open. Norm Johnston stands just inside, frowning at me as if I'm some vagrant off the street, looking for a handout.

"I tried to reach you at the office and your cell," I tell him.

"I called in sick," he tells me. "There's a security company coming out to install an alarm system."

I nod. "I need to talk to you about those notes."

"Why? Has something happened? Did you figure out who's sending them?" His expression is frightened and grave as he ushers me into a foyer with a high ceiling from which a chandelier dangles. To my right, a glass-and-iron console table holds a porcelain vase filled with fresh flowers. Norm and his wife divorced shortly after their daughter's death. Carol got the bank account and moved to Pittsburgh, where her parents live. Johnston got the house and the opportunity to live up to his reputation as a womanizer. I'm reminded that when it comes to murder, the deceased is rarely the only victim.

I follow him to a comfortable living room with leather furniture and an oversized wood coffee table. The flat screen is tuned to a morning television program out of Columbus.

"Have you received any more notes?" I ask.

"No. Why?"

"Jules Rutledge was murdered a few hours ago."

"Wh—what?"

"She'd been receiving notes, Norm. Just like the ones you showed me."

He stares at me, blinking, the color draining from his face. "But . . . Jules? Dead? How?"

"Stabbed to death. In her home."

"Oh my God. Ohmigod." He sets his hands on either side of his temples. I can't tell if he's trying to block out my voice and the news I've just relayed or deny that it's happening.

"Norm, did you know them? Jules Rutledge and Dale Michaels?"

"No," he says defensively.

"There's got to be a connection. At least between you and Rutledge," I say. "The notes you showed me are exactly the same as the ones I found at her gallery."

"Oh Jesus," he says. "Jesus."

The pattern of denial is clear. Blue Branson. Julia Rutledge. Jerrold McCullough. And now Norm Johnston. Each of them adamantly denied being friends with the others. Why?

"Norm, if you knew them, now would be a good time to tell me," I press. "Two people are dead and there's no doubt in my mind there's some connection to you."

He tries to cover his discomfiture with a laugh, but this time the sound that squeezes from his throat more resembles a whimper. "Look, I may have had a beer or two with them, but I didn't run with them. We weren't friends."

"You mean recently?"

"No. When we were young. High school, for chrissake."

"So then, what's the connection?"

"I don't know. Maybe all of this is . . . random."

"This is not random." I take a breath, ratchet back my impatience with him, and soften my voice. "I can't help you unless you help me."

"What do you want from me?" he cries.

"The truth. All of it."

"I've told you everything I know."

I pause long enough to let him absorb everything that's been said. "Norm, I haven't put all of this together yet, but I think these two murders may be related to a cold case from back in 1979," I tell him. "The Hochstetler case."

"I remember it. That Amish family. But I was only a teenager at the time."

"Did you know the Hochstetlers?"

He hesitates. "No."

"Do you know anything about what happened the night that family was murdered?"

"Of course not." He makes a sound of disbelief. "What the hell are you insinuating?"

"I'm not insinuating anything. I'm trying to solve two homicides, get a killer off the street, and maybe keep you safe in the process."

"I had nothing to do with that." His lips peel back, exposing small, artificially white teeth. "How dare you accuse me of—"

"I didn't accuse you of anything."

From two feet away, I can hear his molars grinding. "This is outrageous. I ask you for help, and you come into my home unannounced and start making wild accusations, all because you haven't the slightest clue how to do your job! I'm a sitting member of the council, for God's sake."

"Norm, I need you to level with me. If there's anything you're not telling me, you need to come clean. Right now."

He stares at me, his mouth open, his chest rising and falling. "I've told you everything I know."

"I'm not going to let this go," I tell him. "Do you understand?"

A quiver runs the length of his body. In the periphery of my vision, I see his right hand curl into a fist. And I know he's struggling to control a temper run amok. That if he loses the battle, I'd better be prepared to defend myself. I'm not sure what it says about me, but I'm pretty sure I'd take a hit for the opportunity to arrest him.

"You fucking bitch. I'm sick and tired of your incompetence. First my daughter is killed because of you and now this. I swear to God, I'll have your job for this."

I try hard to let the words roll off me, especially the insinuation about my being responsible for the death of his daughter. But I don't quite succeed. My heart is pounding; I can feel the pulse of it in my neck. Adrenaline jigs in my midsection, powerful enough to make my hands shake.

"You do what you have to do," I tell him. "This isn't going to go away."

He strides to the door and opens it. "Get the fuck out of my house."

I stand there for a moment, looking at him. "Watch yourself, Norm. I mean it."

He snarls another expletive at me as I go through the door and step into the pouring rain.

CHAPTER 15

I'm nearly to the station when my phone erupts. I check the screen to see that I've received a text from the coroner: *Michaels autopsy complete. Will be at my office until noon.* Groaning inwardly, I make a U-turn and head back toward Pomerene Hospital.

No matter how many times I make this journey to the morgue, it never gets any easier. Dread is a dark and silent presence that steps onto the elevator and rides with me to the basement. The doors swish open to a tiled corridor. My boots echo as I pass a yellow and black biohazard sign and a plaque that reads: MORGUE AUTHORIZED PERSONNEL. At the end of the hallway, I push open dual swinging doors and traverse a second hall to the clerk's desk, but Carmen is nowhere in sight. Early lunch, I think, and I'm reminded that I've yet to have coffee.

I go through a second set of swinging doors. The autopsy room is straight ahead. To my right is a small alcove, where the biohazard protection supplies are stored. I glance to my left and through the mini-blinds of his glassed-in office, I see Doc Coblentz sitting at his desk, eating a burger the size of a small tire.

I enter his office. "Sorry to interrupt," I tell him, relieved he's not eating in close proximity of a dead body.

"This is the only place I can enjoy red meat in peace." He blots his mouth and rises. "My wife has me eating rabbit food. Beets and carrots." He extends his hand and we shake.

"You work all night, Doc?"

He nods. "The dead are blissfully quiet."

"Okay." But I can't help but grin. "You finished the Michaels autopsy?"

He sobers. "We just received Julia Rutledge."

"Any idea when you might get to her?"

"As soon as I can." Taking a final bite of the burger, he motions toward the alcove. "You know the drill."

I go to the alcove, where his assistant has set out disposable shoe covers, a blue gown, hair cap, and latex gloves. Doc Coblentz is waiting when I emerge and, I find myself wondering how he does what he does. No matter how well prepared I think I am, I'm never ready to witness this cold and clinical side of death. While the blood and bodily fluids have been rinsed away, the incised skin hidden from view, there is no eradicating the hideousness. I can't look at a body without thinking of the life that person lost or the loved ones he left behind.

Entering the autopsy room is like stepping into a cave where some grotesque beast stores its kills. Ensconced in gray ceramic tile, the room is maintained at a cool sixty-two degrees. But despite the state-of-the-art HVAC system, the smells of formalin and decaying flesh are ever-present reminders of why this place exists. It's a large room, about twenty feet square. Stark fluorescent light pours down from several overhead lamps onto stainless steel counters. There are a dozen or so white plastic buckets. Gleaming instruments lie atop stainless steel trays, the uses of which I don't want to ponder. Two deep sinks with arcing faucets are butted against the far wall, next to a scale used to weigh organs.

"What's the cause of death?" I ask.

"Strangulation due to the compression of the carotid arteries causing global cerebral ischemia."

I follow the doc to a gurney situated beneath a lamp that's been pulled down close. A green sheet marred by several watery stains covers the body. I brace an instant before Doc Coblentz peels away the sheet.

I steel myself against the sight of the massive Y-incision cut into Dale Michaels's torso. The flesh is blue gray with a sprinkling of silver hair on a chest that's sunken and bony. A few inches above his navel, a neat red hole the size of my pinkie stands out in stark contrast against the pasty skin.

"So he was still alive when he was hanged from those rafters?" I ask.

"Correct. There was a good bit of bleeding from both gunshot wounds, which tells me the heart was still beating when he sustained them."

"There were *two* gunshot wounds?"

"Sorry to do this to you, Chief, but you need to see this." He draws the sheet down to mid-thigh, revealing more of Dale Michaels than I ever wanted to see. A shriveled penis and scrotum are nestled in silvery pubic hair. There's a wound there, too, and I can barely force myself to look. My eyes skim over jutting hip bones and the tops of skinny thighs. But Michaels was not a thin man. The abdomen bulges and is slightly gelatinous with fat.

The urge to look away is powerful, but despite my aversion, I don't.

"For simplicity's sake, I'll refer to them as Wound One and Wound Two." Using a wooden, cotton-tipped swab, he indicates the hole near the navel. "On Wound One, we've got an entry wound here. The slug penetrated the stomach wall between the greater curvature and the pyloric canal and lodged near the spine."

"Did it paralyze him?"

"Probably not, but the trauma so close to the spinal cord may have temporarily immobilized him."

"Looks like a small caliber." But I'm finding it increasingly difficult to focus on Dale Michaels's brutalized body. "A .22 or maybe a .25." I look over at him. "Is the slug intact?"

"I have one slug, which I've bagged for you. The other was a through and through."

I make a mental note to get with the CSU that processed the scene. If the second slug wasn't found inside the body, maybe it's still at the scene, in a wall or in the ground.

"Going on to Wound Two." Using the swab as a pointer, he indicates the hole near the groin. "The missile entered the anterior aspect of the left thigh, just to the left of the genitalia. It fractured the superior ramus of the pubis, tore through the neck of the bladder, and left the body through the perineum, compromising the entire genitourinary tract."

"Jesus," I hear myself say, but I'm keenly aware that the buzzing of the overhead lights seems inordinately loud as I stare down at a hole the color of raw meat. Despite the chill, I feel sweat break out on the back of my neck.

I swallow hard. "So there's no slug for the second wound."

"Correct."

"Was he alive when he sustained it?"

"Yes." Doc Coblentz shifts his attention to the neck. "Interestingly, the vertebrae are free of any fractures." He indicates the throat area, where the rope dug a deep groove into the flesh.

"What does that mean?" I ask, but I already know.

"I would venture to guess he was hoisted up from the ground as opposed to being dropped down from the rafters," he tells me. "Unconsciousness would have occurred in a relatively short period of time, probably one or two minutes. Death occurred when the oxygen and blood flow to the brain were cut off. Most of the damage you see here occurred postmortem, gravity working against the weight of his body."

I think about that for a moment. "Would he have survived the gunshot wounds if he hadn't been hanged?"

"Well, both were serious, penetrating wounds. But there were no major arteries involved. Hemorrhage was present, but not life threatening. If he'd received prompt medical attention, and barring any preexisting medical conditions, he would have survived."

Some of the tension leaves me when he pulls the sheet up and covers the body.

"Any sign that he was engaged in a struggle or physical confrontation?"

"No."

"Tox?"

"Won't be back for two or three days."

"What about that Amish doll, Doc? Do you know if it was put into his throat before or after his death?"

"Before. There were abrasions on the upper part of the pharynx, along with a minute amount of bleeding. It wouldn't have been a comfortable ordeal for the victim."

"I get the sense there was a lot of rage involved with this crime."

"I agree." He shrugs. "The level of brutality . . ."

I think about that a moment and then ask, "Do you have anything preliminary on Julia Rutledge?"

Doc Coblentz shakes his head. "I performed a cursory exam upon her arrival. As you've probably already deduced, she sustained several stab wounds, including a deep chest wound. I can't give you a cause of death until I get her on the table."

"What about the object in the wound?"

He turns to a stainless tray on the counter behind him and picks up a plastic evidence bag. "I knew you'd want to see it, so I extracted it first thing."

It's an Amish peg doll exactly like the one we found in Dale Michaels's mouth. I know what's inscribed into the base before I look: HOCHSTETLER. I pass the bag back to the doc.

"I'll get it couriered to the lab ASAP," he tells me.

I thank him and start toward the alcove. As I remove the biohazard gear and toss it into the receptacle, it strikes me that for the first time in the course of my career, the autopsy of a murder victim has raised more questions than it answered.

CHAPTER 16

It had been a long time since Jerrold McCullough was afraid. He'd lived a long, full, and sometimes difficult life. He'd lost a two-year-old daughter when he was twenty-six years old. He'd spent some time overseas in Bosnia when he was in the military. At the age of forty-two, he survived a serious car accident in which he'd lost a limb—and nearly his life. He lost his wife of twenty-four years to cancer several years back. Yes, Jerrold McCullough had faced his fair share of adversity. Each time that bitch fate dealt him a blow, he'd conquered it and come back from it a smarter, stronger, if lonelier, man.

But as life had proved, there were some things you didn't come back from. Sure, you went on with the business of living. You fell in love and got married. You had children and you brought them up right. But through it all, you knew your life was one big fat lie.

The rain had been coming down for five days now, and the creek behind his house crested last night. By dawn, the brown, churning water had encroached an-

other twenty feet into his backyard. If the rain didn't
let up soon, he figured by midnight it would overtake
the deck, where in summer, he kept the barbecue and
lawn chairs. It was hard to believe that roaring
monster was the same creek he'd swum in with his
kids when they were young. The same creek where he
caught that eight-pound largemouth bass—the one no
one had believed him about. The same creek where
he and his wife had gone skinny-dipping after getting
drunk the day their last child went off to Ohio State.
That had been ten years ago now and he still smiled
every time he walked by that deep swimming hole.
He figured if he was going to die, he'd just as soon it
be here, where he'd raised his family.

He'd found the second note last night when he came
home from his Lions Club meeting. It was on plain
notebook paper and had been left in his mailbox.
You're guilty. He'd known it was coming; he hadn't
been surprised. What had surprised him was the fear.
He was only fifty-four years old, and frankly, he
wasn't through living yet. But what could he do? Go
to the police? Tell them a dead woman was sending
him notes?

He hadn't seen her since that night in his driveway.
He'd never admit to it, especially to the others, but
he believed in ghosts. In fact, he knew they existed.
He'd been seeing little two-year-old Tessa for years.
On occasion, he still saw his wife, too, only the way
she'd looked before the cancer ate her up. And so
when he saw Wanetta Hochstetler, standing in the
driveway, looking at him with that accusatory expression, he hadn't questioned his eyesight, blamed it on
the bad light, or even doubted his sanity. He accepted
it as truth because he'd always believed that sooner
or later, a man paid for his deeds.

That didn't mean he was going to go down easy. He was a fighter by nature, and by God he'd just as soon live for another twenty or thirty years. He wanted to pass this house and property on to whichever of his children came home to Painters Mill, once they realized the Holy Grail wasn't in Dallas or Sacramento or Atlanta. So far none of them had been takers, but they would. Sooner or later, everyone came home.

He poured coffee into his BEST GRANDPA IN THE WORLD mug, added a dollop of milk, and then opened the patio sliding door and stepped outside. Cold drizzle fell from a glowering sky the color of granite. Something inside him sank when he noticed the water was just ten feet from the deck now. He'd put a lot work into it. He'd sunk pressure-treated four-by-four posts into three-foot-deep post holes and filled them in with concrete he'd mixed himself. He's used treated two-by-sixes for the decking, two-by-fours for the rail. Damn shame that the water was going to take it all, but then, that was the nature of the creek.

Pulling up the collar of his jacket against the chill, he walked to the edge of the deck. He sipped coffee and listened to the water take down another tree upstream. When he turned to go back inside, she was coming up the steps. Not little Tessa. Not his beloved Luann. But Wanetta Hochstetler. She was wearing an Amish dress and dark head covering pulled low and shadowing her eyes. Black shawl over her shoulders. Her shoes were covered with mud.

He dropped the mug. Coffee splashed on his pants. He glanced down where it lay in pieces, and the word GRANDPA stared up at him. It saddened him because in that instant, he knew he'd never see his grandchildren again.

He looked at her and shook his head, suddenly tired. "I know why you're here," he said.

"Do you?" She stepped onto the deck.

He took an involuntary step back when he spotted the pistol in her hand. A .22 revolver. Something resembling doubt drifted through the back of his mind. If she was a ghost, why did she need a gun? Why was there mud on her shoes?

He looked into her eyes. "I told them not to do it. I didn't want any part of it."

"Liar." Keeping the weapon poised at his chest, she stepped closer. "It was you."

"Things got out of hand," he said. "We didn't mean to—"

"You're guilty," she said. "Just like the others."

"Please, don't kill me." He heard pleading in his voice and it shamed him. "I have children."

"You're a child killer." She shuffled left, motioned toward the steps with the revolver. "Walk."

Heart pounding, he obeyed. Upon reaching the base of the stairs, he hesitated, thought about running to the front of the house and calling for help. But she jabbed the weapon toward the deck closer to the creek. "There," she said. "Go."

He started toward the deck, wondering what she had in mind, wondering if it would be painful, if she would murder him the way she had the others. . . .

Upon reaching the deck, he turned to her. He noticed the length of rope in her left hand and a hot streak of panic ran through his body. "What are you going to do?"

She raised the pistol slightly. The revolver cracked. Agony zinged in his knee. His leg buckled. Crying out, he hit the ground hard. Dizzy with shock and pain, he clutched his knee, glanced down, saw blood between his fingers. "But you're . . . you can't . . ."

The pain took his breath. He couldn't speak. He couldn't tell her she was a ghost and ghosts didn't need guns.

Another shot snapped through the air. Pain exploded in his other knee. He screamed and then flopped around in the mud like a hooked fish. "Don't," he panted. "Dear God, please don't."

He tried to scream for help, but the sound that squeezed through his lips was the howl of a wounded dog. He lay on his side, wheezing, and looked up at her. "You're not a ghost," he croaked.

Rope in hand, she started toward him, a smile curving her mouth.

When you spend the entirety of your professional life in law enforcement, there are certain things you come to know. I've handled my share of firearms over the years, both handguns and rifles, and I know first-hand that without practice, good marksmanship is tough to come by—even by police officers. Half the cops I know couldn't hit the broadside of a barn, especially in a high-adrenaline or shoot-from-the-hip type of scenario.

I also know that the targeting of the genitalia in the commission of a crime speaks to some kind of symbolism. I've seen it done in gangland murders in which some thug wants to make a point. But I've also seen it in revenge crimes involving sexual assault. The question in the forefront of my mind is this: Did Michaels's killer target his genitalia, or was he simply a bad shot?

I enter the reception area to find half a dozen pails of different shapes and sizes on the floor between the reception area and the coffee station. My first-shift dispatcher, Lois Monroe, is in the hall with her headset clamped over her ears, a mop in hand. A steady drip from the ceiling plunks into an old paint can, keeping perfect time with a funky Linkin Park number on the radio.

"Be careful where you walk, Chief." Propping the mop against the wall, she strides to the reception desk and plucks messages from my slot. "I ran out of buckets an hour ago."

I look at the menagerie of containers set out to catch the deluge and I try not to laugh, because it's a hell of a lot more likely that I'll get a rash of excuses from the town council as opposed to a new roof.

"Call everyone and tell them there's a briefing in half an hour," I tell her.

She arches a brow. "Productive day so far?"

"If my tail were the prize, I'd have hit the jackpot." I glance toward the hall, where a puddle is taking form on the tile floor. "I have a Tupperware container in my office," I tell her.

"I'll take it."

"Make sure the computer equipment and phone systems don't get wet."

"Got it covered, Chief." She grins. "Literally."

Ten minutes later, my computer is booted and I've got the technician from the crime lab on the phone. "The coroner says Dale Michaels sustained a through-and-through gunshot wound," I tell him. "Did you guys find a slug at the scene?"

"Metal detector found one that had penetrated the soil," he tells me.

"Caliber?"

"Twenty-two."

"Intact?"

"Enough for us to analyze striations, which we're working on now. If we've got matching striations in the database, we'll know by tomorrow."

"Anything else?"

"We found a long hair on the victim's clothing that doesn't belong to the victim."

I think of Belinda Harrington. "The daughter found the body. It could be hers."

"Interestingly, this hair was naturally blond, but dyed brown."

"That's a switch." And it rules out Harrington as the donor, since her hair is red. "You get enough root for DNA?"

"Working on it. Again, it's going to be a few days. We're a little jammed up here."

"Keep me posted."

"You know it."

After thanking the technician, I end the call. I grab a yellow legal pad from my drawer and take a few minutes to write down everything I know about the cases, which isn't much—at least in terms of concrete information. I have no viable suspects. No motive. No murder weapon. In terms of physical evidence, I have two Amish peg dolls, that link Dale Michaels's murder to the murder of Julia Rutledge—and may or may not tie both murders to a thirty-five-year-old unsolved cold case. I have the notes, which tie the Rutledge case to Norm Johnston. I also have the data from Dale Michaels's iPhone—the list of incoming and outgoing calls he made before his murder. And the text to Blue Branson. But how does it all tie together?

I go to a second page and write down what I remember from my conversation with a dying Julia Rutledge: *When I asked, "Who did this to you?" she replied with: "We didn't mean to." I pressed and she responded with: "Kill her." When I asked who, she said, "Ghost."*

I'm staring down at my notes, trying to decide how to put all of it into meaningful order when Lois peeks her head in. "Everyone's here, Chief."

"Thanks." Gathering the three files and my legal pad, I start toward the meeting room to find that my small department has already converged at the rectangular table, including my third-shift dispatcher, Mona, who should be home sleeping. My chest swells a little when I notice everyone's in uniform. T.J. and Skid are embroiled in a conversation. Glock is thumbing something into his phone. Pickles is nursing a mug of coffee, a legal pad and pen in front of him.

I take my place behind the half podium at the head of the table. "I want to give everyone a quick briefing on what we've got so far on the Michaels and Rutledge murders," I begin. "Doc Coblentz just completed the Michaels autopsy. Cause of death was strangulation from hanging. In addition to being hanged, the victim sustained two gunshot wounds. One to the abdomen. The other to the genital area, which was a through and through."

"Ouch," Skid interjects.

That earns him a few nods from the other men in the room.

"The lab retrieved a slug. We're looking at a .22 caliber. They're working on matching striations now." I look around the room. "At this point, no one knows if the gunshot wound to the genitals was on purpose or by chance. I think you know that if it's the former, we could be looking at the work of a gang or revenge for a sex crime.

"Regarding Michaels's iPhone: We've run all the

names through LEADS and we're working our way through the list. So far I've interviewed three of the individuals he made his final calls to: Blue Branson, Jerrold McCullough, and Julia Rutledge. As you know, Rutledge was murdered last night, which I'll touch on in a moment. All three individuals have alibis and claim no knowledge of the victim or the crime.

"Interestingly, Michaels sent a text to Blue Branson shortly before his murder." I look down at my notes and read: "'Meet is on. Will call 2 let you know outcome.'" I turn my attention back to my team. "Blue Branson says he doesn't know anything about the meeting and he doesn't recall receiving the text."

"You believe him?" Glock asks.

"He showed me his phone," I tell him. "He wasn't lying about having not read the text. But I don't believe him one hundred percent."

"Is he a suspect?" Skid asks.

"He's a person of interest."

"Emphasis on 'interest,'" Glock mutters.

A few chuckles ensue, and I resume the briefing. "We were able to tie the two homicides together by way of similar objects found at both scenes." I hold up a photocopy of the Amish peg doll. "This figurine was found in Dale Michaels's mouth. A second figurine was found inserted into a knife wound inside Julia Rutledge's body. Both figurines have been sent to the lab to see if we can come up with latents or other identifying marks. We're not releasing any of this to the public." I tap the surface of the podium for emphasis. "The information doesn't leave this room. Everyone got that?"

Everyone nods. Glock gives me a thumbs-up.

"What are your thoughts on those Amish dolls, Chief?" Pickles asks.

"We believe both dolls were made by a member of the Hochstetler family, back when they had that furniture operation in the 1970s. As most of you know, the Hochstetler family were victims of a crime back in 1979. We don't know if the dolls left at the scene are in any way related to that incident or if they were left for some other reason."

"One of the kids survived that night, didn't they?" Skid asks.

I nod. "Fourteen-year-old William Hochstetler was the only survivor. He was adopted and legally changed his name to Hoch Yoder. He still lives in the area."

"You talk to him?" Skid asks.

I nod. "He claimed he was home. His wife alibied him. He remains a person of interest." I let the statement hang and go back to my notes. "Aside from the phone calls and the text, we have nothing concrete that ties Blue Branson or Jerrold McCullough to Dale Michaels, but in the coming days, we're going to be putting some pressure on them. Hoch Yoder, too."

I scan the faces of my team, speaking from memory now. "A couple of other interesting developments that are not for public consumption. A search of Julia Rutledge's gallery netted three threatening notes." I pull out copies and hand them to Skid to pass around. "Councilman Johnston has also been receiving notes of a similar nature."

A murmur of surprise goes around the table at the mention of Johnston. Glances are exchanged as I pass a copy of the notes Norm gave me to Skid. "I want patrols stepped up in Norm's neighborhood. If possible, I'd like for us to keep a presence at his house."

"Is Councilman Johnston somehow involved in this?" T.J. asks.

"I don't know," I say honestly. "He hasn't been as forthcoming as I'd like, but I'll keep some pressure on him and we'll see what happens."

When no other questions come, I look at Glock. "I want you to pick up Jerrold McCullough. Bring him in. Let's sweat him a little."

"Yes, ma'am."

"T.J., you've been on for two shifts. You probably ought to go home and get some sleep."

"Aye."

"Pickles, you're on full-time until further notice."

"No problem." The old man nods, not quite able to hide his pleasure.

I bring my hands together. "Everyone else, I hope you don't have any plans for the weekend. Mandatory OT until we get this guy."

The groans that follow are token. I know my officers want this killer off their streets as vehemently as I do.

I spend an hour putting my notes into a Word doc, writing reports and rereading every detail of both the Michaels and Rutledge cases. I spend another thirty minutes combing through the Hochstetler file. By the time I hand everything off to Lois, it's nearly 2 P.M. I look at my phone, and I find myself thinking about Tomasetti and how we left things. I desperately want to talk to him. My pride reminds me that I'm angry with him. It's not enough to keep me from picking up the phone.

He answers on the first ring. "I wasn't expecting to hear from you."

"I miss you," I say without preamble.

Surprise produces a certain echo over a phone line.

I hear that echo now, intriguing and painful at once. "Cat got your tongue, Tomasetti?"

"Yup." A thoughtful pause ensues. "Are you all right?"

"Yes," I say automatically, and then add, "no. It's been a tough day."

"Anything I can do?"

"Just . . . be there when I get home."

I can almost hear his thought processes working. He's trying to peg my frame of mind. My reason for setting my pride aside and calling him when I was otherwise pissed. Why, when it's so unlike me to show him that I need him, that I'm so willing to admit it. I'm not sure I could explain any of those things even to myself.

My second line lights up. On the display, I see Glock's name. "I have a call," I tell him. "Gotta take it."

He sighs. "You'll be home later?"

"I'll try." I punch the button for my second line. "You pick up McCullough?" I begin.

"I would have. If I could find him."

The news drags my attention away from Tomasetti and back to the case. "Where are you?"

"His place. He's not here. Front door was standing wide open. I figured that warranted a welfare check, so I took a look inside. Nothing out of place, but there's no sign of him."

"Shit, Glock, that's not good." I think about that a moment. "Car there?"

"Yeah."

"He could be with a friend." But neither of us is assuaged. "Look, I'm going to go talk to Blue Branson, and then I'll head your way."

"You want me to go with you? Meet you there?"

"I want you to find McCullough. Check with his friends and family and neighbors. See if anyone knows where he is or if they've seen him. For all we know, he's down at the VFW playing bingo."

"I'm on it."

But we both know that's a best-case scenario. With two of his friends dead and ties to a deadly cold case creeping steadily into the picture, I'm not sure we'll find Jerrold McCullough alive.

CHAPTER 17

Blue Branson lives in a modest single-story bunga-low with dormer windows, a homey little porch, and crisp white trim. A six-foot privacy fence separates his property from Brewer's Salvage Yard, which is situated on the lot next door. I turn into the driveway, plow through slightly mushy gravel, and park a few yards from the front door.

I get out and pass by his Mustang as I make my way to the house. Within the glow of the porch light, drizzle floats down. Opening the storm door, I knock.

A moment later, Blue appears; he doesn't look surprised to see me. "Chief Burkholder."

"I guess you knew I'd be back," I begin.

He doesn't respond, and I remind myself he's no greenhorn when it comes to dealing with the police. Most people talk too much when they get nervous, usually to their detriment. Not Blue. He looks at me coolly, eye contact steady, as if trying to decide if he should invite me inside or send me packing.

"What can I do for you?" he asks.

"You heard about Julia Rutledge?"

He sighs, looks away for a moment. "I heard."

"Jerrold McCullough is missing."

His gaze jerks to mine. I see both shock and concern on his face. He steps back and opens the door wider. "Come in."

I enter a comfortably furnished living room. Starving artist paintings on the walls. A newish flat screen mounted above the hearth. The air smells of some spicy aromatic I can't quite place. Classical Spanish guitar hums from speakers on either side of the TV. A sleek laptop hums atop a TV tray next to a half-eaten bowl of ice cream. Blue has shed his sport coat. The sleeves of his shirt are rolled up, exposing forearms that are covered with tattoos—a strange mosaic of blue and red and green on flesh browned by the sun.

He notices me looking at his arms, but he doesn't seem to mind. He motions toward a newish sofa. "Have a seat."

I don't take him up on the offer. "Have you seen or spoken to Jerrold McCullough?"

"No."

"What about Julia Rutledge?"

"I haven't seen her." He grimaces. "I heard she was stabbed to death in her home. Is that true?"

I don't answer. "Where were you last night between eleven P.M. and five A.M.?"

"I was at the Grace Victory Church in Glenmont. Black Creek flooded out some homes, and there were five families in need of shelter. I helped Pastor Bergman get everyone set up in the rec room."

"You were there that entire time?"

"Yes, ma'am."

"You know I'm going to check."

"That's fine." He tugs his phone from his pocket, taps the screen a couple of times, and recites the number for the Grace Victory Church.

I pull out my notepad and write it down. "Can anyone else vouch for you?"

"There were ten or fifteen volunteers around all night. Once we got those families picked up, we delivered food and blankets and set up cots. I had at least one person with me all night."

"So you say."

"I didn't have anything to do with Julia's murder." He tilts his head. "Do you think something has happened to Jerrold McCullough?"

"I don't know." I stare hard at him, waiting for him to say more. He doesn't give me anything. He stares back, completely unperturbed by the silence and the tension slicing the air between us. "What do you think, Blue? Do you think something happened to him?"

"I have no idea. I'm worried about him."

"Do you think if you'd come clean about whatever it is you're hiding, Julia Rutledge might still be alive?"

It's a harsh, unfair question, but I let it stand, hoping to rattle him. He doesn't react to the unspoken implication, but I don't miss the quiver in his hand when he runs it over his goatee. "I'm not hiding anything. I didn't kill Dale. Or Julia. And I have no idea where McCullough might be. You have my word."

"Do you know Norm Johnston?"

"Councilman Johnston?" He looks flummoxed. "I've met him a few times."

"Have you spoken to him recently?"

"No."

I nod, letting the silence ride. After a moment, Blue shifts his weight from one foot to the other. "If we're done here, I'd like to get back to work."

I lean forward and whisper. "I know you're hiding something. I'm going to find out what it is."

His expression doesn't change. "Good night, Chief Burkholder."

I tap the front of his shoulder with my index finger. "Don't leave town."

"I'm not going anywhere."

I leave him standing in his living room with his bowl of melted ice cream and a decidedly troubled expression.

It's after 6 P.M. by the time I arrive at Jerrold McCullough's place. I find Glock standing on the front porch, and we spend an hour or so walking the property on the chance the man fell or somehow injured himself and is unable to respond. But we don't find any sign of him. Earlier, Glock was able to reach one of McCullough's grown children, a son who lives in Sacramento. Jerrold Jr. hasn't heard from his father in over a week. He didn't sound too concerned. When I try McCullough's cell phone, my call goes straight to voice mail.

We're standing in the backyard, twenty yards from the shore of a very swollen Painters Creek, looking out at the woods. It's raining again and I can hear the water crashing over rocks and rushing around the trees that grow along the flooded bank.

"You don't think he fell into the water, do you?" Glock asks.

"I think it's probably premature to start dragging the creek." I say the words lightly, but the notion that at some point it could be necessary bothers me. "He's not even officially missing yet."

"Yeah, but you're worried or you wouldn't be here."

I sigh because he's right. "Did anyone you talked to mention his favorite watering hole?"

"He's been known to stop in for a beer at McNarie's. I thought I'd swing by on my way home."

I nod, but I don't think he'll find McCullough at the bar. "Apparently, we're the only people who seem to be worried about him."

"That's pretty sad." Glock grimaces. "You think he flew the coop? Maybe he had something to do with the murders."

"It's possible, but I don't think he's our guy." I consider that a moment. "For one thing, he's an amputee. He doesn't use a prosthesis."

"That we know of."

"Look, I'm going to put out a BOLO."

Around us the rain increases, fat drops slapping against the trees and the saturated ground. Despite the fact that we're both getting wet, neither of us seems to notice.

"I don't think we're going to figure this out tonight," I say after a moment.

He nods. "I'm going to swing by McNarie's."

"We'll pick up Blue tomorrow," I tell him. "Put some pressure on him."

Glock gives me a mock salute and then turns and starts for his vehicle, leaving me in the pouring rain with the sound of rushing water in my ears and my own thoughts echoing in my head.

I'm on my way home when I pass by Old Germantown Road. On impulse, I hit the brakes, back up, and make the turn. It's fully dark now, and my headlights reveal fog hovering above asphalt that's pitted and cracked. The vegetation is slowly devouring the road so that it isn't much wider than a single lane. Not many people use this road since the new highway went through. The county no longer maintains it, and I imagine in a few years the land will reclaim it completely.

The Hochstetler farm—what's left of it—sits on a hill a half mile down. The house burned to the ground and was never rebuilt, but some of the trees survived and now look as if they're standing sentinel—or waiting for the family to return. The old German-style round barn that Willis Hochstetler transformed into a furniture showroom still stands. I remember my *mamm* and *datt* talking about how the farm had once been a showplace with its white four-rail fence and wraparound porch adorned with hanging Boston ferns. Camera-wielding *Englischers* traveled for miles to park at the end of the lane and shoot photos.

The place fell to ruin after the family was killed. The tourists stopped coming. The Amish spoke of the things that happened that night only in whispers. But I heard the stories. When I was a teenager, rumors abounded. Ghost stories mostly. And a few sightings of Wanetta Hochstetler walking the hilltop, calling out for her children. Some said if you came out at midnight and listened, you could hear the screams of the children as they were burned alive.

Those stories scared me when I was a kid. But as I entered my teenage years, I became intrigued and even partook in several illicit visits myself. Tonight, as I approach the beat-up mailbox and turn into the muddy lane, I feel all those old stories creeping up on me.

I park in knee-high weeds with my headlights illuminating the place where the house had once stood. Leaving the engine running and the headlights on, I grab my Maglite and get out. I pull on my slicker as I start toward what had once been the side yard. I didn't know the Hochstetlers; though they lived in the same church district as my own family, I was too young when they died to remember any of them. But I feel the loneliness of this place. The lingering sadness. A sense of injustice.

All that remains of the house is the brick chimney and the eight-foot-deep crater where the basement had once been. The walls have eroded and crumbled over the years. Saplings and weeds grow up from the basement floor, which is now filled with what looks like several feet of water. At some point, someone used plywood and sawhorses to cover the pit—probably for liability reasons—but the wood has long since collapsed. The only thing left is the remnants of a single caution flag, as faded and shredded as the memory of the people who once lived here.

I think of Hoch Yoder, and I wonder if he ever comes back here. I wonder if he's stood where I'm standing now and grieved for the family he lost. I wonder if he's been able to embrace the age-old Amish tenet of forgiveness.

I jump when a sudden gust of wind sends droplets of rain from the branches of a pine into the water below. The sound seems inordinately loud in the silence, and I get a prickly sensation on the back of my neck. Turning slowly, I fan my light in a 360-degree circle, but there's no one there. No vehicle. No lights.

Thrusting my flashlight out ahead of me, I start toward the silo and barn. My pants are damp from the hip down from walking the McCullough property earlier and, now, from wading through weeds. I reach the rusty silo first. Once upon a time, it had been painted silver, but rust has eaten through the paint.

The hatch stands open. I hear it squeaking as the breeze rocks it back and forth. Bending, I shine my light inside. There's a hole in the roof where the wind has peeled away the shingles. I see yellow cornstalks rotting on the ground and a rat the size of a ground-hog looking at me from the ledge of the concrete footer.

"Shit," I mutter, and continue to the barn. It's a German-style building, most of which were con-structed in the early 1900s and used for dairy opera-tions. Today, the odd-looking structures are akin to covered bridges and much loved by tourists and afi-cionados of unusual architecture. There are several in the area, but none are used in the manner in which they were intended.

Upon reaching the barn, I walk the exterior perim-eter, keeping beneath the overhanging roof until I reach the front door. Trespassers have broken most of the windows. Pushing open the door, I shine the beam inside. The elements have destroyed much of the floor; the wood planks are buckled and rotting in places. Some have splintered and collapsed, and I can see into the crawl space beneath.

I'm not exactly sure what I expected to find here tonight. Nothing, really. But as a cop, there's some-thing intangibly useful about visiting a crime scene, even if the scene is ages old and any evidence has long since faded.

As I walk back to the dry warmth of my vehicle, the wind passing through the trees sounds very much like the cries of dying children.

CHAPTER 18

The first thing I notice when I pull into the gravel lane of the farmhouse is that Tomasetti left the porch light on for me. As I drive around to the rear, I see his Tahoe parked in its usual spot. Butterflies flutter in my stomach when I think of how we left things. I'm not sure what I'll find when I go inside. I have no idea if he's angry or sorry or somewhere in between. I don't know if he's seen Ferguson. Or if he listened to what I had to say.

I unlock the back door to see that the light above the stove is on. The kitchen smells of coffee and vanilla potpourri, and for an instant, I'm over-whelmed with a sense of homecoming. I'm standing just inside the door, taking off my jacket, when the light flicks on.

On the other side of the kitchen, Tomasetti stands at the doorway, looking at me. "Are you hungry?" he asks.

He's wearing sweatpants and a T-shirt. His feet are bare. Hair damp from a recent shower. I take a breath, and even from several feet away, I discern the scent of his aftershave.

"I could be," I reply.

Amusement flashes in his eyes, but he doesn't smile. "I brought home sandwiches from Leo's Deli."

Leo's is a mom-and-pop eatery in Wooster, and in the last months has become our favorite "quick" dinner. "What kind?"

"Paninis. They're in the fridge."

I'm staring at him, but I can't seem to stop. I'm not hungry and I couldn't care less about the sandwiches, from Leo's or elsewhere. What I do care about more than anything else in the world is this man standing before me. Instead of responding, I ask the one question I swore I never would. The one question that strips me bare. The one that requires the truth from him. A truth I fear because I know he'll give it, no-holds-barred, and I have no idea what it will be.

"Do you love me, Tomasetti?"

He's not an easy man to read, but I perceive surprise in the way his eyes dart away, in the way he shifts his weight away from me, as if there's a part of him that would like nothing more than to slink back into the darkness and not deal with this. With me. But it's too late to take back the words.

"You know I do," he tells me.

"Actually, I *don't* know or I wouldn't have asked. Sometimes you say things, and I'm not sure you mean them."

"I've never lied to you, Kate."

"You haven't lied. But you haven't been completely honest, either."

"I don't know what that means."

"It means we've been dancing around some issues we need to deal with."

When he says nothing, I feel the blood leave my head. A physical reaction that takes me a moment to identify. I'm scared, I realize. I'm afraid I'm not handling this the right way. That I'm going to say something wrong. That we're going to somehow blow what we have and he's going to walk away.

"Tomasetti, there's a part of you that you refuse to share with me. A part you keep tucked away, unavailable. That's not honest."

"I told you about my past. I told you what I did. I told you I wasn't going to be easy."

"I don't care about easy."

He shrugs. "That's the best I can do right now."

"I don't believe that."

"What do you want from me?"

"I want all of you. I don't think that's too much to ask."

"I'm not sure what we're talking about here."

"I don't want to share you with them anymore." Taking a step closer, I press my hand to my chest. "I'll never rate and I'm not sure I'll ever garner the kind of love you had for them."

"That's not true," he says with some heat.

"I'm sorry you lost them. I'm sorry they were hurt and your life was devastated. But they're gone now, and I'm here. I'm alive and I want to build a life with you. You have to choose."

At first I think he's going to turn around and walk away. Instead, he rounds the table and starts toward me. He doesn't rush, doesn't give me a clue as to what he's thinking or feeling. His eyes are level on mine, but I don't know if he's going to rail against the words I've just thrown at him—or admit they're true. My heart is like a drum against my ribs. My head feels light, a head rush from standing too fast. Sweat slicks the back of my neck and palms. For a crazy instant, I consider turning around and running out the door and into the night. But the intellectual side of my brain reminds me of what's at stake. However it turns out, I need to finish it.

He touches my arms first, his fingers wrapping around my biceps. Then he's pushing me backwards, one step, two. My back hits the doorframe, the knob bumping my hip with so much force that the picture on the wall rattles.

His eyes lock with mine. In the depth of his gaze, I see a jumble of emotions, none of which I can read. The kiss that follows isn't gentle. Yet I sense the fragility of the moment, something intangible slipping from my grasp even as something else settles more securely inside me.

"You're wrong," he tells me.

"Prove it."

As he lowers his mouth to mine, I experience a fleeting sense of defeat followed by the realization that I'm no longer in control of the situation—or my life. That maybe I haven't been for a long time and I was a fool to believe I could maintain that grasp. It stuns me to realize I'm willing to accept that. For the first time in my life, I've relinquished my heart and given someone else the power to hurt me. The thought terrifies me because I know there's a part of him I don't trust not to do just that.

CHAPTER 19

Sleep is a precious commodity in the course of any homicide investigation, mainly because the first forty-eight hours are so crucial in terms of solving the case. I know better than to allow the things going on in my personal life to interfere with my job. But I have a feeling I'm not the first cop to let it happen anyway. Luckily, I'm pretty good at operating on little sleep and staying focused when I have other issues zinging around inside my head.

Tomasetti and I didn't get much settled last night, not in terms of talking, anyway. We didn't broach any of the topics I brought up. I didn't ask for some magic solution and he offered none. We didn't even talk about the case—and I would have very much appreciated his insights. Despite all of that, this morning I'm feeling optimistic that the kinks we've encountered will smooth out. I'm going to have to trust him and I'm going to have to be patient. Neither of those things comes naturally to me, so I'm going to have to work on them.

It's 7 A.M., and I'm already buzzed on coffee and in that mental zone I find myself in when I'm embroiled in a case. In addition to the two homicides, I've been unable to account for Jerrold McCullough for nearly twenty-four hours. It's possible he became frightened and left town. But I have a bad feeling in my gut.

Questions and scenarios pummel my brain as I climb into the Explorer. Ten minutes later, I'm on the gravel track that runs parallel with Painters Creek, heading toward McCullough's place. I slow for the bridge, and I'm dismayed to see that the water is just a foot from the center span. There aren't many homes in this area, but if any more rain falls, the road will be under water.

I park next to McCullough's Riviera and cut the engine. I can see his house from where I'm sitting. The porch light is on, but there are no lights on inside. I hail Mona on the radio.

"I'm ten twenty-three Jerrold McCullough's place."

"Roger that, Chief."

"Will you do me a favor and call the mayor. Tell him I think we're going to have some flooding out here and we should probably put out some kind of bulletin to let folks know."

"Will do." She pauses. "Glock just brought in doughnuts. Do you want me to save you one?"

"That's affirm." Smiling, I get out.

The first thing I'm aware of is the roar of the water from behind the house. Painters Creek is usually a meandering stream with deep fishing holes and shallow crossings where the water trickles over rocks. This morning it's latte brown and swollen to three times its normal size. The rain has stopped, but the sky to the west is black and ominous looking, telling me there's more on the way. What I wouldn't do for just one day of sunshine . . .

I pause to look through the driver's-side window of the Riviera. I see a pile of magazines in the backseat. A Coke can on the floor. A Netflix movie that probably needs to be dropped at the post office. I take the same path Glock and I took last night, hopping between pieces of plywood and chunks of concrete to avoid the mud. I reach the porch and knock hard on the storm door. "Jerrold McCullough! It's Kate Burkholder with the Painters Mill PD. Come to the door, please. I need to speak with you!"

I shout the words not only to be heard above the roar of water, but because it's still early and I know there's a possibility McCullough is asleep. That would be a best-case scenario. I don't believe he came home last night. I don't believe he's here now. I knock a second time, using the heel of my hand. Upon his arrival yesterday, Glock found the door open. But for security reasons, we locked it when we left.

When there's no answer, I brave the mud and go around to the rear of the house. I pause at the living room window, cup my hands and try to see inside. But the curtains are pulled tight, so I continue around.

The sight of the creek gives me pause. The water has encroached thirty feet into the yard, swirling amid mammoth tree trunks, carrying debris—logs and branches and trash—as it rushes toward its end journey to Sugar Creek and the Tuscarawas River. And I know in my heart there's no way McCullough would have left when flooding is a threat to his home. He's an I'm-going-down-with-the-ship type, even if we'd called for a mandatory evacuation.

"Jerrold McCullough! Police Department!"

I look out across the water. Fifty feet away, a good-size log is jammed against a stand of trees that, so far, have withstood the force of the current. The branches have captured a sizeable amount of debris: leaves and brush and what looks like an old tire. Nearer, the wooden deck is inches from being completely submerged now. When the creek is at normal levels, the deck is twenty feet from the bank and the perfect place to lounge in a chair with a book or maybe barbecue brats and burgers. I know it won't be long before the torrent gobbles it up and sends it downstream. I'm about to head back to the Explorer, when I notice something pale bobbing just beneath the surface a foot or two off the deck, and I get a bad feeling in my gut.

I edge closer to the water for a better look. The ground is muddy and slick and I know that even shallow rushing water can knock someone off their feet. I stop inches from the water's edge and crane my head forward. The bad feeling augments to a hard rush of adrenaline when I see a pale face and silver flowing hair inches beneath the surface.

"Shit!" I stumble back at the grisly sight, slip in the mud, and end up on my ass.

Quickly, I scramble to my feet and grapple for my lapel mike. "Ten fifty-two."

"Go ahead."

"Adult male. In the water. Submerged."

"You still at the McCullough place?"

"That's affirm."

"Fire and rescue's on the way, Chief."

The preservation of life is always the first priority in any emergency situation. But I know it's too late for the paramedics to help. The victim is completely submerged, and I know that soon I'll be dealing with a dead body. Worse, I'm pretty sure the victim is Jer-rold McCullough.

CHAPTER 20

Tomasetti left his office in Richfield at 10 A.M. and headed directly to northbound I-77. Without the hindrance of rush hour traffic, he arrived at the Cuyahoga County Corrections Center in less than thirty minutes. Inmate visitation is designated by sex and last name, but Tomasetti had obtained special permission for today's visit. It didn't hurt that he'd gone to the police academy with the associate warden, who'd cleared it through director of corrections. He wasn't above using his connections to get what he wanted.

He'd been inside many correctional facilities in the course of his career. They all had the same feel, a closed-in space that smelled of dirty shorts, industrial-strength cleaner, and high school cafeteria food. All of it permeated with an overt sense of desperation, the knowledge of men incarcerated and the awareness that most of them are violent.

The walls were painted an institutional two-tone gray. To his left was the control center, a reception office of sorts with a bullet-resistant barrier window and security transaction tray. A uniformed corrections officer sat inside, his thick fingers pecking at a keyboard.

Tomasetti approached the window and leaned close to catch the officer's attention.

"Sign in." Without looking up, the officer dropped a clipboard with a sheet attached to the tray and shoved it toward Tomasetti. "If you're preregistered, I just need two forms of ID."

Tomasetti removed his badge and set it in the tray. "I think this'll do it."

The corrections officer, whose name tag read D. NELSON, finally looked up. He didn't seem too impressed by Tomasetti's credentials. "If you have a firearm on your person, you'll need to check it with the officer in the cage."

"No problem." Tomasetti signed his name and filled in the date, leaving off the part about his being with BCI, and shoved the clipboard back to the officer.

The man glanced at it, looked at Tomasetti, and then picked up the phone. "Have a seat," he said, and motioned toward a row of waiting-room chairs that lined the opposite wall.

Tomasetti took the nearest chair, using the time to check his e-mail and voice mail—none of which were from Kate. Two minutes later, a buzzer sounded. He looked up to see his old academy mate, Stan McCaskill, standing at the door, looking at him as if he wasn't quite sure who he was.

"I'll be damned," he said. "John Tomasetti."

"Hey, Stan." Tomasetti rose and crossed to him, extended his hand. "It's been a while."

"Twenty years, give or take." He opened the door wider, ushering Tomasetti inside. "What are you doing these days?"

"I'm with BCI."

He nodded approvingly. "So what's your business with Kinnamon?"

"Cold case I'm about to close." Tomasetti tapped the file at his side. "Just need to ask a few questions, and I'll be out of your hair."

They went through a windowless steel door, down a tiled hall, and then reached the cage, a glassed-in office where two corrections officers controlled the door locks and access to the interior of the jail. McCaskill set a blue form on the security transaction tray and shoved it toward the other man.

The man inside looked down at it and then gave Tomasetti a quick once-over. "You'll need to check your firearm here."

"Sure." Once again, he placed his badge in the tray. Then he removed his weapon from his shoulder holster and set it in the tray as well.

The officer tore off a ticket and sent it back to him. The locks on the door across the room snicked open.

"Here we go." McCaskill took him through it and motioned Tomasetti into a small interview room. "You need audio? Escort?"

Tomasetti shook his head. "Just Kinnamon."

"I'll get him for you."

The room was like a hundred other interview rooms Tomasetti had been in over the years. Twelve feet square. Gray walls. Windowless. Not even an observation window. Institutional tile floor. Air temp hovering somewhere around sixty-two degrees. Discomfort helped to thwart stonewalling. The table was four feet long and a couple of feet wide with an off-white Formica surface that was etched with scratches from lawyer's briefcases. A single *Fuck You* was carved into the corner. Three cheap blue sled chairs covered with stain-resistant fabric that wasn't that stain resistant surrounded the table.

There was a camera mounted in the corner, just below ceiling level. No glowing eye, but that didn't mean someone didn't have video running. But there was no intercom. No phone. No visible wires. None of those things guaranteed the conversation he was about to have with Vince Kinnamon was private or wouldn't be secretly recorded. Tomasetti wasn't exactly the trusting type, but there was no way around the risk.

McCaskill didn't keep him waiting. Tomasetti had barely settled in when the door opened and the corrections officer produced Kinnamon. "Step inside," he said.

Tomasetti took the other man's measure as he shuffled in. Orange prison jumpsuit. Off-brand sneakers. No chains or restraints. Tomasetti had met him a couple of times over the years, but if it hadn't been for the name tag embroidered into the fabric, he would have been hard-pressed to recognize him. The inmate shuffling into the interview room looked nothing like the man who'd once owned a five-thousand-square-foot house in Edgewater. Three months in jail had taken a heavy toll. He'd dropped sixty pounds. His once-tanned face had the telltale prison pallor. The only thing that was the same were his eyes. They were black as tar and radiated a cunning that could raise the hairs on the necks of even the most seasoned cops. Today, those eyes revealed nothing of what he was thinking as they latched on to Tomasetti.

Up until his arrest, Vince Kinnamon had been a

dangerous man. A killer with a weakness for hard drugs, a penchant for violence, and no conscience to keep him from acting on the most primal of urges. The Cleveland PD suspected him in a plethora of crimes ranging from heroin distribution to murder. Kinnamon's luck ran out three months ago, when he'd been busted by the feds for laundering money through his Downtown Cleveland bar, The Red Monkey. He'd been put before a federal grand jury, which had quickly handed down an indictment. He'd been incarcerated and, deemed a flight risk, denied bail while he awaited trial. Rumor had it that even in prison, Kinnamon was still connected. Still powerful. Tomasetti was counting on both those things.

McCaskill gestured toward the chair on the opposite side of the table from where Tomasetti was sitting. "Kinnamon. Sit down. There." He turned his attention to Tomasetti. "How much time you need?"

"Ten minutes max."

The corrections officer pointed at a button that resembled a doorbell set into the wall. "Just hit the buzzer when you're through, and we'll come get him."

"Thanks again."

The door clicked shut. Without looking at Kinnamon, Tomasetti opened the file and looked down at the blur of black and white that had nothing to do with the purpose of his visit today.

"You don't look like a fed," Kinnamon said.

"They treating you okay here at County?" Tomasetti asked the question without looking up.

"Fucking hacks. They treat all the inmates like shit. What's it to you?"

"When's your trial?" Tomasetti flipped a paper. "May?"

"June."

He looked away from the file, made eye contact with Kinnamon. "Looks like the feds have you by the balls this time, Vince. Money laundering. They take that shit seriously."

Kinnamon regarded him across the table, saying nothing.

"How did they get you, anyway?" he asked.

"Some fucking rat." Kinnamon waved off the question. "I still don't know who you are."

"Let's just say I'm the bearer of interesting news."

Kinnamon stared at him, saying nothing at first, but he wasn't doing a very good job of concealing his interest. "What's that supposed to mean?"

"You heard Joey Ferguson's conviction was overturned, didn't you?"

"I heard. Good for him. What does that have to do with me?"

"How do you think he managed that?"

"The Cleveland cops are a bunch of fuckups."

For the span of a full minute, neither man spoke. The only sound came from the jiggle of Kinnamon's foot against the chair. Tomasetti could feel the other man's curiosity, his misery, his desperation.

"Official word is he got off on a technicality," Tomasetti said. "But I heard Joey Ferguson walked because he turned over on you. He ratted you out. Fucked you over." He leaned back in his chair and contemplated Kinnamon. "That means he gets the house on the lake. A pretty wife. The kids. And a boat. You get life in a six-by-six-foot cell."

The other man said nothing. But Tomasetti didn't miss the color that climbed up his neck or the way the muscles in his jaws quivered with tension. "Who the fuck are you? And why would you come in here and tell me that shit? You got some beef with Ferguson?"

Tomasetti closed the file and got to his feet. "Good luck with your trial."

Kinnamon hissed something, but Tomasetti pressed the call button, shutting him out. When the door opened, he left the room without looking back.

CHAPTER 21

Half an hour later, I'm standing twenty feet from the bank of a raging Painters Creek, watching a volunteer firefighter retrieve McCullough's body from the water. Next to me, Skid slurps at an extra-large McDonald's coffee, watching the scene as if he's sitting cross-legged in front of the television watching an old episode of *Jonny Quest*. Behind us, two paramedics from Pomerene Hospital stand beneath the branches of a black walnut tree that does little to shield them from the rain.

"Chief?"

I glance behind me to see the coroner approach, sliding a little in the mud as he comes down the slope from the front of the house. He's eyeing me as if it's my fault he's out tromping around in such inhospitable weather and he's holding me personally responsible. His eyes slide toward the life preserver–clad firefighters as he starts toward us.

"I wish people would choose better weather in which to die," he grumbles as he reaches us.

Skid chuckles into his coffee.

The doc doesn't smile. "Any idea who it is?"

"I think it's the homeowner, Jerrold McCullough," I tell him.

"Chief!" The nearest firefighter looks over his shoulder at me. "You might want to see this."

Skid lowers the cup from his mouth and looks at me. "You want me to go, Chief?"

"I got it." I cross to the water's edge, where the two firefighters, both of whom have safety tethers attached to their life vests, are standing in hip-deep water. "What is it?"

"This guy didn't just fall off the deck and get tangled in that rope," he shouts to be heard above the roar of the water. "His hands are bound."

In light of the other two murders, I shouldn't be surprised, but there's always something intrinsically shocking about murder. "He's tied to the deck?"

"Looks like."

The deck seems to be shielding them from the worst of the current. Still, it's a dangerous retrieval. Without those tethers, one slip could send a man into the water, where even the strongest swimmer would be swept downstream.

A third rescuer approaches me with an orange life vest. "Here you go, Chief."

All I can think as I put my arms through the straps is that I don't want to go into that swirling, dark water. The firefighter doesn't seem to notice my trepidation as he produces a black nylon tether strap and clips it to my vest with a carabiner.

The firefighter in the water looks over his shoulder at me. "I've never seen anything like this."

At the bank, I look back at Skid. "Grab the camera, will you?"

Nodding, he starts up the incline toward his cruiser.

Trying not to slip in the mud, I enter the water. Cold creeps over the tops of my boots and grips my feet with icy hands that streak up my legs with enough force to chill my entire body. No one had any spare wader boots, so I'm destined to go through the day with wet feet. Another step takes me into a foot of swirling brown water. Even though it's shallow, the current tugs at me, like a child pulling on my pant leg to get my attention.

I'm about four feet downstream from the deck. Tea-colored water rushes around the wood piers. The two firefighters are taking the brunt of the current; I can see it washing around their legs. One of the men has looped a rope around the nearest pier and is using it to hold on to.

Water inches over my knees and slaps against my thighs as I wade closer to the deck. When the farthest firefighter steps aside, I get my first good look at the body. I see a blue-white face with cloudy eyes. A gray strip of what looks like duct tape over the mouth. Hair flowing like some exotic fish fin just below the surface. The victim is wearing a white tank undershirt and blue jeans that have been nearly pulled from his body by the force of the water. Bare feet. My eyes seek out his hands, but they're bound behind his back, cotton rope whipping with the current.

"See that?" The firefighter points. "Hands are tied. Looks like duct tape over his mouth and wrapped around his head. I thought you might want to see it before we cut him loose."

"Let me get a few shots," I tell him.

Gripping the tether with my left hand, I wade back to the shore. "Skid!"

He places the camera in my palm. Wrapping the

strap around my wrist, hoping I don't fall and ruin it, I work my way back out to the body. I stop two feet away, brace my feet against the pull of the water, and start snapping photos. It's difficult to make out the details because of the murkiness and glare. The raging current is whipping the body back and forth with such force that I hear it striking the deck's pier.

I leave the water and shoot a dozen more photos from different angles as the firefighters cut the body loose. The rope drags behind them like a dead snake as they carry the victim to shore. Doc Coblentz and a young female technician, who's staring at the body as if she's expecting it to turn into a zombie at any moment, spreads a black zippered body bag on grass that's been pulverized to mud. The firefighters lay the victim in a supine position atop the vinyl.

When the two men step away, I move closer and look down at the body. The face is discolored and swollen, but not so much that I don't recognize him. "It's Jerrold McCullough," I say.

One of the rescuers comes up beside me. "Looks like he's been submerged awhile," he says as he removes his life vest.

I look at Doc Coblentz. "Any idea how long?"

The doc shakes his head. "Skin hasn't begun to slough. Not much in the way of bloating. If I had to guess, I'd say less than twenty-four hours. I'll get a liver temp once I get him to the morgue."

Skid's gaze snags mine. "That means he was there last night when you and Glock were here, looking for him."

"The water hadn't yet reached the deck," I say. "If he was alive and conscious, he heard us."

"Kate, look at his knees." The coroner glances up at me from where he's kneeling next to the body.

I kneel beside him and watch as he indicates holes in the man's trousers at both knees. Using scissors, he cuts away the wet fabric and reveals neat round bullet holes in both knees. "Looks like gunshot wounds," he says.

"Holy shit," Skid mutters from somewhere behind me.

The doc studies the wounds. "I won't be sure until I get X-rays, but it looks like on the left knee, the bullet hit the patella. On the right, it looks as if it penetrated the soft tissue between the patella and tibia."

"Was he alive when he was shot?" I ask.

"There's bruising. Swelling. I would say yes, he was alive when he sustained those two wounds."

I look down at the body and try not to wince at the images prying into my brain. "Doc, can you cut away that duct tape?"

Using surgical-grade scissors, the coroner cuts the duct tape and peels it away. I work an evidence bag from my belt and hold it out. He drops the length of tape into the bag.

McCullough's mouth is open. I see blue lips and yellowed teeth. A small dark object at the back of his throat. "There's something in his mouth," I say.

"Some kind of foreign object." The doc looks over his shoulder at the technician. "Hand me those pliers."

The technician passes the instrument to the doc. We watch in silence as the doc inserts the pincers and pulls out the Amish peg doll. "Just like the others," he says.

From behind me, Skid hands him another evidence bag and the doc drops it inside.

I hand the camera to Skid. "Get some photos of that, will you?"

"Yep."

The doc continues with his preliminary exam. "No irregularities in the clothing," he says.

Steeling myself against the ghastliness of the body, I kneel for a closer look. "Wrists are scored."

"At some point, he was conscious and struggled," the doc says. "From the looks of that bruising and the abrasions, probably for quite some time."

I look toward the deck and try not to imagine the panic and terror Jerrold McCullough endured before his death. The killer had crippled him. Bound him. Gagged with the peg doll stuffed into his throat. Then he'd tied him to the pier, struggling, until the rising water had drowned him.

"This was personal," I say to no one in particular. "Someone wanted him to suffer."

"I'd say they succeeded," the doc mutters.

I make eye contact with Skid and we move away from the doc and firefighters. Out of earshot, I tell him, "I want you to pick up Blue Branson for questioning."

"You think he did this?" he asks.

"I honestly don't know. But I want you to pick him up. Sweat him a little. See what oozes out."

He nods. "Where are you going?"

"I'm going to pick up Norm Johnston."

I leave Skid standing on the muddy bank with his mouth open.

I sit in the Explorer for several minutes, shaking with cold, heat blasting, trying to decide how to handle Johnston. The optimism I felt earlier has been depleted by the things I've seen and the knowledge that this killer isn't going to stop—until someone stops him. If my theory is correct, and these murders are related to the Hochstetler case, Blue Branson and

Norm Johnston—perhaps even Hoch Yoder and his wife—are in danger.

Or else one of them is a murderer.

It takes me ten minutes to reach the Painters Mill City Building, a two-story redbrick structure built at the turn of the century. I take the elevator to the second floor, where the town council meeting room and offices are located. I find Norm at his desk, a mug of coffee and a bagel piled high with cream cheese sitting on the leather blotter in front of him.

He looks up when I enter his office. He doesn't look like he got much sleep last night. And he doesn't look happy to see me. "What do you want?" he asks.

When I was in the police academy, one of the first concepts I learned was "the force continuum." The term basically outlines the ten levels of force a police officer uses to gain and maintain control of a person or situation. It begins with a uniformed presence and verbal commands and goes all the way to the use of deadly force. No cop wants to become involved in a scuffle or fight, or God forbid, a shooting, whether justified or not. But while a good cop will do everything in his power to avoid escalation, he can never let himself be intimidated by it.

I don't bother with a greeting. "I need for you to come to the police station with me."

"What?" A humorless laugh erupts from his throat. But I don't miss the way his eyes flash to the hallway behind me, telling me he's more worried about someone overhearing than he is at the prospect of a trip to the station. "What's this about?"

"Jerrold McCullough is dead." I say the words brutally.

"Oh my God." The color drains from his face. "How?"

"He was murdered," I tell him. "I need you to come with me to the station."

"But . . . why? I had nothing to do with it. For God's sake, I'm not a suspect, am I?"

"You can either come with me voluntarily or I'll cuff you and you can ride in the cage. It's your choice." I glance over my shoulder at the mail person pushing a cart down the hall. "The latter is guaranteed to get the tongues wagging. I don't think you want to make a scene."

Snarling something beneath his breath, he grabs the bagel and hurls it into the trash. "When my lawyer gets finished with you, you won't even be able to get a security job."

I motion toward the door. "Let's go."

CHAPTER 22

An hour later, I'm sitting in the interview room across the table from Norm Johnston and his lawyer, a young hotshot by the name of Colin Thornsberry. I've met him several times over the years, and each time I like him a little less. He's an attractive man just shy of thirty, with a weakness for expensive clothes, a cocky attitude, and the manners of a chimpanzee.

I brought several files with me, including the Hochstetler case file, though I don't need any of them. They're nice and thick and official-looking. I set them down on the table with a thud.

I turn on the digital recorder, recite the date, and identify all present. I then glance down at the card in my hand and recite the Miranda rights to Norm.

"Do you understand those rights, Mr. Johnston?" I ask as I pass the card to him.

"I don't need those rights read to me," Johnston says. "I'm not some criminal off the street. I'm a town councilman. A respected member of this community."

"We got it," Thornsberry snaps at me, overruling him.

"I know what you are," I tell Johnston.

I see both men looking at the file tab, reading the name scrawled in black marker, and for the first time Thornsberry doesn't look quite so cocky. Taking my time, I open the Rutledge homicide file, giving both men a flash glance at one of the crime scene photos. I pull out the manila folder that I'd tucked inside and set it in front of me without opening it.

"Look, Chief Burkholder, I don't know what you *think* you know about my client," Thornsberry says, "but I'm familiar with your tactics. I'm aware of how you operate, and I won't tolerate my client being railroaded by your overzealous policing."

I look at Thornsberry. "Are you finished?"

His mouth tightens. "I think you should get to the point so Mr. Johnston can get back to his duties as councilman."

I open the folder and remove copies of the notes Johnston gave me and pass them to him. "Do you recognize these notes?" I ask.

The town councilman jerks his head. "Yes. Of course. I gave them to you. Someone's been stalking me."

I pull out a copy of the notes I found at Julia Rutledge's gallery and hand them to Norm. "A few hours after Julia Rutledge was found stabbed to death in her home, a search of her gallery turned up these."

Thornsberry gestures toward the notes. "The only thing these notes prove is that your department should have provided police protection for my client when he requested it, instead of dragging him in here to the police department for questioning."

I don't look away from Johnston. His forehead is

shiny with sweat. He can't seem to stop staring at the notes that had been sent to Julia Rutledge, as if he's reading them over and over.

"Norm, do you have any idea who sent those notes to you?" I ask.

"I have no idea." He shakes his head. "It's got to be related to council business. Someone who disagrees with me on some issue. As chief, I'm sure you know it happens."

"Do you have any idea why Julia Rutledge was receiving similar notes?"

"Of course not."

I look down at the copies of the notes in front of me, and I reach each aloud. " 'Dale sends his regards from hell.' 'I know you were there.' 'You could have stopped them.' 'Murderer.' " I turn my attention to Johnston. " 'You knew.' 'You looked the other way.' 'You're next.' Any idea what they mean?" I ask.

I hear the sticky sound of a dry mouth when he licks his lips. "I don't know."

"I think these notes tell a story," I say. "They certainly raise some questions."

Thornsberry all but rolls his eyes. "Chief Burkholder, you have no proof that these notes are anything but threats sent by a seriously delusional and dangerous individual."

I ignore him, zero in on Johnston. "I can't get into specifics because there are certain details about the case that we're not releasing to the public. But I have evidence that may link the murders of Dale Michaels, Julia Rutledge, and Jerrold McCullough to the Hochstetler case." I hold up my copy of the notes and shake it at him. "These notes connect those cases to you."

"That's crazy. I had nothing to do with any of those crimes." Johnston chokes out the words, jerks his attention to his attorney, prompting him to jump to his aid. "Can you stop this?"

I speak before Thornsberry can reply. "You want to know what's crazy, Norm? I believe you. But I think you know something that, for whatever reason, you feel you can't tell me."

Johnston's eyes slide from Thornsberry to me. "Something about what?"

"Maybe you know something about the Hochstetler case." I'm casting a long line into deep water, and Thornsberry knows it. But I can tell by Johnston's response, he hasn't yet realized it.

"That's outrageous," he says. "That happened ages ago. I was a kid, for God's sake!"

Thornsberry steps in. "Chief Burkholder, unless you've got proof of that, I suggest you curtail that particular line of questioning."

I don't take my eyes from Johnston. "Maybe it's something innocent. Some piece of information that you haven't realized is important." I pause. "Were you there that night? Do you know who was?"

"Who told you that?" Johnston demands.

"Norm," the attorney warns.

"What happened, Norm? Did you get in over your head? Did you somehow find out about something you shouldn't have?"

"For God's sake, no! I was sixteen years old. A minor!"

"You keep reminding me of your age as if it somehow excuses some bad decision you made."

"Chief Burkholder, that's quite enough," Thornsberry says.

"All right." I nod at the attorney and take a chance, stretching boundaries, choosing my words carefully. "I'm going to let you in on a little secret. I talked to some people who hinted that you might know something about that case."

Johnston's eyes jerk in their sockets. "Who told you that?" He looks at his attorney. "They're lying."

It doesn't elude me that he doesn't deny it. "It's an ongoing investigation," I tell him. "I can't get into details, but I'm going to get to the bottom of it, and your cooperation will go a long way toward keeping you safe from harm."

Johnston gets to his feet. His face is red, his teeth clenched. I scoot my chair back, keeping a safe distance between us in case he decides to come over the table and take all that rage out on me.

"You got your information wrong," he snarls. "I was not there that night. And I am not going to take a fall because of something someone else did."

"Norm, take it down a notch, buddy," Thornsberry says.

I ignore him, my attention riveted to Johnston. "If you were involved in any way, you know I'll find out sooner or later."

"Don't say anything incriminating," Thornsberry adds quickly.

"I didn't do anything wrong." Johnston doesn't take his eyes off me. A drop of sweat rolls down his temple. His nostrils flaring with every breath. "For God's sake, do you think I'd have brought those notes to you if I had?"

I don't answer. "Listen to me, Norm. Three people are dead. You've been receiving notes. You're a target. Please help me keep you safe."

He lowers his head and pinches the bridge of his nose between thumb and forefinger. "For God's sake."

"Norm, if you cooperate—if you tell me what you know—I'll do my best to help you." My words aren't quite true. If he incriminates himself, I'll nail him to the wall. It isn't the first time a cop has lied to a suspect to get the truth. That's how the game is played.

"Be quiet, Norm." Thornsberry places his hand on Norm's arm. "My client and I need a quick conference to discuss this."

Johnston shakes him off. He shifts his gaze from me to Thornsberry and then back to me. "I'm not admitting to doing anything illegal. I did nothing wrong. But before we go any farther, I want immunity from prosecution. And I want protection."

I hold his gaze. "You know I'll do whatever I can." The lie flies off my tongue with the fervor of truth. I owe this man nothing. Not the truth. Lease of all immunity from prosecution.

"We're going to want that in writing," Thornsberry says.

"I'll have your statement typed up so you can sign it. I'll need to get the county attorney involved." I look at Johnston. "Tell me what you know."

"It's about the Hochstetler . . . thing. I heard some . . . . rumors about what went down that night."

I give him a reassuring look. "What happened?"

"Be careful what you say," Thornsberry warns.

Some of the tension leaches from the councilman's body. His shoulders sag. "I worked part-time at their furniture shop for a few weeks. Sweeping floors or whatever Mr. Hochstetler needed me to do. I was sixteen, a couple of years older than Billy. Anyway, one day Billy starts bragging about how much money they made. He said his dad didn't like using banks and kept thousands of dollars in cash at the house." He looks away. "I told Blue Branson. . . ." His voice trails.

"When did this happen?"

"A week or so before . . . that night." He heaves a

sigh. "I think Blue and his friends went in to rob them."

"Who was involved?"

"I think they were all involved to some degree. Blue Branson. Dale Michaels. Jerrold McCullough."

"What about Julia Rutledge?"

"She wasn't in on the planning, but I think she was there."

"What role did you play?"

"Chief Burkholder, I may be guilty of exercising poor judgment as a sixteen-year-old kid, but I was not at the Hochstetler farm that night. I didn't know about any of it until Blue asked me to meet them at the turnaround a half mile from the Hochstetler place at four A.M. He said they needed someone with a fast car. I had this jacked-up GTO that could outrun every cop in the county. At that point, I knew there was something going down. I knew it was big. That it was daring and probably illegal. But they didn't trust me enough to tell me what it was."

"Did you meet them?"

"I got scared and didn't show."

"What happened?"

"I don't know," he tells me. "But when I heard about that family on the news, I fucking threw up. I couldn't believe they could do something like that. It was the most horrible moment of my life."

"Do you think they went in with plans to murder that family?"

"I can't imagine that. I mean, they weren't . . . criminals. They certainly weren't . . . killers. They were good kids from decent families. The *good* crowd. Football players. Jules was a cheerleader. Pudge had already earned a scholarship to the University of Michigan." He rubs the back of his neck.

"I think they went in and . . . I don't know . . . some-one must have panicked. Whatever happened was probably an accident."

Anger rushes hotly into my gut. I can understand how a teenager could be frightened or intimidated. What I don't understand is how this man who has worked and lived in Painters Mill his entire life could remain silent about a heinous crime for thirty-five years.

"Do you know who shot Willis Hochstetler?"

"No."

"What happened to Wanetta Hochstetler?"

He shakes his head. "I swear I don't know."

"The things that you do know," I say slowly, "would you be willing to testify in a court of law?"

"Yes." He gives a single hard nod. "I didn't do any-thing wrong. I'm in the clear. That's why I felt I could come to you."

I lean back in my chair and look at him, seeing him in a completely different light. He repulses me. I'm aware that Thornsberry has gone silent. "Is there any-thing else I need to know about any of this?" I ask. "Anything else you'd like to tell me?"

Johnston raises his gaze to mine. "Two days after . . . that night, Blue Branson and Jerrold Mc-Cullough asked me to meet them down at the covered bridge. They beat the hell out of me. They broke two of my fingers. Broke my nose. A couple of ribs." He looks away. "They basically told me they'd kill me and my parents if I ever said a word to anyone."

"That's intimidation," Thornsberry asserts.

I nod, but my mind is reeling. I stare at Thorns-berry, who can't quite meet my gaze. I can't look at Johnston; I'm not sure how to handle this, how to feel. While he wasn't directly complicit in the crimes that were perpetrated that night, he had some advance knowledge. Yet he hadn't known enough to stop it. Still, once news of the crimes became public, he could have gone to the police. He's had thirty-five years to come forward and didn't.

Gathering the file, I rise and turn off the recording device. "Under Ohio code," I tell both men, "prior knowledge of a crime could mean a complicity charge."

"I didn't know anything! I did nothing wrong!" Johnston rises, but Thornsberry presses him back into the chair.

"Chief Burkholder." Across from me, Thornsberry rises. "He was a minor. Sixteen years old. He'd been intimidated and physically assaulted." He lowers his voice. "That's not to mention we have a deal. On tape."

"I'll get with the prosecutor," I tell him. "In the interim, I'll have a statement typed up for Mr. Johnston to sign. We'll talk about a deal after he signs it. For now, Norm, you're not to leave town. Do you understand? One foot over the line, and I will throw everything I've got at you."

Johnston slumps in his chair. "I was a victim, too," he says.

"The prosecutor won't bring charges," Thornsberry tells me. "My client did not break the law. In fact, he just solved a major case for you."

"I guess it's about time, isn't it?" I pick up the file and start toward the door.

Thornsberry blocks my way, smiling, my best friend now. "Because of my client's position as councilman— and the unlikelihood of any charges being levied against him, I'd like to keep this discussion confidential until an official agreement is reached."

"This was not a discussion," I tell him. "It was an interrogation." I go around him.

"Chief Burkholder!" The councilman slaps his hands down on the tabletop. "Please. My reputation!"

I feel nothing but disgust when I look at him. "All of this is going to come out. If I were you, I'd resign my position on the council now, before they remove you." I open the door. "Have a nice day, gentlemen."

When it comes to a homicide investigation, information is never a bad thing. Sometimes even faulty information can lead to something usable. I should be pleased; I now know who was at the Hochstetler farm that night. There's no statute of limitations on murder, so I'll be well within the realm of my duties to arrest and hold Blue Branson.

But in terms of the things I've learned about the people I thought I knew, I'm left trying to make sense of something that's absolutely senseless. All of them—Dale Michaels, Julia Rutledge, Jerrold McCullough, even Blue Branson—were pillars of the community. They were neighbors. The kinds of people you smiled at on the street. Yet they'd lived in this town and kept their dark secrets the entirety of their adult lives. How is it that no one ever really knew them? And while I may have solved a thirty-five-year-old cold case, I still have three unsolved homicides on my hands.

A tap at my office door draws me from my reverie. I look up to see Glock walk in. "I just put Branson in the interview room, Chief, if you're ready to talk to him."

I give him the details of Johnston's confession. "I'll get with the county prosecutor and see how he feels about charging him with a complicity charge. But

Johnston was a minor and intimidation was involved. At the very least, he's finished as councilman."

He nods, but I can see his mind already moving on to the other cases. "Do you think Blue's responsible for these more recent murders? I mean, if one or more of them decided to blackmail him. That's a pretty strong motive."

"I thought of that. But they would have risked incriminating themselves. Plus, he's got an alibi for the Rutledge murder."

"He could have hired someone."

"Maybe. But I don't know, Glock. Something doesn't feel right about that."

"So who else do we have?" He thinks about that a moment. "Hoch Yoder?"

"According to the police report, Hoch stated the perpetrators wore masks. He never saw their faces."

"Maybe he's been doing a little investigating on his own and figured it out." Glock shrugs. "Or someone said something to him."

"Maybe." Lowering my head, I rub at the ache building behind my forehead. "We're overlooking something."

"What about the missing woman?"

"You mean if Wanetta Hochstetler survived and came back for a little revenge?" I say.

"If Johnston is telling the truth, that means Dale Michaels, Julia Rutledge, Jerrold McCullough, and Blue Branson murdered her husband and caused the deaths of her children."

"I agree that's a powerful motive, but Wanetta Hochstetler would be almost seventy years old now."

"Stranger things have happened. If she had some way to subdue them. A stun gun. Something like that."

"Or help." But I'm not sold on the theory. "I'm going to talk to Blue, see if I can get him to admit to being there. Even if he doesn't, we've got enough for an arrest."

Glock nods. "Let me know if you need me to beat his ass for you."

I rise from my desk. "You always know just the right thing to say."

"That's what everyone tells me."

I find Blue Branson sitting at the same table where I spoke to Norm Johnston and his attorney just an hour ago. Thornsberry's Polo aftershave still lingers in the air.

Blue's wearing his trademark black suit jacket, white shirt open at the collar. The big silver cross glints at his throat. Creased black trousers brush the tops of his wingtip shoes. Before coming in, I turned the heat up and changed out the cushioned chairs with the old wooden ones from the storage room. Comfort never makes for a productive interrogation. That said, I'm not sure those old police tactics will work on Blue Branson.

I hand him the laminated Miranda rights card and recite them to him from memory. "Do you understand your rights?"

"I do."

I round the table and sit opposite him. "Jerrold Mc-Cullough is dead."

He starts slightly, then looks down and shakes his head. "God bless him," he whispers, and then looks at me. "How?"

"Murdered." I pause and then ask, "Where were you between three P.M. yesterday and six A.M. this morning?"

"I was at the church with two volunteers from noon until eleven o'clock last night. Then I went home. Alone."

I pull my pad from my pocket. "I need the names of the volunteers."

"Rick Baker and Ralph Sanderson."

He gives me their contact info, and I write down their numbers.

"If you're wondering if I killed McCullough," he says, "the answer is no."

"Your alibi for the time when Julia Rutledge was murdered checked out."

"I didn't kill anyone."

For a minute or two, neither of us speaks. I break the silence with, "The last time we spoke, I told you I was going to find out what you were hiding."

"And I told you I have nothing to hide."

I stare hard at him. "You're a good liar for a pastor."

He stares back, unflinching.

"I know you were at the Hochstetler farm the night Willis Hochstetler was shot and killed. I know the others were there, too. You went in to steal cash. It should have been an easy hit. Amish family. Pacifists. A quick in and out. But something went wrong, didn't it?"

Shock resonates in his eyes. He opens his mouth as if to speak, but no words come.

"I'm sure you're aware that there's no statute of limitations on murder," I tell him.

"I think I'd like to call my lawyer."

"I think you're going to need one." I look down at the file in front of me; letting the silence work. Then I ask, "Do you know who murdered the others?"

"No."

"What happened to Wanetta Hochstetler?"

A ripple moves through his body. His fingers twitch on the table in front of him. But he doesn't reply.

"Did you kill her, Blue? Was it an accident? Did you bury her body somewhere? Leave her for dead?" When he doesn't respond, I add, "I will get to the bottom of it. You help me now, and I'll do what I can to help you."

"I didn't kill anyone."

Setting my hands on the table between us, I partially rise and lean toward him so that my face is only a foot away from his, close enough to smell the meaty odor of his skin. "I have a witness who can put you at the scene. It's over. You're done. Do you understand?"

He stares at me, saying nothing.

I move away, work the handcuffs from the compartment on my belt. "Stand up and turn around. Give me your wrists."

Blue Branson rises and turns his back to me and offers his wrists. I thought I'd draw some small sense of satisfaction from this moment—solving a thirty-five-year-old open case and taking a killer into custody—but the only thing I feel in the pit of my stomach is a great deal of emptiness.

CHAPTER 23

Someone always knows something.

When I was a rookie patrol officer in Columbus, I partnered up with a veteran cop by the name of Howie Sharpe. He was old school and just six months away from retirement. I worked my first major case with Howie. A six-year-old girl, little Melissa Sussman, had gone missing, and the entire police department worked around the clock to find her. Like so many missing child cases, Melissa's story didn't end happily. But I learned more in the course of that case than at any time in my career. Howie always told me: "Someone always knows something." It was one of his favorite idioms, and that case proved it true, albeit too late for the child.

I never forgot that weeklong frenzy of good old-fashioned police work. I never forgot little Melissa Sussman or the life that would never be. And I never forgot the things wise old Howie—who got his retirement, by the way—taught me.

I'm at my desk, combing through the Hochstetler

file for the dozenth time when it strikes me how few Amish people were interviewed in the course of the investigation. Ron Mackey had been the chief of police back then and retired shortly after. I didn't know him personally, but I've heard that in the late '70s there was a good bit of friction between the Amish and "English" communities. Most disputes were over the use of slow-moving vehicle signs, building codes, and taxes. I can't help but wonder if, because of the tension and that cultural divide, Mackey ruled out turning to the Amish for help.

Ten minutes later, I'm in the Explorer and heading toward Bishop Troyer's farm. He's been the bishop for as long as I can remember, but I don't know if his tenure goes back to 1979. Even if it didn't, he probably had a grasp on what was going on in the Amish community. I'm hoping he can tell me something I don't already know.

I make the turn into the narrow gravel lane of the Troyer farm and park near the sidewalk. Most of the Amish in Holmes County have extraordinarily neat yards with shorn grass and manicured shrubs. Many go so far as to plant flowers, display potted plants, and landscape their yards. Not the Troyers. Both the front and back yards are plain. No flower-beds or potted plants or even shrubs. Just a small garden and a birdhouse mounted on a fence post in the side yard, but even that is unadorned.

I'm midway to the house when someone calls out my name. I turn to see the bishop trudging toward me from the barn. I haven't seen or spoken to him since last fall, when I was working the Borntrager case. Though it's been only a few months, he looks years older. I've never seen him use a walking stick, and I can't help but notice that his legs seem to be even more bowed.

"Bishop." I start toward him, wishing him a good morning in Pennsylvania Dutch. *"Guder mariye."*

"I'm surprised you still speak the language," he says, a hint of reproach in his voice.

I withhold a smile. Bishop Troyer may be old, but he's got a keen mind and a sharp tongue. He's clad in black trousers. Black jacket. White shirt. Flat-brimmed black hat. His long beard is wiry and gray with small bits of alfalfa hay in it. I stop two feet away from him. "I'm sorry to disturb you at home, Bishop, but if you have a few minutes, I'd like to ask you some questions about Willis and Wanetta Hochstetler."

"I've not heard those names in a long time," he says. "Such a terrible thing. So many young lives lost. It makes the heart hurt." His gaze meets mine. "Why do you ask of them now?"

"I'm working on another case that may be related." I pause. "Were you bishop back then?"

He shakes his head. "Eli Schweider was."

"Is he still around?"

"Eli lives in the house next to his son's farm out on Rockridge Road."

"I know the one," I tell him. "Not too far from Miller's Pond."

"He's very old now, Katie. Ninety years old, I think. His *fluss* is bad and he's frail." *Fluss* is the Pennsylvania Dutch word for "rheumatism."

"Danki," I tell him, and start toward my vehicle.

"You watch your manners with him, Katie Burkholder," he calls out after me.

"Don't worry, Bishop. I'll behave myself."

I leave him standing on the sidewalk with his walking stick in his hand, a frown on his face.

Minutes later, I turn onto Rockridge Road. Half a mile in, I pass by a plain metal mailbox with the name SCHWEIDER finger-painted in black on the side. I turn into the gravel lane and bounce over potholes as I head toward the big white farmhouse. I crest the hill only to notice the smaller cottage-style home on my left, and I realize it's probably the original farmhouse, where the elders would live now.

I drive past the larger house and park near the cottage. Though it's midday, the sky is low and dark and spitting rain. As I pass by a mullioned window, I see the glow of lantern light inside, telling me someone is there. I step onto the porch, knock, and wait. I'm about to knock a second time in case Eli Schweider is hard of hearing, when the door creaks open.

I find myself looking at a bent, white-haired man who's at least a foot shorter than me. Tiny eyes peer out at me from the folded-leather creases of eyes set into a face that's brown from the sun and mottled with age spots. Wire-rimmed glasses sit on a lumpy nose, and he tilts his head back to look at me through Coke-bottle lenses.

"Who's there?" comes a crushed-gravel voice.

"I'm Kate Burkholder, the chief of police of Painters Mill."

He stares at me long enough for me to notice cloudy irises that had once been blue, and a mat of drool in a beard that reaches all the way to his belt. "You're an *Englischer.*"

"Yes."

"I have no business with you."

He starts to close the door, but I stop him. "Please,

Bishop Schweider. Bishop Troyer sent me." The statement is out before I can amend it. I add in Pennsylvania Dutch, "I just need a few minutes of your time."

As always, my fluency in the language garners his attention. "Burkholder is a good, strong Amish name."

Raindrops begin to tap on the ground behind me. When he doesn't invite me inside, I ask, "May I come in? I promise not to stay too long."

He shuffles back and I step into a small room with low ceilings and exposed beams. The odors of woodsmoke and toasted bread fill the air. But the room contains the slightly unpleasant smells of mildew, cedar, and old things, too. From where I'm standing, I can see into a small kitchen with stone walls and a two-burner stove. Atop a table, a mug of something hot sits next to a paper plate with a single piece of toast.

"I've interrupted your lunch," I begin.

He doesn't respond. I don't know if it's because he didn't hear me or he chose not to. Turning his back to me, he shuffles toward the kitchen, sliding his feet across the wood planks a few inches at a time.

"You speak *Pennsilfaanisch Deitsch* and yet you're an *Englischer*," he says. "There's something wrong with that."

"I left the Amish when I was young."

He tries to look at me over his shoulder, but his neck is too stiff. He continues shuffling toward the table. "Who is your father?"

"Jacob Burkholder."

He turns and looks at me. "You must be Little Katie."

I smile. "Not so little anymore."

"What is it you need?"

"I'm working on a case. From a long time ago. It's about Willis and Wanetta Hochstetler."

A quiver goes through the old man's body, as if he'd been hit with a brisk wind and the cold took his breath away. "They are with God," he says. "The children, too."

"Except for William."

"God spared Billy." He starts toward the table, shuffling. The soles of his shoes scrape across the floor, sounding vaguely like a saw through wood. "Are you going to catch the men responsible, Katie Burkholder?"

"I've taken one man into custody. The others were murdered."

"God will make the final judgment."

His progress is slow and uncomfortable to watch. I have to resist the urge to help him into the chair. I wait until he's settled in before continuing. "Did the police talk to you about what happened that night?"

"The English police." He says the words with disdain. "They don't care about the *Amisch*. Not then. Not now."

"I care."

He meets my gaze, but he is unmoved. "What is it you need from me?"

"Is there anything you can tell me about the night Willis Hochstetler was killed?" I ask. "Do you know of anything unusual that happened in the days before or after? Or did you hear any rumors?"

"What happened in the house that night was *gottlos*." *Ungodly*. He sets down the toast as if realizing it's covered with maggots. "When we found the boy, he was . . . shattered. It was a painful time for all of us."

"Did you know Wanetta and Willis?"

"I baptized them when they joined the church. I spoke to them many times. Saw them at worship." He nods. *"Willis es en faehicher schreiner." Willis was an able carpenter.* "Wanetta—" He shakes his head.

"What about her?"

"I talked to William after . . . what happened. He was a boy. Only fourteen years old and innocent. But even then, he knew things."

"Like what?"

He raises his gaze to me. "Those men . . . they took Wanetta. They used her. Soiled her. Forced her to break her vows to her husband. Her sacred vow to the church."

The words, the meaning behind them, light a fire of outrage inside me, a mix of anger and disbelief and the sense of unfair judgment levied upon the innocent. "She had no choice in the matter."

He raises rheumy eyes to mine. "Some things are so broken, they cannot be mended. It is the way of the world."

"I don't agree with that."

He gives me a sharp look. "I thought it best that she didn't return."

I stare at him, incredulous, and so taken aback by his narrow-minded arrogance that for a moment I'm rendered speechless. "I don't understand."

"It's not for you to understand. It's done. In God's hands."

Before I realize I'm going to move, I'm hovering over him. "Do you know something about what happened to her?" Despite my efforts, my voice has risen.

His eyes roll back in their sockets slightly when he looks at me. "A few years after Willis and the children were killed, I received a message from the bishop of the Swartzentruber Amish in Pennsylvania."

The Swartzentruber clan are the most conservative Amish. The group emerged after a split of the Old Order back in 1917 over a conflict between two bishops regarding *Bann und Meidung*, or "excommunication and shunning." Several Swartzentruber families live in Painters Mill. Generally, they're stricter with regard to the use of technology, rejecting conveniences like milking machines and indoor plumbing. Their buggies are windowless. Even their dress is plainer, especially for the women.

"What message?" I ask.

"One of the families in Cambria County had taken in an Amish woman who'd been in an accident and had severe injuries. The woman had no memory. She didn't know her name or where she lived. The family nursed her back to health, fed her, clothed her, and opened their home to her." He looks down at his gnarled fingers. "Months after she arrived, the woman began to remember things. She was fluent in *Pennsilfaanisch Deitsch*. She knew she had a husband and children and wanted to come home. The Swartzentruber family began contacting Amish bishops all over Pennsylvania and, later, Ohio."

"The woman was Wanetta Hochstetler?"

"All I can tell you is that she was not the woman who had been married to Willis Hochstetler."

I can't tell if he's speaking figuratively or literally. "What happened?"

"The Swartzentruber Amish do not permit a community telephone booth, as we do here. It took several weeks, but she was finally able to contact me."

"You spoke with her?"

"On the telephone." He hesitates. "She didn't know that Willis and the children had passed. When I told her, she became very distraught. She accused me of lying and used ungodly words." He touches his left temple. *"Sie is ganz ab."* *She was quite out of her mind.*

"Did you go to the police?"

"Why would I? We are Amish. It was an Amish matter."

"But they would have—"

"There were bad feelings between the Amish and the English police." He shrugs. "I don't know how it would have been for her, coming back, after everything that happened. There had been talk."

"What kind of talk?"

"That she'd left her husband and children. That maybe she didn't want to come back."

"But she had a son," I say. "William."

"The boy was with an Amish family. A *good* family that had welcomed him into their lives and given him a home. This woman was . . . *narrish.*" *Insane.* "It was for the best. For the boy. He needed to be protected from what she had become."

"That wasn't your choice. It wasn't your decision to make."

"I left it in the hands of God."

I look at him, this grizzled, disapproving old man, and I want to rail at him, call him a son of a bitch. I want to tell him the woman could have sustained a head injury or suffered a stroke. But I hold my tongue. "How long ago did you speak with her?"

"Many years," he says.

"She was living in Pennsylvania at the time?"

"Yes, but many of the Swartzentruber Amish have left that area for New York. Too many disputes with the government."

"What was the name of the family that took her in?"

"I don't know."

"Do you remember the bishop's name?"

He shakes his head.

I sigh. "Where in Pennsylvania? What's the name of the town?"

"Cambria County," he tells me. "Near Nicktown."

CHAPTER 24

My head is reeling with the bishop's disturbing revelations as I get into the Explorer and start down the lane. It's difficult for me to believe an Amish bishop could be so cruel. Is it possible Wanetta Hochstetler is still alive? Did she, as a damaged and broken woman, try to return home to her family, only to be shattered by news that they were dead? Or that she wasn't welcome?

But there are other, darker questions pulsing at the back of my brain. Did Wanetta Hochstetler find her way back to Painters Mill? Did she have something to do with the murders of Dale Michaels, Jules Rutledge and Jerrold McCullough? The people who murdered her husband, caused the deaths of her children and destroyed her life? It doesn't seem likely. She was thirty-four years old when she was kidnapped; that would put her at around seventy now. The more recent murders required a good bit of strength—too much for a woman that age. Too much for a woman of *any* age.

But I know better than to discount a female perpetrator based on strength alone. If she's determined and armed—or insane as the bishop asserted—anything's possible.

I pull over in the parking lot of a carryout on the west side of town and call Glock. He picks up on the first ring with his usual, "Hey, Chief."

I summarize my conversation with Bishop Schweider.

"You think she's got something to do with these murders?" he asks.

"I don't know. She certainly qualifies in terms of motive, but she'd be old now. I can't see her pulling off three murders."

"She might've had help." He pauses. "Hoch Yoder."

I tell him about my conversation with Hoch. "Pay him a visit. Tell him you're following up. See if you can get anything new out of him. Put some pressure on him. Rattle him a little. At this point, I think it's best we don't let on that she might still be alive."

"Where are you going?"

"Nicktown, Pennsylvania. It's about four hours away. The Swartzentruber Amish don't use community pay phones, so I'm going to drive over there and see what I can find out."

"Chief, are you sure you don't want to take someone with you? Any of us are happy to tag along."

I don't believe "tag along" is the exact term he had in mind, but he's being magnanimous. With three people dead, he's worried that I won't have backup if I need it. There's a small part of me that agrees with him, but with my department strapped tight and the threat of flooding in the forefront of our minds, I don't take him up on the offer. "The Swartzentruber

Amish generally don't like dealing with outsiders, especially the government. Best if I go alone."

"Do me a favor and be careful, will you?"

"You know it."

The rolling hills, farm fields, and woodlands between Painters Mill and Nicktown make for beautiful scenery, even if the weather doesn't cooperate. But I barely notice the countryside as I head east and push the speedometer over the limit. I can't stop thinking about Wanetta Hochstetler and what it could mean if she's alive. I have no idea if she's perpetrator or victim or somewhere in between, but if I can find her, she might be able to shed some light on exactly what went down that night thirty-five years ago—or the more recent murders.

But it's been over thirty years since Bishop Schweider spoke to her; there's a possibility I won't find her. She may have died of natural causes or left Cambria County for Upstate New York with the other Swartzentruber Amish. If I was dealing with any other group of people, it might have been wiser for me to call ahead, try to get someone on the phone or, perhaps, speak to the local PD. But I know the Swartzentruber Amish would not speak to me by phone. While this trip and the hours I'll sink into it may be a long shot, I have to try.

I hit construction east of Pittsburgh and a thunderstorm as I enter Cambria County. By the time I pull into the town limits of Nicktown, it's after 4 P.M. and I'm in dire need of coffee. The town is a postcard-pretty village with large homes and a main street lined with spruce and maples that will be budding in a few weeks. Since I have no clue where to begin my search,

I pull in to the gravel lot of the first restaurant I come to, Lucy's Kountry Kitchen.

The dinner hour hasn't yet begun, so the place isn't crowded. An older couple sits at a table near the window. A man in a DeKalb cap broods over a mug of coffee in the corner booth. Leaving my umbrella at the coatrack near the door, I walk to the counter and take a stool. A middle-aged woman in a pink golf shirt, black pants, and a black apron approaches me from behind the counter.

"What can I get for you?" she begins, giving me only half her attention.

"Coffee, please."

"You're in luck. Just made a pot."

There's a pass-through window that opens to the kitchen behind her. Beyond, a cook clad in white scrapes the grill to Zac Brown Band's "Free."

"You want cream with that?" The waitress sets a ceramic mug in front of me.

"Sure."

She pulls two containers of half-and-half from her pocket and drops them on the counter.

I smile at her. "Any chance I could get a piece of that cherry pie to go with the coffee?"

"You bet."

Two minutes later, I'm midway through the pie and on my second cup of coffee. The waitress, whose badge tells me her name is Daisy, is several feet away, wiping down the pastry display case.

"How long have you lived here in Nicktown?" I ask.

She looks at me over her shoulder. "All my life."

"You like it?"

"It gets kind of boring, but it's a good place to raise a family." She saunters to the counter where I'm sitting and, taking advantage of my company, begins refilling the containers of artificial sweeteners.

"Kids?" I ask.

"Four. Oldest is in high school now. Hard to believe. Seems like yesterday when he was running around here, filling the salt and pepper shakers for me."

"They grow up fast." I extend my hand and introduce myself. "I'm the chief of police over in Painters Mill, Ohio."

"Oh. A cop. Hi." Grinning, she wipes her hand and we shake. "My husband and I were over that way couple of years ago. He photographs covered bridges. A lot of Amish there."

"Are there many Amish in this area?"

"Used to be. Swartzentrubers, mostly. But they started moving out a couple of years ago. Didn't like all the government rules and regulations and were always getting into trouble. You know, with zoning and such because they don't use indoor plumbing and people were complaining about the sewage. Stuff like that."

"I hear a lot of them are moving to Upstate New York."

She nods. "Kind of hate to see them go, to tell you the truth. Nice Amish girl used to bring us pies, but she left with her family six months ago. And of course, the tourists always meant business for us here at the restaurant."

"Are there any Amish left?"

"Two families that I know of." She shrugs. "They keep to themselves, so I'm not really sure."

I sip my coffee. "I'm looking for an Amish woman who went missing thirty-five years ago from Painters Mill. I believe she was injured and somehow ended up with a Swartzentruber family near here."

"Oh gosh, thirty-five years is a long time. I was ten years old."

"Do you remember hearing anything like that? Rumors, maybe?"

"Sorry, but I sure don't."

"Is there an Amish bishop or elder still around I could talk to?"

She looks at me over the tops of her glasses. "I don't know about a bishop or elder, but there's an Amish family lives down the road from my husband and me."

"Can you tell me how to get there?"

"Sure." She tears a sheet from her order pad and turns it over, sets it on the counter between us. "It's not too far." She grins. "Kind of hard to get lost in Nicktown."

I watch her draw a crude map. "It's only about five miles from here. Take Castine Road and then make a right at the flashing caution light." She looks through the window toward the parking lot. "What are you driving?"

"Explorer."

"Four-wheel drive?"

I nod.

"Good, 'cause you're going to need it. The Swartzentrubers don't use gravel. Their lane is dirt, and with all this rain, you're going to sink in something awful." She slides the map toward me. "There you go."

"Thanks for the map." I look at my empty plate. "And the pie."

She smiles. "I hope you find what you're looking for, Kate Burkholder."

I'm feeling a little more optimistic when I leave Lucy's Kountry Kitchen and head north on the main drag.

It's four thirty now; I've devoted half the day working a hunch that has a high probability of turning into a wild goose chase. But the coffee and sugar helped, and my cop's gut urges me to keep going.

Daisy's directions are perfect right down to the distances. I make the turn on Castine Road and then hit the flashing caution light just a few miles down and make a right onto a dirt road. She was right about the mud, too. I encounter deep ruts and standing water, and twenty feet in, the Explorer bogs. I throw it into four-wheel drive and muscle through. Half a mile down, I come to a dirt lane. There's no name on the mailbox, but the plainness of the house and outbuildings beyond tells me it's an Amish home, so I turn in.

The house is white with a tin roof that's striped with rust. It looks as if the place originally had a wrap-around front porch, but over the years—probably due to a growing family or the addition of elderly parents—the porch was transformed into an extra room. The barn is also white, but in need of paint. A rail fence surrounds a muddy paddock, where several Jersey cows chew their cud, watching me.

Growing up Amish, I never thought twice about living on a farm. I've always been an animal lover, and having livestock was one of the things I enjoyed most. The only thing about rural life I hated was the spring mud, which was always made worse by manure. I park behind a windowless black buggy with steel-clad wooden wheels, telling me this is, indeed, a Swartzentruber farm.

Resigning myself to muddy shoes and wet feet, I get out and tromp through several inches of mud toward the side door. Despite my best effort to keep my shoes clean, I leave clods of mud on the concrete steps as I ascend to the porch. I knock on the door and wait.

Around me, the air is heavy and wet with the smells of manure and wet foliage. I'm looking down at my muddy boots, thinking about going into the yard to wipe them on the grass when the door swings open. I find myself looking at a middle-aged Amish woman wearing an ankle-length gray dress and a dark winter bonnet.

"Guder middag," I begin, wishing her a good afternoon.

She mumbles the same, but her eyes widen as she takes in my non-Amish clothes.

"I'm Kate Burkholder from Painters Mill, Ohio," I say in Pennsylvania Dutch. "I'm looking for a missing Amish woman, and I'm wondering if I could ask you a few questions."

"Voahra." Wait. The woman turns and walks away.

I stand on the porch, relieved that she didn't close the door. The smells of kerosene and woodsmoke waft out. No matter how many years pass, those are the smells that take me back to my youth of endless days spent on a farm much like this one. Through the dimly lit living room, I see an old woman sitting at the kitchen table, sewing or mending some piece of clothing. She leans back just enough to make eye contact with me and then goes back to her work without acknowledging me further.

I'm a full minute into my wait and thinking about knocking again when a man approaches. He's dressed in black except for a white shirt. In keeping with the Swartzentruber ways, his long beard is untrimmed. His face is deeply lined and grim, but I guess him to be in his mid-forties.

"May I help you?" he asks in Pennsylvania Dutch. I introduce myself. "I'm looking for an Amish woman who disappeared about thirty-five years ago from Painters Mill," I begin. "It's possible she was injured and may have suffered some memory problems."

He eyes me with open curiosity, and I know he's wondering about my use of Pennsylvania Dutch. But I know the Amish too well to take for granted that it will garner his cooperation. I'm as much an outsider as any camera-toting *Englischer*. Still, it can't hurt, and I'm certainly not above using whatever means I can to get him to talk to me.

"I've traveled a long way," I tell him. "Please. The woman has a son back in Painters Mill."

"I'm Eli Zook." He doesn't offer his hand. "I have an uncle in Painters Mill."

"What's his name?"

"William."

"I know William and his wife, Alma." When he doesn't open the door, I try to keep the conversation going. "I understand many of the Swartzentruber Amish are leaving Cambria County."

"That is true. We live simply. The government people don't care if we make it to heaven or not." He sighs. "God provided for us in New York, and I intend to follow my conscience. We will go soon."

"You've lived here your entire life?"

He nods.

"Do you know anything about this Amish woman who would have arrived in the area about thirty-five years ago? Her name is Wanetta Hochstetler, but I don't know if she used that name."

My heart sinks when he shakes his head. "I was just a boy back then. I don't recall."

He starts to close the door, but I set my hand against it. "Mr. Zook, are there any other Amish families in the area I could talk to? The woman I'm looking for may have been taken in by one of the families. It's important that I find her."

"Grossmuder!" He calls out over his shoulder, then tosses me a look. "She's nearly deaf, so you will have to speak up."

I look past him to see the old woman look our way. "You're lucky to have your grandmother," I tell him.

"She is my wife's *grossmuder,* but we are happy to have her." He calls out to the woman again. *"Mir hen Englischer bsuch ghadde,"* he tells her. *We have non-Amish visitors.*

With excruciating slowness, the woman sets her mending on the tabletop and scoots away from the table. *"Es waarken maulvoll gat."* *There's nothing good about that.*

Her voice is like sandpaper against stone, coarse and wet and abrasive, but it makes me smile. I like old people with attitude.

One side of Zook's mouth hikes, and he lowers his voice. *"Sie hot die hose aa."* *She wears the pants in the family.*

The old woman shuffles across the wood plank floor. When her eyes meet mine, I see instantly that despite her advanced years, they are clear, as is her mind. *"Sell is nix as baeffzes."* *That's nothing but trifling talk.*

Zook nods. "The *Englischer* doctor calls it selective hearing loss."

Waving off his words, the woman reaches us and gives me a slow once-over. "What's this about a missing *Amisch*?"

Leaving out the details of the crime, I explain to her what might have happened to Wanetta Hochstetler. "She may have been injured or had some memory problems. Do you remember anything like that happening about thirty-five years ago?"

"I remember plenty." Nodding, she looks from her grandson to me, and in that instant she doesn't look quite so cocky. "There were lots of stories. About her. Terrible stories."

"What kinds of stories?"

"Joe Weaver and his family found her. He owned some land near Ebensburg. Didn't live there, but kept hay on it. He was out there with his family one day and heard something in the well. Kids thought it was a cat some fool had thrown down there. But it wasn't. It was an Amish woman, and she was in a bad way."

"Injured?"

"*Ja*. Bad, too. Joe took her to the midwife."

"Not the hospital?"

"Joe had no use for English doctors." She says the words as if they explain everything. "Joe and his wife knew she wasn't from around here—the clothes and such, you know. Still, she was Amish, so they took care of her."

"Did he call the police?"

"He didn't have much use for the English police, either. I don't know if it's true, but I heard the woman was slow in the head. Didn't know where she was from. Joe and his wife took her in to their home. Clothed her. Fed her. Did their best to teach her the Swartzentruber ways."

"Didn't they worry that she had a family somewhere?" I ask. "Someone who was worried about her?"

"I wouldn't know the answer to that."

"What became of her?"

"She left the Amish a few months after they took her in. Stole some money from Joe. It was a bad thing."

"Is she still around? Would it be possible for me to talk to her?"

"She passed a couple of months ago."

The words hit me like a cold, buffeting wind. All I can think is that I've come all this way for nothing. "So she stayed in the area all these years?" I ask.

"Last I heard, she lived over in Nanty Glo, south of here. There's a trailer home park off of Blacklick Creek."

"What name did she go by?" I ask.

"They called her Becky. Used the last name of Weaver." Her expression darkens. "I'm no friend to the gossipmongers or busybodies. But there was talk about that woman."

"What kind of talk?"

"That she wasn't as nice as she wanted everyone to think, and she remembered a lot more than she let on." The old woman looks at her grandson. *"Wu schmoke is, is aa feier."* Where there's smoke, there is fire. "That's all I've got to say on the matter."

CHAPTER 25

One of the things that separates a good cop from a great cop is the ability to sift through the bullshit you're fed in the course of your job and get to the usable information sprinkled throughout. I've always had a pretty good handle on that particular skill set, some of which is old-fashioned common sense. As I turn onto the highway, I'm forced to admit I'm not sure what to make of the story Zook's grandmother relayed about Wanetta Hochstetler. Is it possible she lived out her days here and never made her way back to Painters Mill?

Nanty Glo is a sleepy little town about half the size of Painters Mill. From the looks of things, the bad economy has hit this town particularly hard. A smattering of vacant storefronts peppers the downtown area. Large homes that had once been grand look tired and downtrodden. The town almost has a postapocalyptic feel. Within minutes, I've passed through downtown and I'm in a rural area that's hilly and thick with trees. I'm looking for a gas station to ask for directions to the trailer park when I spot the sign for Blacklick Creek Road. Braking hard, I make the turn.

A quarter mile down, I see the sign for the Glad Acres mobile home park. I turn in and I'm met with a gravel lane that's blocked with a chain and a sign that probably once warned off interlopers with NO TRESPASSING, but the letters have long since faded. I stop the Explorer and get out. I barely notice the lightly falling rain or the cackle of a rookery in the treetops, and I approach the chain. I can tell by the slope of the land that there's a creek at the base of the hill.

There are some places that, due to time or circumstance, have earned their state of deterioration. Glad Acres has no such claim. It had never been pretty. The park comprises a single street with four ancient mobile homes lined up like crushed railroad cars in pastel colors streaked with rust. Several have broken windows; at least one is missing a door. At first I think the entire park has been abandoned. Then I notice the bumper of a car parked on the far side of the last trailer.

Stepping over the chain, I start toward the trailer. It's not yet 6 P.M., but the overcast sky and fog make it seem like dusk. Light glows at the window. As I pass by the vacant trailers, I see fingers of fog rising from the ground, and I sense I'm being watched. I reach the last trailer and take the wooden steps to the door and knock.

The door opens almost immediately. I find myself looking at an older woman in a housedress and camo jacket. "That 'No Trespassing' sign is there for a reason," she says in a cigarette-rough voice.

For an instant, I'm tempted to point out that the sign is illegible, but I don't think that will help my cause, so I smile and show her my badge. "I'm sorry to bother you. I'm the police chief in Painters Mill, Ohio. I'm looking for someone. Would you mind answering a few quick questions for me?"

"Since you're a cop, I reckon I don't have a choice."

"How long have you lived here?"

"Going on thirty years now." She motions toward a rusted-out swing set lying on its side on the slope that leads to the creek below. "Used to be nicer. People had kids. Jobs."

"What happened?"

"Coal mine closed. Folks got laid off. Moved away."

"You rent this place? Or own it?"

She frowns at me and shakes her head. "I own the whole park. Goddamn property taxes keep me broke, but that's the government for you."

"I was told there was an Amish woman by the name of Becky Weaver who used to live here. Do you know her?"

"I knew Becky. Lived here for twenty or so years. She died a couple of months ago."

"Do you know how she died?"

"Heart attack or stroke or something. She was a strange bird, that one."

"How so?"

"Well, for one thing, she wasn't sure if she was Amish or English. Wore them Amish dresses and bonnet thingie, but let me tell you, there wasn't nothing godly about her. Kept to herself mostly, but she had her share of men come over, and they weren't there to fix the plumbing." She speaks with a great deal of animation, and I realize she enjoys her gossip. "I always thought it was wrong of her to be that way with that girl around, but —"

"What girl?" I cut in.

"Her daughter. Ruth."

"She had a daughter?"

"That's what I just said."

"Who was the father?"

"Never asked and she never said. She wadn't much for small talk."

"How old is her daughter?"

"Early thirties now, I'd say. Lived here until a few years ago, but she visited every so often. Ain't seen her since her mama passed, though."

The information pings inside my head, a rubber ball with no place to land. "Do you know where the daughter lives now?"

"No idea."

"Did either of them have jobs?"

"Not like regular jobs. They cleaned houses and such, but it was kind of hit-or-miss."

"Did they clean for anyone in particular?"

"I wouldn't know. We weren't exactly friendly."

"Were you her landlord?"

"Yes, ma'am, I was."

"Do you have a file? Maybe an application she filled out? An address or phone number for the daughter? Anything like that?"

"They wasn't real forthcoming with information. And I don't keep them kind of records, anyways. Alls I know is Becky paid on time every month, and usually in cash."

"Is there anything else you can tell me about either woman? Or anything that might help me find Ruth?"

The woman shrugs. "Not really. Only talked to Ruth a handful of times over the years and she was about as strange as her mama. Looked like her a little bit, too."

Nodding, my mind whirling with this new bit of information, I eye the three abandoned mobile homes. "Which trailer was theirs?"

The woman points. "Blue and white one in the middle there. Not sure how the window got broke. Damn teenagers, probably."

"Do you mind if I take a look inside?"

"Knock your socks off. It ain't locked, and I sure don't think she left any valuables behind. Just close the door when you're done. Don't need no raccoons tearing things up."

"Thank you." I turn away and start down the stairs, but think of one more question. "What last name did Ruth go by?" I ask.

"Weaver. Ruth Weaver."

The interior of the trailer reeks of rotting food and backed-up sewage with the underlying redolence of moldy carpet. I'm standing just inside the door in a small living room. The kitchen is to my right. To my left is a hall that presumably leads to the bedrooms and bathroom. Leaving the door open for ventilation, I walk into the kitchen. The window is broken. The curtains are rain-wilted and discolored. On the floor, a single mushroom sprouts from threadbare carpet. To my left, a 1970s yellow refrigerator has been tipped onto its face. From where I'm standing, I see what had once been a package of cold cuts and a half gallon of ice cream dried to a sticky goo on the floor. The counters are covered with rat droppings and several mismatched plastic containers. A filthy dish strainer sits in the sink.

Slipping on my gloves, I start with the drawers, quickly going through each one. I find take-out menus. Plastic utensils. What had once been a loaf of bread, but is now an unrecognizable blue-green blob inside the wrapper. In the final drawer, I find an old phone book. Tucked inside, I discover an article from the Painters Mill *Weekly Advocate* newspaper about the murder of Willis Hochstetler, the disappearance of his wife, Wanetta, and the deaths of their four children. Because they were Amish, there are no photos of the family, just the burned-out shell of the house and a chilling headline: MURDER IN AMISH COUNTRY. It's another connection, so I fold the article and put it in my pocket.

I'm not sure what I hope to find. At this point, any information would be helpful. Social security numbers. Aliases used. The addresses of employers or friends. Utility bills. A phone bill. But after a quick search of the two bedrooms, I realize neither woman left anything behind. All I have is the newspaper article and the name of a woman who seems to have disappeared off the face of the earth.

When a case breaks, the last place you want to be is on the road, two hundred miles away from home base. Unfortunately, that's the position I find myself in as I hightail it toward Painters Mill. Once I hit the highway, I call Glock.

"Wanetta Hochstetler was alive up until a few months ago," I begin without preamble. "She's been living in Pennsylvania under the assumed name of Becky Weaver."

"Holy shit. The kidnapped *wife*?"

I relay to him everything I've learned in the last hours. "Evidently, she was injured and may have suffered some kind of head injury or psychological trauma that affected her memory."

"But if she's dead, how does—?"

"She had a daughter. Ruth Weaver. Do me a favor and run both names through NCIC and LEADS, will you?"

"Got it."

"These two women lived off the grid. We don't have any information on Ruth Weaver, no address or phone number, known associates, not even a description. Poke around and see if you can find something. Mona's pretty good on the Internet. Get her to help."

"You think this Ruth Weaver is here in Painters Mill?"

"I think she's there, and I think she's making good on an old debt for her mother."

"Shit." He pauses and I can feel our minds zinging back and forth as we try to process the information. "Where you at?"

"Pittsburgh."

"Pittsburgh?"

"I'm on my way. How did it go with Hoch Yoder?"

"I pulled him in. At the time Jules Rutledge was murdered, he was helping one of his neighbors move cattle and hogs due to flooding. I cut him loose."

CHAPTER 26

Four hours and 160 miles later, I'm back in Painters Mill in the interview room with Glock and Blue Branson. Glock and I spoke several times during my drive, and he relayed the news that neither Becky Weaver nor her daughter, Ruth, were in the NCIC or the Ohio-based LEADS databases. Evidently, the two women kept their noses clean. As a result—and the fact that they were Amish—we have nothing.

Carrying the Hochstetler file, I seat myself across the table from Blue, who's slouched in his chair, staring down at his hands. Glock holds his position at the door, assuming an unobtrusive presence. I set the file on the table and press the Record button on the tape recorder, recite the date and the names of everyone present. I read the Miranda rights to Blue from a printed card and then slide the card across the table to him.

"Do you understand your rights?" I begin.

"I understand."

Using the same tactic I used with Norm Johnston,

I open the file, making sure he can see the label and photos, and rifle through a few pages. "I spent the afternoon in Cambria County, Pennsylvania."

"I don't know where that is," he says in a monotone voice.

"It's near where you and your friends threw Wanetta Hochstetler down that well and left her for dead. Ring a bell?"

Blue Branson has as good a poker face as anyone I've ever met. But he can't conceal his shock. He stares at me, unblinking, his mouth partially open, wondering how I could possibly know.

"She survived," I tell him.

He drops his gaze to the tabletop, his eyes darting, landing on nothing, like a trapped animal about to take some fatal leap to avoid being ripped to shreds by a much larger predator.

"I know you were at the Hochstetler farm the night Willis Hochstetler was killed. I know you and your friends kidnapped Wanetta Hochstetler. I know you took her across the state line into Pennsylvania."

Blue looks up, his gaze digging into mine. I hold my breath, hoping he doesn't ask for his lawyer again, because that would bring the interview—and any progress on the case—to a screeching halt.

"She tell you that?" he asks after a moment.

I'm under no obligation to inform him that Wanetta Hochstetler died two months ago. I don't reveal that bit of information, because I know keeping him in the dark will work to my advantage. "I know what you did, Blue. I know what all of you did. You're going to be charged, and the only thing that can help you now is cooperation. Do you understand?"

Blue studies the tabletop. Beneath his goatee, I see the muscles in his jaws working. After a full two minutes of silence, he raises his eyes to mine. "Is that woman the one who killed them?"

"That *woman*?" I say. "You mean Wanetta Hochstetler, don't you?" I'm humanizing her, hoping to guilt him into cooperating. "She was a young Amish mother with five children and a husband. A religious woman who loved God. She loved her children. She loved her life. You took all of that away from her."

He looks away, but not before I see a flash of anguish in his eyes. He shakes his head as if to rid himself of the memory, of any culpability. "She'd be old by now. Sixty or seventy. How could she kill three people? Men twice her size?"

I don't answer his question. For the span of several minutes, no one speaks. I let the silence ride, hoping it will rattle him. But I know Blue Branson is not easily shaken. I know he's not going to volunteer information without coercion.

"This case is going to go federal," I tell him. "You kidnapped a woman and crossed a state line. The FBI will probably assume jurisdiction. Children were killed in the commission of a felony. That could turn this into a death penalty case. Once those things happen, it's out of my control." I wait a beat. "Tell me what happened that night, and I'll go to bat for you. I'll do everything in my power to make sure your cooperation is taken into consideration by the court." I stop speaking and hold his gaze. "I can't help you unless you help me."

"What will happen to Crossroads?" he asks, referring to his church. "My work . . . it's important. Not to me, Chief Burkholder, but to the people I help."

"I can't answer that."

We fall silent. The room is so quiet I can hear the

tick of the clock on the wall. The muffled ringing of the phone in the reception area down the hall. Several minutes pass, but I'm not inclined to rush this. The longer we're here, the better my chances of walking away with something I can use.

When he finally speaks, his voice is so low and rough, I have to lean closer to hear. "I was there that night."

"At the Hochstetler home?"

"Yes."

"Who else was there?"

"Dale Michaels. Jerrold McCullough." He heaves a heavy sigh. "Jules."

"Was Norm Johnston there?"

He gives me a dark look, and I realize he knows Johnston was the person who'd come forward. "He was supposed to meet us, but didn't show."

"Did he know what was going down?"

"I don't know. I didn't tell him, but I reckon he figured it out."

I nod. "Tell me what happened, so we can put this behind us and decide what we're going to do next."

Another lengthy silence ensues, and then he says, "Johnston told me the Amish kid was bragging about his father keeping a lot of cash at the house."

"Hoch Yoder?"

"Yeah."

"Was Hoch in on it?"

"No. I'm just telling you that because that's how the whole thing started. I told Dale, and we talked about hitting their farm. At first neither of us was serious. We were just a couple of stupid teenagers looking for a thrill, talking about some big score that wouldn't ever happen. We were going to buy a kilo of cocaine with the money. McCullough knew a guy.

He'd cut it for us, and then we'd sell it by the gram. A onetime deal, but we'd triple our money, and that would be the end of it. But Jerrold got pretty excited about the idea. Too excited. He wouldn't stop talking about it. He fired everyone up, made it sound daring and cool, and we'd make a ton of easy money in the process. I mean, the family was Amish, right? They wouldn't defend themselves—and no one would get hurt. No one would ever know, and we'd get off scot-free."

"At some point, you got serious," I prod, "and you worked out a plan?"

"Go in hard. At night. Intimidate them. Get the cash and then get out quick, and no one gets hurt."

"What went wrong?"

"Everything. We were nervous. Scared. We'd been drinking. Liquid courage, I guess. We were all pumped up on adrenaline. I was with Jules for a while back then. We'd . . . been fighting. I was . . . pissed off. . . ." His words trail. "God almighty. I can barely remember."

"All of you were armed?"

"Except for Jules."

"What happened? What went wrong?"

"We went in. Faces concealed. Got the parents out of bed. We were in the kitchen, getting the cash. We hadn't counted on all of those little kids showing up. That was when the woman got . . . hysterical. We were all screaming at her to sit down. We started losing control of the situation. . . ." A single drop of sweat slides from his temple to a crease in his neck, but he doesn't seem to notice. "McCullough panicked and . . . shot him."

"Willis Hochstetler?"

He nods.

"What happened next?"

"We freaked out. I'd never been so scared, and I mean really scared. All of a sudden, everything was real. I couldn't believe McCullough had done it. I went after him, and we got into it. But it was done. The guy was dead."

"What about the woman?"

Blue looks at the wall behind me, as if there's a window there and he can see through the darkness and rain to the promise of freedom beyond. But there is no window. There's no escape for him, and he knows he won't be walking out of here a free man.

"We took her with us."

"Why?"

He shakes his head, doesn't answer.

"Whose idea was it?"

He turns his gaze to mine, and in that instant I see the depth of his shame. The breadth of his disgust and self-loathing. "Mine."

I'm so taken aback, I lose my train of thought. With the others dead, he could have blamed them. Only he didn't.

Time to face the music . . .

He continues, his voice flat and low, like a robot. "We put her in the trunk and just drove. Like I said, we were scared. We didn't know what to do. Somehow we ended up in Pennsylvania. Found a dirt road out in the middle of nowhere. We were going to leave her there. But she got her hands untied and pulled off Dale's mask. She saw his face."

Abruptly, he leans forward, puts his face in his hands, and rubs his eyes. "She got away. Ran into a cornfield. McCullough went after her. By the time I got there, he was on top of her. We raped her."

I stare at him, sickened. "What else?"

He looks at the wall again, at the window that isn't there, and I know he's wishing he were out there, far away, in that imaginary place. "We argued. Figured we could intimidate her into keeping her mouth shut."

"She saw your faces?"

He nods. "We couldn't let her go." He makes a sound, a sigh that ends with a moan. "Dale strangled her right there on the ground."

"Did you try to stop him?"

A long pause. "No."

"You thought she was dead?"

He nods.

"What did you do next?"

"Put her back in the trunk. Drove her to an abandoned farm and threw her into the well."

He paints a scene so vivid, so horrific, I can feel the acid churn in my stomach, the bile climbing up my throat. I can hear Wanetta Hochstetler crying out for her children. Sense her terror and panic. I can hear her tumbling down that terrible shaft. Her body striking the stone walls on the way down. The splash of the final impact. The shocking cold of the water. Had she been conscious? In pain? How long had she lain there before someone found her? Hours? Days?

I look at Blue, and a wave of revulsion moves through me. I'm well aware that there are boundaries a cop can never cross. I know that once he does, there's no going back. I feel myself venturing close to that line now. I'm keenly aware of my .38 pressing against my hip. Of how easy it would be to turn off the recorder, pull my firearm, and put a bullet between his eyes. I have a full confession. There's no doubt in my mind I could come up with a believable story that he attacked me. I'm not the first cop to entertain such a dark fantasy.

I go to my next question. "Which one of you threw the lantern into the basement?"

He gives me a sharp look. "I don't know what you're talking about."

"Hoch Yoder said one of you threw that lantern down the steps, which started the fire that killed those kids. The fire marshal's investigation corroborates that."

"We locked them in the basement, but no one threw a lantern."

"Are you sure? Maybe one of the others did it and you didn't notice?"

"No one threw a lantern into the basement. That's all I got to say about that."

There are more questions to be asked, more details to be recorded. But I need to get out of there. Away from him and the ugliness of the things he's done. I turn off the recorder. Scooting my chair away from the table, I rise and start toward the door. But I stop and turn to him; there's one more question that won't leave me alone.

"You could have lied about it being your idea to take Wanetta with you. Why did you admit to that?"

"There are times when the punishment is less painful than the secret." He pauses, stares hard at me, his eyes pleading with me to listen. "I know this isn't going to end well for me. I know I'm going to jail for the rest of my life. But if you believe anything I've said, believe this: I'm not the person I was back then."

"If you're looking for absolution, you're not going

to get it from me," I say coldly. "You'll have to find another way to live with yourself."

I turn my back on him and go through the door.

Glock follows me to my office. As I settle in behind my desk, he takes the chair adjacent.

"You look like you just lost your best friend," he says.

"I lost something," I tell him. "Another little piece of my faith in humanity, maybe." I intended the words lightly, but that's not the way they come out. "That son of a bitch has been preaching in this town for twenty years. Right under our noses. A rapist and murderer."

"Not the first phony to grace the house of God. Not even the first murderer."

"That's the thing, Glock. He's done so much for so many people. Why did he have to turn out to be a murdering son of a bitch?"

"Maybe he figured that by saving others, he could somehow save himself," he says. "Do you think he's lying about the kids? About tossing that lantern?"

"I don't know. He just confessed to kidnapping and rape and attempted murder. Why stop there?"

He grimaces, gives me a moment to reel in my emotions, then hits me with a questioning look. "What do you know about this Ruth Weaver?"

"Not much. White female. Thirty-five years old." I shake my head. "You guys come up with anything?"

"Nada. No records. No photo. Not even a driver's license."

"I think she's our killer. I think she's going after the people who brutalized her mother."

"Powerful motive."

"We need to put out a BOLO."

"A lot of thirty-five-year-old white females out there."

"Wait." I recall my conversation with the lab technician from BCI. "There was a long hair found on Dale Michaels's body. We don't know if it's from the killer or if he picked it up in the course of his day. It's a blond hair that's been dyed brown. Lab is working on ID'ing the donor now."

"So now we have a thirty-five-year-old white female with brown hair."

"It's all we've got. Let's put out a BOLO. If she's driving without a license or proof of insurance, we might get lucky."

"Could be using a stolen identity."

I try not to groan. "Tell Mona and Jodie to stay on it. Tell them to search for the names Hochstetler and Weaver. First names Wanetta and Ruth. Cambria County, Pennsylvania. Nicktown. Nanty Glo. Tell them to look at everything. Blogs. Photos. Videos. News items. Whatever they can find. I'll take anything at this point."

"Got it." Glock jots notes in the small pad he keeps in his uniform pocket. Without taking his eyes off the pad, he asks, "Chief, might not be a bad idea to try and smoke her out using Blue."

"I thought of that, but there's this pesky little detail called procedure. Could get sketchy with the lawyer, too." I feel his eyes on mine, but I don't look at him. I don't want him to know I'd already seriously considered it.

"Wouldn't be the first time cops used a witness to nab a bad guy."

I meet his gaze and we stare at each other across the spans of my desk, our minds working over the logistics as we were considering doing something we shouldn't be considering. "It's a bad idea. Lots of things could go wrong."

"On the other hand," he says slowly, "it might be our best hope of getting our hands on Weaver. We keep it simple. Drive him back to his place and stay with him, out of sight. Make sure he's visible. See what happens."

"Things could go bad pretty fast, Glock. Blue could make a run for it. Weaver could take a shot at him."

"So we put a vest on him."

"Maybe an ankle monitor . . ." I pinch the bridge of my nose. "I did not just say that."

Glock grins. "Yes, you did. Sheriff's Department has an ankle monitor, Chief. I can run over there and pick it up."

My smile feels like wax on my face. "You're not making it easy to say no."

"This woman, this Ruth Weaver, is working fast," he says. "We know Blue is a viable target. It could work."

I give a nod, but the decision leaves a jittery sensation in the pit of my stomach. "Put Blue back in a cell and go get that ankle monitor." I look at my watch. "Meet me back here in an hour. I've got to break the news to Hoch Yoder."

CHAPTER 27

It's 11 P.M. by the time I turn into the gravel lane of Yoder's Pick-Your-Own Apple Farm. The shop is closed this time of night, so I continue down the lane to the house and park adjacent a white rail fence. A single upstairs window glows with lantern light. After shutting down the engine, I leave my vehicle and go through the gate and take the sidewalk to the front of the house and knock.

I wait several minutes before the door opens. Hoch Yoder thrusts a lantern at me, his eyes widening upon spotting me. "Chief Burkholder. *Was der schinner is letz?*" *What in the world is wrong?*

"I'm sorry to bother you so late, Hoch. I need to talk to you." When he hesitates, I add. "It's important."

"Of course." He opens the door wider and beckons me inside.

I follow him through a darkened living room and into the kitchen. I take the same chair I took last time I was here. He goes to the counter, removes the globe of a second lantern, and lights the mantle.

"Hoch?"

I glance toward the kitchen doorway to see his wife, Hannah, enter. She's wearing a blue sleeping gown with a crocheted shawl over her shoulders. She looks from her husband to me. "Is everything all right?"

"I have some news for Hoch," I tell her. "About the case from 1979."

They exchange looks, and then Hannah joins him at the counter, sets her hand on his arm. "I'll make cider."

Giving her a nod, he crosses to the table and sits across from me. "Did you catch them?"

"I believe all but one of the people responsible for what happened that night is dead."

"Dead? But . . ." Realization dawns on his face. "You mean those people who were murdered?"

I nod. "The fourth man is in custody. He confessed."

"Confessed? Who is it?"

"Blue Branson."

"The *Englischer breddicher*?" *The English preacher?* Incredulity rings hard in his voice. "But why . . . He . . . *Mein gott.* I have no words."

"Hoch, I can't go into much detail, because the investigation is ongoing. But . . . I have some information for you."

Hannah approaches the table with three mugs of cider. "Chief Burkholder," she begins, "are you certain about Pastor Branson?" She sets the mugs in front of us. "He seems like such a decent, God-loving man. He donated a hundred dollars when Chubby Joe Esh's house burned last year. He came out and worked alongside the Amish to help rebuild."

"I have his full confession." I turn my attention

back to Hoch. "I know what happened to your mother. Some of this will be difficult for you to hear, but I think there are some things you need to know."

He opens his mouth, but no words come. For an instant, his lips quiver, like a mute man trying to speak. "It's terrible?"

"It's bad," I tell him. "I'm sorry."

Hannah sinks into the chair next to him, sets her hand on his forearm again, and squeezes so firmly, her knuckles turn white. "We value the light more fully after we've come through the darkness," she murmurs in Pennsylvania Dutch.

Bolstered by her words, Hoch looks at me and nods.

As gently as possible, leaving out most of the sordid details, I convey to him the account of events that Blue relayed to me earlier. "She passed away two months ago," I finish.

He blinks at me, hurt and confusion twisting his features. "But if she was alive, why didn't she come back?"

"We may never know." I shrug. "Maybe she suffered a traumatic brain injury. Sometimes those kinds of injuries can affect memory, and in some cases, the patient's personality. She may not have remembered who she was or even her name."

"Blue Branson did that to her?" he asks, incredulous. "Forced her and then left her for dead?"

"Yes."

Next to him, Hannah lowers her head and puts her face in her hands. "She is with God now. At peace. We can take comfort in that."

The Amish man sets both elbows on the table and looks down at the untouched mug of cider in front of him. "She was alive. All this time."

"Hoch, I know this is difficult, but there's more."

"There's more than that?" He raises his gaze to mine. "Isn't that enough?"

"Was your mother with child when she disappeared? Had she mentioned it?"

"With child? No." He says the word with a defensiveness that tells me he knows where I'm going with this.

"I believe your mother had a child. A daughter."

"*What?* But . . . When?" Making a sound of distress, he sets his fingers against his temples and massages. "I have a sister?" He raises his head. My heart twists when I see a tremulous smile on his lips. *"A sister."*

"Hoch, it's more complicated than that. We're looking for her. We think—"

"Looking for her? You mean the police? But why?"

"I'm sorry, but I think she may be involved with these murders."

He goes still. "You think she *killed* those three people?" His gaze searches mine. In their depths, I see his mind digging into all the dark crevices of the past. Remembering things he's been trying to forget. "How old is this woman who claims to be my sister?"

"She's about thirty-five years old."

Hannah goes to the sink and begins to wash her mug.

I see Hoch's mind working over the time frame, and I know he's doing the math. "So this woman . . . she could be my half sister."

"It's possible."

"My mother endured much suffering."

"Yes. You, too."

From her place at the sink, Hannah looks at me over her shoulder, and I see tears on her cheeks. *"Sell is en shlimm shtoahri." That is a terrible story.* "It breaks my heart."

"I'm sorry." I look at Hoch. "Can I talk to you alone?"

Wariness enters his eyes. At first I think he's going to refuse; then he nods at his wife. "Leave us for a moment, Hannah."

She bows her head slightly, dries her hands on a dish towel, and leaves the kitchen.

When we're alone, I say, "In your statement, you told the police that one of the men threw the lantern down the steps and into the basement, causing the fire that killed the children."

"Yes, that is true."

"Blue Branson claims none of them threw the lantern. That they forced all of you into the basement without any light."

He blinks at me, unspeaking.

That he doesn't deny Blue's assertion stirs a small ping of skepticism, of pain—and compassion. "Hoch, I'm not here to lay blame. You were the victim of a crime that night. I just want to make sure I have all the facts and that those facts are correct because it will have a bearing on the case. Is Blue telling the truth about the lantern? Is it possible the lantern was already in the basement and the children lit it?"

"Why does it matter?" he snaps. "They're with God now."

"It matters because if Blue was the cause of that fire, he'll be charged with four additional counts of homicide."

The Amish man lowers his face into his hands and emits a single sob. "My brothers and sisters . . . they were frightened of the dark. Mamm kept a lantern on the workbench where she made soap. I lit the lantern. I thought . . . I thought they would be all right."

I steel myself against a rolling wave of sympathy. For him. For the children. And for the first time, I'm fully cognizant of the guilt he must have felt all these years. "It was an accident, Hoch. The kids may have panicked and somehow knocked it over."

"It's my fault. If I hadn't left them . . . they'd still be alive. I've prayed for God's forgiveness. He has given me comfort. Still, those little ones are gone because of me."

"You couldn't have foreseen what happened. You did your best, and that's all any of us can do. It was an accident. God knows that, Hoch." The words make me feel like a hypocrite; I'm the last person who has the right to talk to this man about God. Still, I believe the words. "You were trying to save your mother's life. That was very brave."

"The children suffered because of me."

"Because of those men. Not you."

Hoch hangs his head. He doesn't make a sound, but tears stream from his eyes. He wipes his face with his shirtsleeve. "I bragged about the money. To the *Englischer.* He was a couple of years older than me, and I . . . wanted to impress him." He utters a sad laugh. "I wanted to be cool. Like him. I told him we had jars full of money."

"Who did you tell?" I ask.

"He's a government man now. Johnston. He worked for my father for a few weeks. I think he must have told the others." Pain flashes on his features. "But it was my fault. I was . . . prideful. That's not the Amish way."

I nod, understanding. "You were a kid. You didn't know someone would act on that information."

"God punished me. I deserved it."

"The only people responsible for what happened are Blue Branson and the others." I reach out and touch his shoulder. "Thank you for telling me what happened. I know it wasn't easy."

He raises his head, his cheeks wet. "I hear them sometimes," he whispers. "When I go out there. I hear them crying for me from the basement."

I don't know what to say to that, so I say nothing.

He blows out a shuddery breath. "What happens next?"

"I'm going to find Ruth Weaver."

The weight of Hoch's grief follows me on the drive back to the station. Guilt is always a bad thing, but it's somehow worse when you're Amish. It's times like this when I need Tomasetti most. He's been on my mind on and off all day, mostly on, despite the fact that I'm fully engaged with the case. I've wanted to call him a dozen times, but each time I somehow convinced myself not to. Finally, sitting in my Explorer outside the police station, knowing I'm not going to make it home anytime soon, I hit the speed dial for our home number.

He answers with his usual, "Hey, Chief."

"Things are heating up with this case," I tell him. "I just wanted to let you know . . . I'm not going to make it home tonight."

"Everything all right?"

I recap the events of the day, and I hear him sigh on the other end of the line. I consider telling him about my plan to stake out Blue Branson's place tonight, but I don't want to worry him, so I don't mention it.

"You've had a busy day."

"Yeah."

"For a moment there, I thought maybe you were avoiding me."

"I was, but now that I'm talking to you, I can't imagine why."

He laughs. "I'm going to have to think about that one."

From my place at the wheel, I watch T.J. pull up in his usual parking slot a few spaces down from where I'm sitting and walk into the station. "Tomasetti, this woman has lived off the grid her entire life. She was homeschooled. As an adult, she didn't get a driver's license. No credit cards in her name. There's not a single photo of her I could find. No one knows anything about her."

"It sounds like her mother's death put something into motion," he says. "Maybe before she died, the mother made some deathbed confession that set this woman off. The daughter, distraught and without a support system, took it upon herself to mete out a little payback."

"What if Ruth Weaver is a result of the rape? What if Wanetta Hochstetler knew it and some part of her hated her daughter for it. What if, over the course of her daughter's life, Wanetta put her on this path?"

"There is a twisted sort of logic to that."

"Hatred can take on a lot of different faces."

"What else do you know about her?" he asks.

"We know she's armed. Probably bat-shit crazy. Determined."

"If I were Blue Branson, I'd be looking over my shoulder."

"He's in custody."

In the interminable silence that follows, I groan inwardly because I know he's just figured out how I'm going to be spending the night. "So when were you going to tell me you're going to camp out at Blue Branson's place?"

"I was going to try to avoid that, if possible."

"And you accused me of not being honest?"

"That's a different kind of honesty."

"Goddamn it, Kate."

"Tell me you wouldn't be doing the same thing," I say defensively.

"Aside from that being a bad idea, you don't have the manpower for that kind of operation."

"We're talking about a woman with a .22 revolver she may or may not know how to—"

"Who's going to be there to cover your back? Pickles? T.J.?"

"Glock."

"I guess that makes everything all right, then, doesn't it?" Sarcasm oozes from his every word.

"Tomasetti, I can't deal with your overreacting every time something dicey comes up with my job. I'm the chief of police. There's a killer out there, and I know who the target is. Staking out Blue's place is the best way to stop her, and you know it."

"What I know is that you should involve the sheriff's office!"

"And have five cruisers parked in front of Blue's place? That's pretty subtle."

We fall silent. My own words and the anger behind them ring in my ears, and I wonder when we came to this, shouting at each other over the phone. I wonder why I'm so angry. Why I can't tell him I'm sorry. Maybe because I know he's right, but I'm going to do this anyway.

"Tomasetti," I say after a moment.

"I'm here."

"We have to stop doing this."

"I know."

"We need to talk—"

"We need to spend some time together," he cuts in snappishly.

"When this case is over, I'll take some time off. We can hang out at the farm and . . . grill hamburgers and drink wine and listen to the frogs."

"And fish."

My anger gives way to a sense of longing so powerful my chest aches. "I'm good at what I do. You're going to have to trust me. There's no one else."

"Who's going to keep you safe, Kate?"

"Glock's a good cop. He's former military and rock solid. We'll be fine."

His sigh tells me he's not assuaged. "Do me a favor and be careful, will you?"

"I always am. I'll see you in the morning."

After we disconnect, I realize we didn't talk about him or how he's dealing with the release of Joey Ferguson.

CHAPTER 28

A little past midnight, I'm in my office with Glock and T.J. I've just briefed them on everything I know about the Hochstetler case and the three recent murders.

T.J. speaks first. "So you think this Ruth Weaver person is going to make a move on Blue Branson?"

I nod. "If we're right and she's targeting the people involved in the rape and attempted murder of her mother, she's got at least one more target."

"Pretty strong motive," Glock says.

"Especially if you're crazy," T.J. adds.

But Glock caught the open-ended nature of my statement. "You said 'at least' one more target. Do you have someone else in mind?"

Rising, I go to the door and close it. Their eyes follow me as I go back to my desk and sit. "Norm Johnston was involved with this group and had previous knowledge of the crimes."

T.J. gapes at me. "*Councilman* Johnston?"

I tell them about my conversation with Johnston. "He had previous knowledge . . . to a degree. I sent everything I have over to the prosecutor, and this is something he's going to have to look at. I don't know if he'll bring charges."

"Even if he didn't know at the time," Glock says, "he found out shortly after. He could have come forward then."

"It's tricky." I tell them about the beating Johnston endured. "There was intimidation involved. He was a minor at the time. Still, under Ohio code, that could mean a complicity charge."

T.J. shrugs. "Hard to believe he kept his mouth shut all these years."

I look from man to man. "In any case, Johnston could also be in danger from this woman." I turn my attention to T.J. "I want you to keep an eye on Norm Johnston's place tonight. Park out of sight. Keep it unobtrusive. Keep your cell and radio handy. Wear your vest at all times."

"You got it."

"Glock and I are going to take Blue back to his place and camp out there. Keep Blue visible and see if she bites."

"Might get kind of dicey if she takes a shot at him through the window," T.J. says.

No one has anything to say about that.

Glock and I find Blue lying on his cot with his back to the cell door.

"Rise and shine," Glock calls out as he approaches the cell.

The preacher rolls to a sitting position, a crease from the pillow marring the left side of his face.

"Do not move." Glock unlocks the cell door and steps into the cell. "Relax and keep your hands where we can see them. All right?"

"No problem," Blue replies.

I step into the cell, the ankle monitor in my hand. "Roll up your pants on your left leg," I tell Blue.

Never taking his eyes from mine, he leans forward and rolls up the hem of his slacks. A meaty white calf the circumference of a telephone pole comes into view. When the hem is rolled up to just below his knee, I cross to him and kneel. "I'm placing a GPS monitoring device on your person," I tell him.

"I see that." Blue watches me place the monitor around his ankle. "Aren't those things for house arrest?" he asks.

"Sure. House arrest," Glock says from his place at the cell door. "Only you're going to have two armed babysitters. So keep your shit cool. You got that?"

"I got it. Where are we going?"

"Your place." I roll down the pants leg. "We believe Wanetta Hochstetler's daughter is going to attempt to murder you."

"Her *daughter*?" Incredulity rings in his voice.

"Maybe she's *your* daughter, Blue."

He stares at me, blinking. His mouth forms words, but no sound emerges from his throat, and I feel a small, cruel sense of satisfaction.

"This is your chance to redeem yourself." I move away from him and stand. "You interested?"

"I'm interested." Regaining his composure, he bends to roll down his pants and then gets to his feet. "Whatever you think of me, I'll help anyway I can."

"That's big of you," I say.

Glock hands me the black Kevlar vest and I pass it to Blue. "I think you know what this is," I tell him. "Put it on. Under your shirt."

He stares at me as he unbuttons his shirt and takes it off. I keep my eyes on his as the pasty skin and sagging flesh of his chest come into view. "How do you know she has a daughter?" he asks.

"I went to Pennsylvania," I tell him.

Setting his shirt on the bunk, he shoves his arms through the openings of the vest. "Are they together?" he asks. "Wanetta Hochstetler and her . . . daughter?"

Instead of answering, I glance over at Glock, who steps forward and tugs the vest closed and smoothes down the Velcro closures.

"So we go to my place and wait for them to show?" Blue asks as he buttons his shirt.

"That's about the size of it." I hand him the keys to his truck. "You're driving. Officer Maddox is riding shotgun. And I do mean shotgun, so don't do anything stupid."

"I think I've used up my quota of stupid," he says.

"You're not going to get an argument from us on that," Glock tells him.

I don't like the idea of Blue getting behind the wheel any more than I like the idea of using him as bait. But despite the heinous nature of his past crimes, I don't believe he has any intention of harming anyone or running. The one thing I do know is that if the sting is going to be successful, Ruth Weaver must believe Blue is alone and free of police surveillance.

We're at the police station, standing outside the interview room. "Here's how it's going to go down," I tell Blue. "Once you reach your house, you'll pull into the garage and park just like you always do. Once the garage door is closed, you and Officer Maddox will go inside. Did you leave any lights on?"

"Nope. Never do."

"Are there any curtains open?"

"Kitchen, I think. There's a window above the sink, and I got a bird feeder out there."

"Since those curtains are open, do not turn on any lights until Officer Maddox takes his position in the hallway outside the bedrooms. Do you understand?"

"Yes."

"I want Officer Maddox's eyes on you at all times, Blue. If you screw that up, the deal is off and we take you back to jail and I'll lobby heavily when it comes time for the prosecutor to file charges. Do you understand?"

"I got it."

"Once Officer Maddox is in position, I want you to turn on all the lights. I want you to open the drapes or blinds. Make yourself visible from outside. If there's a TV in your living room, I want it on and I want you on the sofa, visible through the front window."

He nods.

"What's behind the house?" I ask Blue.

"Woods."

"Lots of places to hide back there," Glock puts in.

"Do you have a back patio?" I ask Blue.

He nods.

"We believe Jerrold McCullough was accosted on his back patio. We found pieces of a broken mug that had been swept over the side. If you want to move around, you can go out onto the patio, as if you're enjoying the fresh air."

At his nod, I address Glock, "I'll be parked next door at Brewer's Salvage Yard. I'll have my cell and the radio. And a pretty good view of Blue's house and front yard, but I can't see the back from there."

Blue speaks up. "You can see the backyard from

the master bedroom." He looks at Glock. "I can show you if you want."

Glock frowns at him. "I'll figure it out. You just do as you're told."

"Give me a few minutes to get into position at the salvage yard," I tell Glock. "There are a couple of places I can park and not be seen from the street or Blue's place."

"You got it, Chief." He gives me a let's-do-this nod. "Watch your back."

"You, too."

Twenty minutes later, I'm in the Explorer with the vehicle wedged between a corrugated fence and the forklift used to move scrap metal. A foot-wide section of fence is missing, which gives me a decent view of Branson's house and front yard. I've been there only a few minutes when I see the flash of headlights and then Blue's Mustang barrels down the lane. The twin headlight beams play over the facade of the house. The security light blinks on and the garage door rolls up. I try, but even with the vehicle illuminated by the garage light, I can't see Glock. So far, so good.

A moment later, the garage door rolls down. Another minute, and a light appears in the front window. My cell vibrates against my hip, and Glock's name pops up on the display. "The eagle has landed," he says.

"Roger that. I'm in place. How's the view?"

"I'm in the rear bedroom. I can see the backyard to the fence from here."

"Good." I pause. "Blue behaving himself?"

"Like an angel."

"Make sure he stays visible," I say. "Going to be a

long night. Let's do everything we can to draw this woman out."

"Got it."

I end the call and settle in for the wait.

By 4:30 a.m., I'm stiff and cold and convinced the entire operation is a bust. Not only am I stretching the rules by involving Blue, but I'm also starting to think I was a fool for thinking it would work. Of course, I went into this knowing there was a high probability that Ruth Weaver wouldn't show. I could spend a week parked in this junkyard, and it could all be a waste. Still, it was worth a shot, but disappointing nonetheless.

I've talked to Glock six times and Mona twice in the last three and a half hours, eaten an energy bar I found in my glove compartment that was a month past its expiration date, and left my vehicle to pee in the weeds next to a totaled '72 Ford LTD.

I'm thinking about throwing in the towel—at least for the night—when my cell vibrates. I glance down to see Mona's name on the display. "Hey, Mona."

"Chief, I'm sorry to bother you, but I thought you should know . . . Hoch Yoder called for you a few minutes ago. Wouldn't say what he wanted, but he sounded . . . strange. I offered to patch him through, but he started talking about souls and forgiveness and then he just hung up."

I pause, trying to ignore the twinge of worry threading through my gut. "Do you know where he was calling from?"

"That Amish community pay phone at Hogpath Road and the township road."

"Did you call him back?"

"I let it ring like twenty times, but he didn't pick up."

I sigh. "There's nothing going on here. I'm going to call this off for now and head out to the Yoder place to make sure everything's okay."

"You want me to let Glock know?"

"I'll call him," I tell her. "Thanks for the heads-up." I hit End and dial Glock. "We need to wrap this up," I say, and tell him about the call from Hoch Yoder.

"You want me to meet you out there?" he asks.

"I've got it. I don't expect any trouble, but I'm a little concerned. He was pretty upset when I told him about his mother."

"Gotcha."

"Take Blue back to the station and put him in a cell." I choose my next words with care because I don't want to seem paranoid. But I know this is one of those situations when paranoid isn't necessarily a bad thing. "Stay with him until I get back."

"Ten four."

I cruise by the phone booth Hoch used on my way to the Yoder place, but there's no one there. The closer I get, the more convinced I become that there's something wrong. I can't imagine Hoch calling the police at four thirty in the morning unless there's a problem. I'm also aware that Hoch, along with his half sister, both have a motive for murder.

The black trunks of naked apple trees blur by as I head toward the farm. I find my eyes combing the ditches on either side of the road, looking for a buggy or pedestrian—anything out of the norm. The fruit stand is closed up and dark, so I speed past and make a left into the lane. Slinging mud, gravel pinging in the wheel wells of the Explorer, I barrel toward the house. A hard stop, and I'm out of the vehicle and jogging toward the house.

Hoch's wife, Hannah, comes through the door as I reach the steps. "Chief Burkholder?"

She's still in her sleeping gown, but has thrown a shawl over her shoulders. Her damp hair tells me she's already been outside.

"Hoch called the police department earlier," I tell her. "Is everything all right?"

She blinks, and I can tell she's struggling to hold back tears. "I can't find him," she blurts. "I woke up twenty minutes ago. I thought he'd gone out to the fruit stand, but he's not there."

"Did he take the buggy?"

"He harnessed the horse, but left the buggy in the barn."

"He took it to the pay phone down the road," I say, thinking aloud. "He must have come back."

"Why would he leave at this hour to call the police?"

"Hannah, is it possible he couldn't sleep and started his chores early? Or is there a place on the property he might go if he's troubled and needs some time alone?"

She shakes her head. "I checked the shop and the fruit stand first thing, but he's not at either place. I called out to him, but he didn't answer. I even tried the dinner bell, in case he was out walking in the orchard. Chief Burkholder, he didn't make coffee. He *always* makes coffee."

"How was his frame of mind after I left last night? Was he upset or acting strangely?"

"He was . . . quiet. He gets that way when he's restless." She pauses, her face screwing up slightly. "Do you think that crazy woman who killed those men would go after Hoch, too?"

"Let's not jump to conclusions just yet." But my own mind has already ventured into the same territory.

She nods, but I can plainly see by the way she's shaking that she doesn't believe me.

"When did you last see him?" I ask.

"Last night. At bedtime."

"What time was that?"

"Eleven or so."

"Do you mind if I take a look around your property?"

She brightens, as if pleased to have something proactive to do. "I'll go with you."

"I'd prefer if you stayed here." I set my hand on her shoulder and give a reassuring squeeze. "In case he comes back while I'm gone."

Wringing her hands, she crosses to the porch and sits on the step, not caring about the damp. "I know God will take care of him. But I'm frightened."

I hit my lapel mike. "T.J.?"

"Hey, Chief."

"Any sign of anyone at Norm's place?"

"Nothing here."

I fill him in on the situation. "Will you take a cruise around the block out here at the Hochstetler farm?"

"Will do."

I disconnect to see Hannah returning from the mudroom off the kitchen with a pair of mud boots in hand. "He didn't take his boots with him. If he'd been going out, he would have taken them."

"Go inside and lock the doors," I tell her. I'm going to take a look around. I'll be back in a few minutes, all right?"

Nodding, she goes back into the house and closes the door behind her. I hold my ground until I hear the lock click, and then I go to the Explorer. It's drizzling, so I pull on my slicker, grab my full-size Maglite, and head into the darkness.

I begin my search at the fruit stand. The structure is small, and within minutes I've determined that Hoch isn't there. The only visible footprints are Hannah's. I leave the fruit stand and take the gravel driveway to the rear of the house, where a ten-foot-wide gate opens to the orchard. The hinges squeak as I open it and go through. Mud sucks at my boots as I follow the two-track path toward the trees where the road splits. I set my beam on the ground in front of me and spot a single set of tracks. The mud is too sloppy for me to discern the size or type of shoe, but they go left, so I follow.

Around me the night is as dark and wet as some underwater cave. The air is heavy with mist, and I can feel the cold weight of it pressing down on me. The tracks take me along a row of mature apple trees. In the darkness, the branches look like black capillaries spread out against the sky. It's so quiet, I can hear the water dripping off of the branches and splattering on the saturated ground.

I've walked about half a mile when I spot the old mill house. It's a small wooden structure with a stone foundation and steeply pitched roof. A whisper of nostalgia moves through me when I realize this is one of the places I used to come with my *datt* when I was a girl before the new mill was built closer to the stand. Twenty-five years ago, the siding had been painted cheery red with crisp white trim. Lush ivy had climbed the walls all the way to the roof, giving it a cottage-like countenance. I remember being intrigued by the wind chimes Mrs. Yoder had hung beneath the eaves. The pretty red paint is long gone now. The ivy clings to the rotting wood like the skeletons of long-dead snakes. It disheartens me to see such a place abandoned and left to the elements.

"Hoch Yoder!" I call out. "It's Kate Burkholder!"

There used to be a big window in the front with a wood shutter that hung down from the top and was propped open with a board. Now, the shutter hangs by a single hinge that squeaks like some injured rodent in an intermittent breeze.

I shine my light along the front of the building. Sure enough, the tracks lead to a stone walkway that's barely visible through the high weeds. I follow them around to the side of the building and find muddy footprints on the concrete stoop.

"Hoch!" I call out, and identify myself again. Holding my flashlight steady, I shove open the door with my foot and thrust the flashlight inside. The smell of rotting wood and wet earth and a darker smell I don't want to name greets me. I get the impression of a single room, fifteen feet square. To my right there are several busted-up bushel baskets and an ancient apple cider press. To my left, the old counter has collapsed into itself. I see half an oak barrel on the floor. Several plastic jugs—the kind used for cider. Ahead I see an old rectangular table and several chairs. Beyond, Hoch Yoder lies on the floor next to an old pot-bellied stove.

"Hoch!" I run to him, drop to my knees beside him. He's lying in a supine position. I know instantly he's dead. His left arm is over his head, his right is bent at the elbow with his hand near his shoulder. His head is twisted to one side. I force myself to look at his face. His flesh is that terrible color of blue gray.

His staring eyes are sticky-looking and beginning to cloud. Still, I reach out and press my finger against his carotid artery. His skin is cold to the touch, like rubber. There's no pulse.

"Oh . . . Hoch."

A .22-caliber revolver lies on the dirt floor a few inches from his right hand. Rising, I turn away from the sight and grapple for my cell phone. Even though we use the ten code system here in Painters Mill, there are certain situations that are best handled off the radio. A lot of people in the area have police scanners. It's never a good thing for them to find out about a death before the next of kin.

"Mona."

"Hey, Chief."

"I'm out here at the Yoder Apple Farm. I found Hoch Yoder. He's DOA. Possible suicide."

"Do you want me to send the coroner?"

"Yeah." I look at Hoch and, in light of the murders, I'm reminded that not every scene is as it appears at first glance. "Give BCI a call, too, will you? See if we can get a CSU out here."

"Got it." A thoughtful pause ensues. "You sound kind of funny, Chief. Are you okay?"

I'm not sure how to respond to that. I'm not okay. I feel sucker-punched because this decent man saw death as a better alternative than life—and his only escape from the truth and the agony of his past. I can't help but wonder if our conversation the night before was the final straw.

But this isn't about me or the way I feel. It's about hatred and revenge and stopping a killer.

CHAPTER 29

According to a poll I read in a magazine a while back, something like 71 percent of people hate their jobs. I'm lucky because I'm one of the minority. In fact, most days I love my job. I love being a police officer. I enjoy my duties as chief and the people I work with on a daily basis. I take pride in what I do, and I take seriously my oath to serve and protect the citizens of Painters Mill. But no job is perfect, including mine. Tonight, I hate my job with a passion.

T.J. is the first to arrive. We spend a few minutes walking the scene, and then I help him mark the perimeter with yellow caution tape. All the while the knowledge that Hannah Yoder is back at the house, frightened and wondering why a second police unit has arrived, beats at the back of my brain. I know that in a few minutes I'm going to bring her world crashing down around her.

I wait until I see the flashing lights of the ambulance coming through the gate before I trudge through the mud toward the house. Usually, when I have to notify an Amish person that their next of kin has died, I'll pick up Bishop Troyer for counsel. This morning, I don't have that option; I can't keep Hannah waiting that long. And I realize with some surprise that the bishop is probably as much help to me as he is to the grieving loved ones.

I hit my lapel mike as I leave the orchard and pass through the gate. "Mona?"

"I'm here, Chief."

"Will you have someone from the sheriff's office pick up Bishop Troyer and bring him to the Yoder farm?"

"Will do."

I find Hannah standing on the sidewalk a few yards from her back porch, watching the ambulance make its way toward the mill house. I take a shortcut through the side yard and traverse the distance between us. "Hannah?"

"Did you find Hoch?" she asks. "Is he all right? Why is that ambulance here?" She pelts me with rapid-fire questions as she rushes toward me, her eyes never leaving the orchard behind me, where the flashing lights of the ambulance are still visible through the trees. "Is he hurt?"

"Hannah, I'm sorry but Hoch is dead."

"What?" She coughs out a strangled sound. "That's not possible. He just went for a walk . . ."

Around us a steady rain pours down from the pre-dawn sky, but neither of us notices the cold or wet. She keeps craning her neck to look around me, trying to see past me, past the trees, as if expecting Hoch to emerge from the orchard and tell us all of this is some big misunderstanding.

"I'm sorry," I tell her.

"No." Her eyes find mine, but I can see there's a

part of her that isn't there. There's a blankness on her face, as if she's gone inside herself, where the pain of this can't reach her. Shock, I think, and I find myself hoping the sheriff's office gets Bishop Troyer here quickly, because I'm not sure I can handle this alone.

"But how?" Her eyes search mine. "Did that woman do something to him? Hurt him?"

From where I'm standing, I can see her entire body shaking. Her shawl is soaked and sagging against her. I reach out and touch her arm. "Let's get out of the rain so we can talk."

"I don't want to talk." She shakes off my hand. "I want to see Hoch."

"Hannah, that's not a good idea."

"Please. I want to see him."

"Bishop Troyer's on his way," I tell her. "We need to be here to meet him." I motion toward the door. "Let's go inside and wait for him, okay?"

She blinks rain from her eyes, looking at me as if I'm speaking some language she doesn't understand.

"It's going to be all right," I tell her.

"That's what Hoch always says," she whispers. "Only it's not, is it?"

"No," I tell her. "It's not."

Looping my arm around hers, I guide her to the house.

It's past noon when I leave the Yoder place, and I'm so exhausted, I can barely see straight as I drive home. I park in my usual spot and drag myself to the door. Inside, I drape my mud-spattered slicker on the coatrack. My boots and slacks are caked with mud, so I take them off at the door and carry both to the laundry room. In the bedroom, I drop my holster and .38 onto the night table next to the bed. I lose the rest of my clothes on the way to the shower and spend fifteen minutes washing away the remnants of a day I'd like nothing more than to forget. I stumble to the bedroom naked and crawl between sheets that smell like Tomasetti. I curl up in the essence of him and tumble into a hard, troubled sleep.

I dream of Hoch Yoder. I'm Amish and my datt has brought Jacob and Sarah and me to Yoder's Pick-Your-Own Apple Farm for apple butter, cider, and a bushel of McIntosh apples. I'm happy to be there, looking forward to playing hide-and-seek. The three of us run into the orchard, calling out to each other, hiding among the trees. I've found the perfect hiding place when the orchard goes silent and dark. I can no longer hear my siblings. Frightened, I leave my spot, but no matter how hard I search, I can't find them. Thunder rumbles and the wind picks up, warning me of a storm. When I look up, the sun is black and the rain is red, falling onto me like blood from the sky.

"Kate. Hey. Kate."

I wake to find Tomasetti leaning over me. One hand braced on the headboard, the other warm against my shoulder. Disoriented, unnerved by the dream still so vivid in my mind, I sit up quickly. Hazy light slants in through the windows and I realize with some surprise I don't know if it's morning or afternoon or somewhere in between.

"Hey." My voice is clogged, so I clear it.

"You were thrashing around." Tomasetti tilts his head as if to get a better look at my face. "Bad dream?"

"Yeah." Not making eye contact with him, I swing my legs over the side of the bed and scrub my hand over my face. "What time is it?"

"After six."

I look at him over the tops of my fingertips and smile. "A.M. or P.M.?"

He smiles back. "P.M."

"I have to go." I start to rise.

But he presses me back. "Whoa."

"I didn't intend to sleep this long."

"That's what you get for staying up all night."

He's wearing an exquisitely cut charcoal suit with a light gray shirt and the tie I bought him for Father's Day last summer. I know he hates that tie; I have the fashion sense of a toad, especially when it comes to dressing a man. But I know he wears it because he loves me.

Lowering himself onto the bed next to me, he puts his arm around my shoulders and pulls me against him. "I tried to wake you for dinner, but you were out cold."

"You know that's no reflection on your cooking, right?"

He smiles. "I picked up a sandwich at Leo's for you."

I make an exaggerated sound of disappointment, wondering if he has any idea how comforted I am by his presence. "You know we're putting Leo's kids through college, don't you?"

"You know his name isn't really Leo, right?"

That makes me laugh.

"That's better."

"Where are you going?"

"Dinner with the brass." He smoothes a strand of hair from my face. "Do you want to talk? I have a few minutes."

I shake my head. "No."

"I heard what happened to Hoch Yoder. It was on

the news." He leans close and presses a kiss to my forehead. "I'm sorry. I know you liked him."

"Are they calling it a suicide?"

"Yeah."

Talk of the case reminds me that I lost half a day and how much I have to do. I try to rise again, but he stops me.

"Wait." Gently, he wraps his fingers around my biceps and turns me to him.

I look up at him. "Tomasetti, I have morning breath."

"Do I look even remotely concerned about that?"

He sets his mouth against mine and I melt into him. My arms go around his neck and I pull him closer. I kiss him hard, using my tongue, wanting more. He kisses me back in kind, and in an instant I'm swept away. It's crazy, but even as he holds me, I feel an inexplicable rise of desperation, of wanting that has nothing to do with physical needs, and I wonder how it is that my love for him can be so all-encompassing.

After a moment, he pulls away. His face is scant inches from mine. His pupils are dilated, his mouth wet. "I have to tell you something." His voice is low and rough, his nostrils flaring, but he isn't smiling. "Before you hear it on the news."

Something cold skitters up my back. "What?"

"Joey Ferguson is dead."

I hear the words as if I'm standing in some vast canyon, and they echo off rocky cliffs. I'm so shocked that it takes a moment for the words to register. "Dead? How?"

"He was shot outside a bar in Cleveland. Execution style. Passerby found his body a few hours ago."

I stare at him, stunned, not sure what to make of

it. The silence is deafening. "Did the cops get the shooter?"

"No."

I'm suspicious by nature, and no matter how much I love him, I know him. I know what he's capable of. And I have no choice but to ask the one question I fear most. "Did you have anything to do with it?"

He takes the question in stride, as if knowing I would ask. "No."

A sense of relief unravels the knot of tension at the back of my neck. Still, I know there's a possibility that he's lying. To protect me. To protect himself.

"All right," I hear myself say.

"I wanted you to hear it from me."

"Who's handling the case?"

"Cleveland PD."

"Are they looking at you?"

"Probably. They won't find anything." He looks down at our clasped hands and then makes eye contact with me. "Are we all right?"

"Yes," I say.

As he walks out the door, all I can think is that they didn't find anything the last time the police looked at him, and Tomasetti had been guilty as sin.

CHAPTER 30

I arrive at the station a little after seven. I'm preoccupied by my conversation with Tomasetti and operating in a fog as I go through the front door. Mona
greets me with her usual cheery, "Hey Chief," as I
make a beeline for the coffee station.

"What are you doing here?" I ask.

"Jodie's flooded in, so I told her I'd cover her shift."
She rises and crosses to me, her hand extended with
a dozen or so pink slips. "I hate to hit you with this
with everything else that's going on, but I just took a
911 from Randy Trask. He says the water's up over
the Tuscarawas Bridge."

"Of course it is," I mutter.

The Tuscarawas Bridge is a covered bridge of historical significance and a Painters Mill icon that spans
Painters Creek and part of a floodplain. "Get T.J. out
there to set up flares. Notify the sheriff's department."
I take the messages and glance through them. "I want
the road blocked and a detour set up." I pour coffee
into my cup, knowing there's always some motorist

who's in a hurry and takes a chance by driving through high water. "Give the mayor a call and put in a call to ODOT."

"Will do." I can tell by the way she's fidgeting that she's got something else on her mind. Before I can ask, she blurts, "Chief, I think I found something on Ruth Weaver."

I set the coffeepot back on the burner and give her my full attention. "Let's see it."

I follow her to the dispatch station. She slides behind her computer and deftly runs her fingers over the keyboard. An instant later, a photo of an Amish woman appears on the screen. I guess her to be about twenty-five to thirty years old. Plain gray dress. Dark bonnet. *Swartzentruber,* I think.

"I found it on a blog site," she tells me. "A blogger posted it eight years ago on a site called *A Lid for Every Pot.*"

"That's an old Amish saying," I murmur.

"I was just messing around and did a search for Nanty Glo, Pennsylvania, and the blog came up. I started reading, and the blogger, a lady by the name of Gwen Malcolm, had driven across Pennsylvania while on vacation and ran across this Amish woman on the roadside selling handwoven baskets. She bought a basket and started talking to the woman and somehow ended up taking the photo, which she used in her blog."

"That's surprising," I say. "That dress and bonnet are Swartzentruber."

"According to the blogger, the Amish woman's name is Ruth Weaver."

I lean closer to the monitor. "Can you enlarge it?"

"Yeah, but we lose resolution." She taps a menu tab, and a larger but grainier photo augments.

I stare at the woman's face, and a vague sense of familiarity grips me. I know it's impossible; I've never met Ruth Weaver. Still, staring at the photo is like having a word on the tip of your tongue that you can't quite conjure. "Mona, I think I've seen her before."

"Here in Painters Mill? Or when you drove over to Pennsylvania?"

"I'm not sure. But her face . . . there's something familiar about her."

"Like passing-on-the-street familiar or you've-talked-to-her familiar?"

"I don't know." I shift my attention to Mona. "See if you can get in touch with the blogger and get your hands on a better photo. Or if she has others, ask her to send them."

"I'll do it right now."

"E-mail it to me."

"Will do."

Half an hour later, I'm in my office on my second cup of coffee, staring at the grainy photo on my twenty-one-inch monitor. I hit the Print key and the printer spits out a not-so-great black-and-white reproduction. Grabbing it out of the tray, I leave my office, and head to the jail cell located in the basement.

Skid is sitting in the chair with his feet on the desk, playing with his iPad. "Oh. Hey." His fleet slide from the desk. "Didn't realize you were here."

I glance at the cell, where Blue Branson lies on his cot, watching me. "Get up," I tell him, crossing to the cell door.

The big man rolls and gets to his feet. His hair is mussed. His face pushed slightly aside. His typically crisp white shirt is wilted. Somehow he looks older than last time I saw him. He looks at me with eyes shot with red as he pulls his black jacket over his shoulders.

"I need you to look at a photo," I tell him.

"All right." He approaches me.

When he's close enough, I produce the eight-and-a-half-by-eleven-inch photo. "Do you recognize this woman?"

He fumbles for his reading glasses, shoves them onto his nose, and takes a good look at the photo. When he raises his eyes to mine, his face is white all the way down to his lips. "Where did you get this?" he asks.

"Who is she?"

"That's Wanetta Hochstetler."

"It can't be." I tap the photo with my thumb. "The photo is eight years old. The woman is too young to be Wanetta Hochstetler."

"I reckon I ought to know, Chief Burkholder. It's her."

I lower the photo, not sure if he's telling the truth or trying to muddy the water. "You had better not be yanking my chain."

"With God as my witness, that's Wanetta Hochstetler."

I leave without thanking him. As I go through the door, he calls out my name, but I don't look back.

On the way back to my office, I peek my head into the reception area. "Mona, call Pickles and tell him I want him in my office ASAP."

It takes Pickles fifteen minutes to appear at my office door.

"How is it out there?" I ask, referring to the weather.

"Bad." He shuffles to the visitor chair adjacent

my desk and settles into it. "Never seen it rain like this."

"I need an ID on this woman." I slide the printed photograph toward him. "Do you know who she is?"

He pulls his reading glasses from his uniform pocket and tilts his head back to look at the photo through the bifocals. "Damn, Chief, she kind of looks like Wanetta Hochstetler."

"The photo was taken eight years ago. It can't be Wanetta. Pickles, I think it's her daughter."

"Daughter? I didn't realize she had a—"

"She does." Sighing because I didn't intend to snap, I tell him about my trip to Pennsylvania."

"Well, damn." He squints at the photo again. "Photo is kind of grainy. But the features are similar. Looks like she might have blond hair beneath that bonnet."

I turn to my computer and pull up the image. "The resolution is a little better here."

He rises to come around my desk and look at the monitor. We stare at it, not speaking.

"Huh." Pickles rubs his chin.

"What?"

He points at the woman's face, his finger hovering an inch from the screen. "You put dark hair on her, and she kind of looks like Hoch Yoder's wife."

"I don't see it." I study the photo, trying to imagine Hoch's wife with brown hair. All the while, something niggles at the back of my mind.

"So we may have an ID on the killer," he says. "You want me to add that to the BOLO?"

I can't stop staring at the photo. *You put dark hair on her, and she kind of looks like Hoch Yoder's wife.* Tunnel vision narrows my sight until all I can see is her face. Everything around me fades away. I can feel my heart thudding against my breast, my pulse roaring in my ears. From somewhere in the backwaters of my mind, I recall my conversation with the CSU technician about a hair found at the scene of the Michaels murder. *This was a long hair. Blond that was dyed brown.* I remember that because it's unusual for a woman with naturally blond hair to dye it brown.

Unless she's trying to hide something . . .

A cold realization augments inside me. I almost can't believe what I'm thinking, because the possibility makes me sick to my stomach. "Oh my God." I stand so quickly, my chair rolls back.

"Chief?"

I jab my finger against the photo. "That's Weaver. I thought she and her mother were living off the grid because they were Swartzentruber. But the real reason is so much more insidious. Pickles, I think Wanetta Hochstetler devoted her life to instilling her hatred into her daughter so that Ruth would come back to Painters Mill and kill the men who'd murdered her family—her children—and destroyed her life."

His rheumy eyes sharpen on mine. "Jesus, Chief, what kind of parent does that?"

"An insane one." I look at him, my mind reeling, still trying to put all the jagged pieces together. The picture that emerges is almost too ugly to consider. "I think Wanetta became pregnant from multiple rapes that night. I think that sent her over the edge. She had the baby, but . . . there was a part of her that hated her daughter. Hated her because of what she represented."

"Son of a bitch. How do you hate a little girl?"

"Pickles, this is so twisted, I can barely get my

mind around it. But you mentioned the woman in that photo looks like Hoch Yoder's wife." I swallow something bitter at the back of my throat. "Do you think it could be Hannah Yoder?

He stares at me, shocked by my words and the story they paint. "But that would mean . . . You think she married her *half brother*?"

"I don't know if I'm right, but it fits." I recall my last conversation with Hoch, and another piece of the puzzle snaps into place. "Hoch told me that a few days before the home invasion, he'd bragged about his *datt* keeping a lot of money at the house. That's why he's always blamed himself for what happened."

Pickles thinks about that a moment. "It sounds like he wasn't the only one who blamed himself. Maybe his mama blamed him, too."

"I can't fathom how her daughter would *know* about what happened. Or how a mother could hold her fourteen-year-old son responsible."

He shrugs. "Maybe one of the men told her. Salt on the wound kind of thing. If you look at what they did to her. Rape is about violence and pain and degradation. What better way to destroy this woman than to tell her that her own son was the one who set everything into motion?"

"Chief!"

I look up at the sound of Mona's voice to see her standing at the door to my office. "I just took a 911 from a driver out on Township Road 1. She drove through some standing water and her car got swept into the creek. She has a bunch of kids with her, and now they're on the roof."

Across from me, Pickles stirs, as if from habit he's ready to go. "Get Skid out there," I tell her. "Call the sheriff's office and fire department, too."

"Got it."

Pickles shifts restlessly. "Damn people never learn about driving through water," he grumbles.

"I've got to get out to Yoder's place." I start to rise.

"Chief. Wait." He leans across the desk, and he reaches out, his eyes filled with determination. "Look, I know I'm a little past my prime, but I don't think it's a good idea for you to go out there by yourself."

"The sheriff's department—"

"With all this flooding, every agency between here and Cleveland is going to have their hands full, and it's only going to get worse."

"Pickles—"

"I can handle it." He growls the word with a good bit of attitude, and for a moment I see him as the cocky young police officer he'd once been. The adrenaline-addicted cop who'd spent months working under-cover and risked his life to do it.

When I hesitate, he adds, "I'm right about that, and you know it."

I sigh and give a resolute nod. "Bring your slicker and your vest."

CHAPTER 31

Ten minutes later, Pickles and I are in my Explorer, bound for the Yoder apple farm. My police radio crackles with activity as my officers and Holmes County sheriff's deputies are dispatched to several high-water areas. I call Glock as I pull onto the highway. "I'm sorry to bother you so late," I begin.

"I figured I was going to get a call from you with all this flooding. What's up?"

"The rain isn't the only thing wreaking havoc." I give him a condensed version of my theory on Ruth Weaver.

"You want me to go with you?"

"I've got Pickles with me. We're heading out there now."

He makes an indecipherable noise in his throat, and I quickly add. "I need you to keep an eye on Norm Johnston. There's a possibility she'll show up there."

"What about Blue Branson?"

"T.J.'s on his way there. I can't imagine Weaver

making a move on the police station, but . . ." I sigh, feeling overwhelmed and uncertain. "She's unstable and tough to predict. Do me a favor and wear your vest, will you?"

"I'll head over to Johnston's now."

I disconnect as I make the turn into the gravel lane of the Yoder place. Rain pelts the windshield as I pass the house and park in the gravel a few yards from the back door. Jamming the shifter into Park, I turn and pull a slicker from the backseat. "We're just going to talk to her. I'm going to knock on the back door. I want you to go around to the front and make sure no one leaves. Don't knock, okay?"

"Got it."

I pull on the slicker and we disembark simultaneously. I wait until Pickles is around the side of the house; then I approach the back door. The rain is coming down so hard, it stings my exposed skin. I can't hear anything over the downpour, and visibility is down to just a few yards.

Ever aware of the .38 against my hip, I use the heel of my hand to knock. To my surprise, the door rolls open, and I think, *Shit*. A police officer must exercise caution when entering any premises. Even in a benign situation, there's a risk of being mistaken for an intruder and getting your ass shot off by an armed homeowner. That's not to mention the rights and privacy issues anytime you enter a home without a warrant or the express permission of the owner. But certain circumstances transcend those things, including concern for the homeowner's well-being. Several gnarly possibilities run through my head as I stand there, trying to decide what to do next. I'm not 100 percent certain Hannah Yoder is Ruth Weaver, which means she could be in danger, too.

"Mrs. Yoder?" I shout. "It's Kate Burkholder with the police department. Is everything all right?"

The pound of rain is thunderous, making it impossible for me to hear anything inside or out. Pushing open the door the rest of the way, I step into the mudroom and call out for her again. "Hannah! Are you home? Is everything all right?"

No response.

I transfer the Maglite to my left hand and draw my pistol, keeping it low at my side. I walk through the mudroom to the kitchen and find it dark and empty. I go right and peer into the living room, but there's no one there. Through the curtains at the front door, I see Pickles's silhouette. Quickly, I ascend the stairs to the second level and check the bedrooms, the closets and the bathroom, but there's no one there. When I come downstairs, I find Pickles standing in the mudroom.

"No one here," he says.

I holster my sidearm. "Let's check the barn."

Exiting through the back door, we slog through mushy gravel and ankle-deep puddles toward the barn fifty yards away. All the while, I keep an eye on the house for movement or light. I slide open the big door and step into the large structure. Like many of the older barns in this part of Ohio, the floor is hardpacked dirt. I notice the buggy immediately. To my right are stairs that lead to the loft. Ahead are two stalls, each occupied by a horse.

"Could she have a second buggy?" Pickles asks. "Another horse?"

"It's possible, but not probable." I walk to the buggy and see mud, still wet, caked on the wheels. "This one's been used recently."

"So if she didn't take the buggy, where the hell is she?"

"Her husband just died. It's possible one of the local Amish families came by and picked her up. They rally when something like that happens." I'm looking at Pickles as I speak. I can tell by his expression that neither of us believes it.

"Yeah and people confuse me with Tom Selleck," he grumbles.

I'm in the process of closing the door when I happen to glance down and see tire tread marks in the dirt. I kneel and set the beam of my Maglite on it for a closer look.

Pickles squats beside me. "Those ain't from no buggy."

I look around, silently cursing the dark and the pound of rain against the tin roof. "I can't think of a single logical reason why someone would have a vehicle out here."

"You think she's got a car?" he asks.

I unclip my cell and speed-dial Mona.

"Hey, Chief." She sounds breathless and stressed. "Phones are lit up like a Christmas tree. People bugging out all along the creek."

"I need you to check with DMV to see if anyone with the name of Ruth Weaver, Wanetta Hochstetler, or Becky Weaver in Pennsylvania or Ohio has a vehicle registered to them. While you're at it, check Hannah and Hoch Yoder, too."

"I'm on it."

"Call me."

I hit End and clip my phone to my belt. "There's one more place I want to check."

Pickles gives me a quizzical look.

"The old Hochstetler place," I tell him.

"I guess it's the perfect night for ghost hunting," he mutters, and we walk back out into the rain.

* * *

Because of water on the road and low visibility, I end up creeping along at thirty miles an hour, and it takes us fifteen minutes to reach the Hochstetler farm. I nearly miss my turn into the lane, brake hard enough to skid, and then jam it into four-wheel drive and slosh up the hill. I traverse mud puddles deep enough to swallow a tire and park several yards from the hollow where the house had once stood. I kill the engine, and in the darkness and flickering lightning, the place looks like the set of some B horror movie.

"Never liked this place," Pickles grumbles.

"You don't believe in all that ghost talk, do you?"

He doesn't answer, and my attempt at humor is lost.

Through the rain-streaked windshield, the old farm has a sad, abandoned appearance. The maple tree that had once stood tall in the front yard is still there but long dead. Some of the branches have rotted and fallen to the ground amongst hip-high brown weeds.

"I don't think there's anyone here," I tell him. "Let's take a quick look around and get back to the station."

He points. "If she's got a vehicle, she might've stowed it in that old round barn over there."

I set my hand against the door handle and look at Pickles. "Just in case, you might want to keep your sidearm handy. She's armed."

Flipping up my hood, I get out of the Explorer. The rain hammers down on me in torrents. I can hear it pinging against the Explorer, the tin roof of the old round barn twenty yards away, and plunking into the standing water in the old basement like hailstones.

My slicker comes to my knees, and the lower half of my slacks and feet are soaked in seconds. Usually, if I'm approaching a scene and I don't want to be visible, I wouldn't risk using a flashlight. But nights are incredibly dark in Amish Country. No streetlights or porch lights. With the thick cloud cover, visibility is nearly down to zero. The last thing I want to do is end up in some hole or ditch, so I pull out my Maglite and we start toward the barn.

I train the beam on the ground, looking for tire tracks or footprints, any sign that someone has been here, but all I see are weeds and mud, stands of saplings, and the occasional piece of trash. The old round barn has stood on this spot for over a century. But for the last three decades, the structure has gone without maintenance and looks every bit of its hundred years.

"I remember when this was a showplace," Pickles says as we go around the side of the building toward the rear. "Old Willis Hochstetler and his pop worked their tails off. Made some damn nice furniture, too. Not the kind of stuff you find today."

We reach the back of the barn. The door has been torn off its hinges and hangs at a perilous angle. I enter first. The smells of rotting wood and rodent piss greets me. I shine my light along the perimeter of the room. Broken windows—either from hail or vandals or both—allowed the elements to invade. The once-gleaming oak floors are warped and rotting in places. The support beams show signs of termites. Mindless graffiti has been spray-painted on one wall in fluorescent orange. A pile of what looks like coyote shit sits on the seat of a rail chair that has the back rest broken off.

"Hate to see this place go to crap like this," Pickles mutters.

"Me, too." I sigh. "I think we've struck out. Let's go."

We take the same route out of the building and start toward the Explorer. We're midway there when Pickles calls out, "I'm going to take a quick look-see in all that brush over there, Chief."

I glance to my left to realize he's referring to the place where the house once stood, which is little more than a partially caved-in pit now. The once-manicured landscaping is overgrown, some of the bushes jutting twelve feet high. A tangle of vines hang down from the branches of a pear tree.

I've got my beam trained on Pickles when I notice the tire ruts in the grass. They're pounded down by the rain, but I don't think they're very old. "Pickles! I've got—"

The *crack!* of a gunshot cuts off my words. It's not loud, and almost drowned out by the rain. Ducking slightly, I jerk my beam back to Pickles, surprised that he hasn't moved to take cover. Then I noticed that he's stooped at an odd angle. The realization that he's been hit registers like a punch to my forehead. "*Pickles!*"

His Maglite drops to the ground next to him. He looks down at it, staggers left as if he's trying to pick it up, then goes to one knee. His right hand reaches out to me. His eyes meet mine. His mouth opens, but he doesn't speak. Then he reels sideways and falls into the pit.

A hundred thoughts hit my brain at once. I have no idea where the shot came from. There's no cover. I know Pickles was wearing a vest, but that doesn't mean he was completely protected from a bullet. I don't know how badly he's injured. I don't know if he's conscious—or dead. And I'm ever aware that he just toppled into water deep enough to drown him.

I hit my lapel mike. "Officer down!" I scream the words, barely recognizing my own voice. "Ten thirty-three! Fuck! Ten thirty-three!"

I fumble for my .38. The slicker hinders me, costing me precious seconds. Then my sidearm's in my hand and I'm sprinting toward the place I last saw Pickles. "Police!" I don't know where the shooter is, but I shout the words anyway.

Movement ahead and to my left draws my attention. I catch a glimpse of a figure in the periphery of my beam. "Drop your weapon! Police!" I take aim and fire three times.

Vaguely I'm aware of my radio lighting up with activity, telling me every cop within ten miles will be here in short order. I don't think Pickles has that kind of time.

Two shots ring out. I hear a *plunk!* and actually feel the concussion next to my foot as a bullet plows into mud inches from where I'm standing. I douse my flashlight, making me invisible but blind. I think the shooter has taken cover behind the outhouse to my left, forty-five feet away. I drop low, moving fast, and head toward the opposite side of the pit, expecting a bullet to slam into my chest at any moment.

I don't have much cover here, either. A few small trees growing out of the pit. The brick chimney. The ten-foot-high stump of a dead tree. The best I can hope for is that the piss-poor visibility will keep her from getting off a good shot.

Sidling right, never taking my eyes from the place where I last saw her, I get as close as I can to the pit. "Pickles?" I call out.

No answer.

It seems like hours since he went into the water,

but it's only been seconds. I know that if he were able, he would have answered. Panic clenches my chest, a fist twisting the air from my lungs. I can't help but think: head shot.

I hit my radio. "Where's my backup!"

"Sheriff's office ETA five minutes, Chief."

"Ten thirty-three! Ten thirty-nine!" I shout the codes, frightened because I know Pickles doesn't have five minutes, and I'm not going to let him die.

I drop to my belly. Cold sinks through my clothes as I slither through mud and weeds to the edge of the pit. My line of sight is hindered by dead vegetation and trees that have taken root. Cursing, I look around for a way get into the pit, but it's dark and raining and I can't see shit.

"*Pickles!* Where are you?"

"Bitch . . . got me."

Choking back a swell of emotion, of hope, at the sound of his voice, I crawl in the direction of the sound. "How bad are you hurt?"

"Bad . . ."

"Can you get out of there?"

"Negative." The word is followed by a groaned, "Shit."

"Help's on the way."

"Chief . . ."

I wait, but he doesn't say anything more. "Pickles?"

I'm on my belly and elbows on the east side of the basement, facing west, toward the shooter's last position, but I see nothing. I don't know if she's moving to a new location or if she's running. All the while, I envision Pickles slipping beneath the water. . . .

Calling out his name, I wriggle closer to the edge. The ground falls away beneath my elbows as I draw near. I risk using my Maglite and flash it on and off into the pit. I get a snapshot of black water that's thick with foliage, rotting wood, and trash of indiscernible sources. A slick of blood two feet away. Pickles face-down in the water.

I slide my legs over the side and jam my fingers into the mud. I try to lower myself slowly, but my fingers plow through mud and I plunge into four feet of icy water. I manage to keep my Maglite above the surface. My feet sink deep into mud and God only knows what else. When I move toward Pickles, I trip over a submerged object and nearly go under.

I lunge toward the place I last saw him. My right hand makes contact. His skin is cold to the touch. He's trembling, thrashing weakly, trying to keep his head above water. "I've got you," I say.

He tries to speak, but he's choking and sputtering.

The crack of a gunshot rings out over the din of rain. I look around wildly, spot movement on the other side of the pit, a silhouette against the sky. I raise my .38 and fire once, conserving ammo, but in the process I drop my flashlight. Cursing, I drag Pickles through the water, stumbling over debris and squeezing through saplings and brush. He's conscious and cries out several times, but there's nothing I can do to ease his pain. My leg hits something solid. When I reach out, I realize I've found the stone steps that were probably part of the original house and led to the basement.

Using every ounce of strength I possess, I haul Pickles onto the steps. He's too heavy to pull completely from the water, but I'm able to get his head and shoulders out. "Pickles, where are you hit?"

"Went in at my armpit . . . angled into my side . . ."

"I need to go get her," I say. "Will you be okay?"

"Go," he whispers.

I don't want to leave him, but we're sitting ducks here. If she spots us, there's no doubt she'll kill us both.

Giving his hand a final squeeze, I rush up steps that are slick with mud. At the top, keeping low, I go right, toward the place I last saw her. Brush tears at my slacks as I make the sprint. If I can get behind her, I might be able to surprise her. I hear sirens in the distance, but I can't tell how close they are. My .38 is heavy and reassuring in my hand, but I'm ever aware that I have only three shots left. Better make them count.

The roar of an engine sounds to my left. I glance over and see headlights. At first, I think a sheriff's deputy has arrived, but the position is wrong. Then I realize it's Weaver. She must have hidden her vehicle in the trees beyond the outhouse, and now she's making a run for it.

I hit my lapel mike, but quickly realize it's dead from being immersed in water. I run to the Explorer, yank open the door, jam my key in the ignition. I grab my radio mike and flick on my emergency lights. "Ten eighty! In pursuit! Old Hochstetler place."

The radio crackles with voices and codes. A sheriff's cruiser is northbound on Old Germantown Road, less than a minute away. I'm turning my vehicle around when the cab is suddenly filled with light. I glance left to see headlights bouncing wildly. Coming directly at me. Too fast. Too close. I jam the shifter into reverse and hit the gas. The Explorer lurches backward, but not fast enough to avoid the collision. Headlights blind me. I see the front end of a pickup truck. Then I'm jerked violently left. The air bag deploys, punching my face and chest like a giant fist.

My head slams against the driver's-side window hard enough to shatter the glass.

I sit there for a few seconds, dazed, unable to move. As the air bag deflates, I regain my senses. I look right and see taillights disappearing down the lane. Weaver's running, I realize, heading toward the road. The Explorer's engine died on impact, so I restart it and stomp the accelerator to the floor.

The wheels hiss as they spin over grass and mud; then the vehicle jumps forward, crashes over something unseen that scrapes the undercarriage, but I don't slow down. Flipping on the wipers, I squint through the rain-streaked windshield. Ahead, I see the red flash of brake lights.

I snatch up my radio. "In pursuit. White Chevy pickup." The vehicle reaches the road and goes left. "Northbound Old Germantown Road."

"Roger that."

The Explorer bumps over potholes and debris and old vegetation. I'm fifty yards behind her. I reach the road, haul the wheel left, and floor the accelerator.

Another voice cracks over the radio. "I got a visual."

A glance in my rearview mirror reveals flashing lights of a Holmes County cruiser. My speedometer registers 80 mph. It's a dangerous speed in such poor conditions, but within seconds, I catch up with her. I nose the Explorer to within a few feet of the bumper. The road here is poorly maintained; the asphalt is pitted and uneven. The ditches on either side are filled with water. I'm thinking about attempting a PIT maneuver when Weaver takes the decision away from me.

The truck makes a hard left toward the gravel entrance of a field, but she's traveling too fast. I stomp hard on the brake. The Explorer slides out from under me. My training kicks in, and I turn into the skid, keeping my eyes on the truck. It spins 360 degrees and slams into the ditch. Water cascades twenty feet into the air.

Jamming the Explorer into Park, I throw open the door. Then I'm running toward the truck, my .38 poised, finger on the trigger. "Get out of the vehicle! Get your fucking hands up! Get on the ground! Right fucking now!" I scream the words in rapid succession. Overwhelm the target. Take control of the situation. Stay alive.

"Drop that weapon!" I scream. "Show me your hands! Do it now!"

My pulse is a jackhammer inside my head. I'm vaguely aware that it's pouring rain, but I don't hear it. I don't feel the wet or cold on my skin. Every ounce of my focus is on the driver's-side door.

"Show me your hands!" I come up behind the vehicle, staying out of her line of vision. Out of the line of fire. My gun hand is steady, but my heart is like a fist punching my ribs from inside my chest.

I reach the rear of the truck, check the bed. Nothing there. Keeping close to the truck, I sidle to the driver's-side door. I look through the window. I can see the silhouette of her inside. Reaching out, I try the door, but it's locked.

"Open the door! Do it now!" My finger snugs more tightly against the trigger, my aim steady at her center mass. *"Open the door!"*

I hear a vehicle skid to a halt behind me. Lights glint off the truck windows. I don't take my eyes off the suspect. "Open the door!"

Movement inside the cab. The passenger door flies open. I stumble back, keep my weapon steady. "Stop! Drop the weapon!"

Then she's out of the truck. She looks at me over her shoulder, and I get my first glimpse of Ruth Weaver's face. Features pulled into a snarling mask. Crazy light in her eyes. And I know she's not going to obey my command.

"Stop or I will shoot you!" I scream.

She hauls ass toward the gravel lane that will take her into the field and, beyond, a wooded area. She's not a bad runner for a woman, but I'm faster. And I'm pissed. I round the front of the truck, splash through the ditch, go up the other side. And then I'm six yards behind her, running full out and closing in fast. "Police!" I shout. "Stop! Now!"

She doesn't slow. Doesn't look behind her. It's too dark for me to discern if she's got the gun in her hand. But I know she's armed. She's already shot a cop. Tried to kill me. One wrong move on her part, and I'll cut her down.

I catch her thirty yards into the field. I dive and throw my arms around her waist, ramming my shoulder into the small of her back. A scream tears from her throat as she goes facedown in the mud. She tries to turn over, but I'm faster and stronger and I'm able to use my body weight to pin her.

"Stay down!" I shout. "Give me your hands!"

She writhes, twisting in an attempt to get her knees under her, but she's not strong enough to dislodge me. Holstering my weapon, keeping my eyes on her hands, I grind my knee into her back. "Stop resisting!"

A cry of rage erupts from her throat as I clamp my left hand around her left wrist. I reach for my cuffs with my right. "You're under arrest."

"Get off me!"

"You shot a cop," I snarl as I crank the cuff down tight. "A friend of mine."

"I hope he dies!"

I shove her face into the mud. I'm still trying to get a grip on her right hand when the deputy arrives. He's panting like a dog as he drops to his knees beside me and helps me snap the cuff into place.

I sit back on my heels, go for my lapel mike, only to remember it's dead.

Noticing I'm without communication, the deputy speaks into his own radio. "Ten ninety-five." He looks at me, taps his left temple to indicate mine. "You okay?"

I get to my feet. "My deputy's been shot. He needs an ambulance."

"They got one out there now."

"He's seventy-six years old." Bending, I grab Ruth Weaver's biceps and try to haul her to her feet. In that instant, I understand how a cop can get caught up in the high adrenaline of a chase, the rage of having one of your own cut down as if his life means nothing.

"Stand up," I snarl.

The deputy goes to the other side of her and helps her rise. He's tossing concerned looks my way, and I make a conscious effort to pull myself back from the edge upon which I'm standing.

This should be a good moment. I made my arrest. Got a dangerous killer off the street. But as the adrenaline ebbs, a hundred other gnarly emotions rush forward. Anger at the utter senselessness of the crimes. Relief that she can't hurt anyone else. But worry for Pickles is at the forefront of my mind. At this point, I don't know if he's dead or alive, and that makes me angry all over again. The need to see him is a desperation I can't contain.

"I need to check on my officer," I tell the deputy. "Can you put her in your cage?"

"Yes, ma'am," he says. "Go."

CHAPTER 32

A strange psychological phenomenon occurs in the seconds and minutes following a high-adrenaline event. I've heard it referred to as the "tachy-psyche effect" and "high-speed-pursuit syndrome." I suppose both terms are apt, but only loosely correct. The shrinks haven't yet coined a term for the emotions a cop experiences later, in the hours after a high-speed chase or physical encounter or officer-involved shooting. Those hours when the adrenaline ebbs and the intellect kicks back in. Most everyone gets the full-body shakes. Some cops get angry. Some laugh or joke in an almost giddy manner or act in some otherwise inappropriate way. I've seen some cops cry—and not just females—even the tough veterans who think they're immune.

The ambulance has arrived by the time I get back to the Hochstetler place. When I get out of the Explorer, I realize my legs are shaking violently. My stomach is jittery. I have tunnel vision, and it's focused on the red and blue lights of that ambulance. I see the silhouette of someone approaching. I don't know who it is, but I don't slow down. I have to reach Pickles because I'm suddenly terrified I'm too late.

"Chief?"

An odd sense of relief sweeps through me at the sound of Glock's voice. "How is he?" I ask.

He falls in beside me, matching my long strides. "Paramedics are working on him now."

"Bad?"

"I don't know. Paramedic thinks the bullet went in through the arm hole at an angle, got him in the side."

"Shit. *Shit.*" I feel his eyes on me, drilling into me, seeing too much, and I'm annoyed because this isn't about me. "He's too old for this. I shouldn't have—"

"Chief, he's a cop. And he's tough. He'll be okay." Then his eyes narrow. "You're bleeding pretty good yourself."

Vaguely, I'm aware of the warmth of blood streaming down the left side of my face. "Let's go see Pickles."

As we approach the ambulance, I spot two uniformed paramedics carrying a litter toward a waiting gurney. I can just make out Pickles' form, his uniform wet and black-looking in the flashing lights. His face isn't covered, and suddenly I feel like crying. I reach them, but they don't stop, so I keep pace with them and look down at my most senior officer. An oxygen mask covers his nose and mouth. His eyes are open, but unfocused. I say his name, but he doesn't respond; he doesn't look at me or give me any indication he heard me. I see a blood smear on a pale, gnarled hand.

I make eye contact with one of the paramedics. "How is he?"

"He sustained a single gunshot wound to the armpit area, penetrated the chest. Vitals are stable. We're transporting him to Pomerene. That's all I can tell you at this point."

"Can I ride with him?" I ask.

He hesitates, then I see him looking at the blood on my temple and he nods. "Sure, Chief. Hop in."

An hour later I'm sitting in the surgical intensive care waiting area of Pomerene Hospital in Millersburg, worried and pacing and trying in vain not to acknowledge the headache gnawing at my temple. The paramedics allowed me to ride in the ambulance with Pickles. I'd known there wasn't anything I could do to help, but I wanted to sit with him or maybe hold his hand. I never got my chance and ended up spending most of the ride trying to stay out of the way.

Upon arrival, Pickles was quickly assessed by the ER physician and, after some tests, rushed to surgery. At that point, I called Glock and asked him to notify Clarice that her husband had been shot. In typical Glock style, he was already en route. I feel incredibly lucky to have such a good team of officers and know they have my back.

I couldn't escape the doctor's notice of my own injury, a gash I must have sustained when my head struck the driver's-side window. And while Pickles was in the OR, the ER doc cornered me and put seven stitches in my head. He had the nerve to try to admit me for observation in case I had a concussion, but I assured him I had someone to keep an eye on me for the next twenty-four hours.

I'm on my second cup of vending machine coffee when I hear the chime of the elevator. I look down the hall to see Glock, Skid, and Mona shuffle out and start toward me. My chest tightens at the sight of them, and for the second time, I fight tears. They are my adopted family, my children and parents and siblings rolled into one, and I've never been so glad to see them in my life.

"How's the old curmudgeon doing?" Glock asks.

"Stable." I tell them everything I know, which isn't much. "They took him in to surgery. Doc said bullet went low and damaged his spleen."

"You don't need your spleen," Skid says quickly.

"My grandmother had hers taken out two years ago," Glock says, "and she's doing fine."

"I thought your grandmother was in prison," Skid says.

Our laughter feels a little forced, but I think all of us appreciate it because we're worried and scared and no one can think of a better way to deal with it.

Mona touches my arm. "Clarice okay?" she asks.

"She's waiting for him outside recovery," Glock replies.

I turn my attention to Glock. "T.J. holding down the fort?"

"He wanted to be here, but there was no one else."

"Where's Ruth Weaver?" I ask.

"Holmes County transported her and booked her in."

"I need to go talk to her."

"Figured you would. We've got it covered here if you want to go."

I had no business leaving my suspect or the scene of a shooting. But there's an unwritten rule in law enforcement whether you're the chief or a beat cop: When one of your own gets hurt, you drop everything and you go.

"Call me," I tell him.

"The instant I hear anything."

I've just started toward the elevator when the door swishes open and Tomasetti steps into the hall. My steps falter at the sight of him. His eyes take in the length of me, a grim, determined look on his face. His eyes narrow on the bandage at my temple, and he starts toward me.

"Kate . . ." He tries to frown, but only manages to look worried. "For God's sake, are you all right?"

"I'm fine."

He reaches me, and his arms engulf me without hesitation. He squeezes too hard for too long, then sets me back and sighs. "I guess you're going to make me ask what's underneath that bandage."

"You mean besides a mullet?"

He lets out a laugh.

I can't help it; I smile. I'm happy to see him, relieved that he's here. "It's only seven stitches."

"Only seven?" He leans close and kisses the top of my head. "You scared the hell out of me, you know that?"

Of all the things I expected him to do, that wasn't it. "Driver's-side window wasn't that hard, I guess."

"Not as hard as your head, evidently." He smiles back at me. "Do you have a concussion?"

"No."

He eases me to arm's length, his hands grasping my biceps with a little too much force, and looks down at me. "You didn't call."

"I was about to." The words sound automatic, so I add, "I didn't want you to make a fuss."

He looks past me at the rest of my team, who are standing in a group just outside the waiting area. "How's Pickles?"

"Stable."

"That's a good sign."

"I hope so. Seeing him . . . like that scared me, Tomasetti."

"I'm familiar with that particular emotion."

I move away from him and press the elevator down button. I know I should be more focused on him and what I just put him through, but I've got tunnel vision when it comes to this case. If anyone understands, I know Tomasetti does.

"Who called you, anyway?" I ask.

"Glock." He comes up beside me, and we watch the lights as the elevator car makes it way to our floor. "I wish it had been you."

"I was a little busy."

"So where are we going?"

Only then do I remember I left my vehicle back at the Hochstetler farm. I look at him, trying not to feel like an idiot. "Did anyone ever tell you that you have good timing?"

The door swishes open, and he ushers me inside. "All the time."

An hour later, Sheriff Mike Rasmussen, Detective Jessup Price with the Holmes County Sheriff's Department, and I are sitting in an interview room at the sheriff's office in Holmesville, Ohio, which is about fifteen minutes north of Painters Mill.

"How's your officer?" Rasmussen asks as we wait for the corrections officer to bring in Ruth Weaver.

"Stable," I tell him. "He was still in surgery when I left the hospital."

He taps his temple. "You get that tattoo there in the wreck?"

I nod. "That's two counts of attempted murder of a police officer."

"The more the merrier." He sighs. "She's not going anywhere anytime soon."

"Has anyone talked to her yet?" I ask.

He shakes his head. "Just ID info. She has not been Mirandized. We basically put her in a holding cell and waited for you." He motions toward the small audio recorder. "When you're ready, just hit the On button there, and you're good to go."

"I appreciate that, Mike."

"This is your deal."

The door opens. Ruth Weaver steps into the interview room. The last time I saw her, she looked like a hundred other Amish women I'd met over the years. Now she dons blue scrubs that are at least two sizes too large and flip-flops, the kind you might pick up at the local dollar store. Her hair is down and still damp from the rain. I see the blond roots peeking out at her scalp. Her hands are cuffed in front of her, for comfort during the interview.

Interestingly, she doesn't look shaken; she hasn't been crying. I don't think she's looking for anyone to feel sorry for her or help her. She was ready for this, she knows she's on her own, and she's completely at ease with both those things.

A trim female corrections officer has a firm grip on her biceps and motions toward the only vacant chair, opposite the table from me. "Sit down."

When Weaver is settled into the chair, the corrections officer steps back and takes her place at the door. The sheriff and Detective Price scoot their chairs away from the table slightly, keeping their notebooks handy, and give me the floor. I lean forward, press the On button of the recorder, and recite the date and names and titles of everyone present.

I focus my attention on Weaver and recite the

Miranda rights from memory. "Do you understand those rights?"

The detective tugs a laminated card from an inside pocket of his jacket and slides it across the table to her.

She nods without taking the card. "Perfectly."

When I was a rookie patrol officer in Columbus, I was lucky enough to partner up with one of the best interrogators in the department. His name was Cooper aka "Coop" and he was a natural, charismatic and personable. Within minutes, he could have even the most hardened criminal believing they were destined to become best friends. But Coop was also the kind of cop who, once he had gained the trust of a suspect, could rip out his throat and never lose his smile in the process. During the short period of time we worked together, Coop gave me the best advice I'd ever received on interviewing: A suspect will never tell you anything they don't want to. The key, he said, is to *make* them want to. I never forgot that gem of advice. And while I'll never be the interrogator Coop was, because of him, I became a better cop.

"I don't know whether to call you Hannah or Ruth," I begin.

"You can call me Ruth."

I look at her, searching for some semblance of Hannah Yoder, loving and supportive wife of Hoch Yoder. The Amish woman who'd comforted her husband and brought us cider and cookies. Tonight, there's no trace of her. It's as if in the last hours, she's become another person. The familiar stranger I've never met. A stone-cold killer capable of marrying her own brother in order to carry out some twisted agenda.

"I know you murdered Dale Michaels," I tell her.

"I know you murdered the others, too. Jerrold Mc-Cullough and Jules Rutledge."

She accepts my statement with a chilling calm and without defending herself. I hold her stare, and I realize that while she's not foaming-at-the-mouth crazy, she is insane—and a sociopath. The lives she took—the suffering she caused—mean nothing to her. A mission to be achieved. An errand to be checked off her to-do list. There's a vital part of her missing. The part that makes us human and sets us apart from the animals. Ruth Weaver isn't human, at least not in any meaningful way. She's an animal—the kind that kills and eats its young.

"We've got your DNA, Ruth. All the evidence we need to put you away for the rest of your life," I tell her. "We've got you dead to rights on multiple charges. Do you understand that?"

I give the words time to sink in, but she doesn't argue or deny or defend. She doesn't try to make excuses. Her expression doesn't alter. She doesn't seem too concerned about any of it. "I understand."

"Did you kill William, too?" I ask after a moment.

Her only reply is a cold stare and a slight curve of her mouth, and I can't help but think that she's enjoying her fifteen minutes of fame. This game that's finally reached its climax. A lifetime of hatred come to fruition. Like a serial killer whose overriding desire is to get caught so she can confess her sins to the people who fully appreciate her special skill set.

"Why now?" I ask. "After all these years?"

"Because she died. It was time."

"Your mother? Becky Weaver?"

"Yes."

"How did you find them?"

"I kept tabs on them." She shrugs. "I used the computer at the library. There were photos over the years. In the newspaper and such. The art gallery. The housing development. The church. It wasn't easy, but I'm a patient woman and I had plenty of time."

I nod. "Why did you kill them, Ruth? I'm trying to understand."

For the first time, emotion flickers in her eyes. Hatred? Satisfaction? "I killed them because they deserved it. Because they got to live their lives. They were happy, with spouses and families. They got to have all the things they took away from her." She tilts her head, her eyes gleaming with a cunning that raises the hairs on my arms. "Why is that so hard for you to understand?"

"You could have gone to the police." I nod toward Rasmussen and Jessup. "Myself and these other police officers would have worked around the clock to find them and bring them to justice. We would have done it for you. And for your mother."

"The *Englischer* police?" Her laugh is a musical sound that defies any emotion. "Do you know what they did to her, Chief Burkholder? That night? After they killed her husband and children?"

"I want you to tell me."

She leans forward, the cuffs at her wrists clanging softly against the tabletop, her eyes intent on mine. "There are no words to describe the things she endured. No words to convey the horror and agony and unbearable grief of that night." Her voice falters. "She wasn't a person to them. She was nothing. A rag to be used and tossed aside. Those men—those *boys* who had everything—they used her. For hours.

They did things that broke her mind. Her body. Her faith. The spirit that lived inside her. They made her want to die."

"Your mother told you this?"

"She told me everything. Every sordid, violent detail of how they used her. On the ground. In the mud. They beat her and kicked her. Spit on her. Urinated on her. Do you have any idea what that does to a person?" She tosses her head to get the hair out of her eyes. "They put her in the trunk and drove her to Pennsylvania. They strangled her. She played dead. But she was still conscious when they threw her into the well."

Despite my efforts not to, I feel something for this woman. I feel more for Wanetta Hochstetler. Compassion. Pity. Empathy. A sense of outrage at what had been done.

I think of Blue Branson sitting in the jail cell, and I loathe him. "Why did you kill Jules Rutledge?" I ask. "The woman?"

"You think because she was a woman she isn't guilty? Really, Chief Burkholder? Are you that naïve? Let me tell you about Jules Rutledge. She stood by, watching and laughing as the men took turns brutalizing my mother. She was no different, no better. Worse, perhaps, because she was a woman." Her gaze meets mine with such intensity that I have the sense of being sucked down into a bottomless black pit, a vortex, and I know something terrible awaits me at the end of it. "They deserved what I did to them. All of them. I have no regrets. My mother always said God would mete out their punishment and that punishment would be just. But she was Amish. I listened to her, but I never believed it. I knew that one day, I would be the one to make things right."

I think of my own past—the things that happened to me and the things I did about it—and I struggle not to draw parallels, however thin.

"The fall into the well broke her spine," she tells me. "She had no idea how long she lay there, hours or days. But it wasn't her day to die. Eventually a local Swartzentruber family came by." Her mouth curves again. "Sent by God, according to her." But she waves off the notion. "The Amish family heard her cries and pulled her out. They took her to the midwife. Of course, word got around. Eventually the *Englischer* police were called, but my mother couldn't remember who she was or what happened to her. She couldn't even remember her name. The police assumed she was a local and eventually forgot about her.

"The Swartzentruber family—the Weavers— took her in. Gave her food and clothing and a place to sleep. But there was no love lost between them. You see, my mother . . ." She lowers her voice as if she's about to utter words best not spoken too loudly. *"Sie is weenich ad." She was off in the head*.

"Six weeks later, she found out she was with child." The twisting of her lips is a grotesque mask in the glare of the fluorescent lights. She's an attractive woman, but there's something ugly beneath the surface of that pretty face, like a hideous scar camouflaged by makeup. "A few years after she gave birth to me, the Swartzentrubers began moving to New York. They were having some trouble with the government. Mamm didn't go with them."

"Why not?" I ask.

"By then she'd started to remember things." Absently she raises her cuffed hands and touches her head. "Like who she was. Her family. What happened to her that night. She went to the bishop and told him everything. He'd heard about an Amish family in Ohio, the missing wife, the dead husband and children that perished in a fire. He called the bishop in Ohio. That was when she found out they were all dead. That . . . changed something inside her. And it wasn't for the better. She left the Amish, became bitter and full of hate. I was only five years old—an innocent—but I knew she hated me, too. And I knew my life would never be the same."

"What did she do?"

"Over the months and weeks, as her memories returned, she told me everything. The bedtime stories I heard at night weren't about bunnies or bears or horses. They were about violent men and children burned alive. Every day I learned something new and terrible. About my *datt*. About my brothers and sisters. And about William. *Especially* William. The one who, because he was so very prideful, brought evil into their home."

"You were only a child. You couldn't have understood."

"I understood enough. Later, when I was older, I understood more. I understood what I had to do to make things right."

"Your mother wanted revenge?"

"She wanted justice. God's justice." A hint of a smile pulls at her mouth. "I wanted revenge."

"Ruth, as an adult, surely you know she was mentally damaged, injured. She used you. Brainwashed you. An innocent child."

"Not so innocent, Chief Burkholder. You see, my mother was never strong. I took care of her. She needed me more than I needed her. She made me strong because she knew I possessed what she did not. I had the strength to do what needed to be done."

"Did you murder Hoch Yoder?"

She waves off the question. "I didn't have to. He suffered with the melancholy. Had for years. I knew it was only a matter of time before he ended it. One little push from me, and he was all too happy to oblige."

"Ruth, he was your half brother. And yet you married him."

"My mother blamed him for the deaths of her children. I did what needed to be done. I have no regrets."

"Did he know?"

One side of her mouth trembles, as if she's withholding a smile. "He knew enough."

I lean back in my chair, trying to digest everything I've heard. It's not easy. I've interrogated dozens of criminals over the years, and many of those interviews left me feeling unsettled and disturbed. But I can honestly say none of them ever made me feel as sick inside as I do at this moment.

"You have no idea which of them is your father, do you?" I ask.

A quiver goes through her body. Her hands slowly curl into fists. Only then do I realize I've found her weak spot. She was borne of violence, and the question of her paternity has left her twitching inside like a nerve exposed to air.

"My father is Willis Hochstetler."

"You were born nine months after that night, Ruth. You don't know who your father is. It could be any of them. Dale Michaels. Jerrold McCullough. Blue Branson."

"I made them sorry for it, didn't I?" she says.

"You're going to be charged with three counts of first-degree murder and two counts of attempted murder of a police officer. You're not going anywhere for a very long time."

"So be it. My work is done."

Needing to get out of there, I turn my attention to the detective. "We're finished here." I rise, round the table, and bend so that my mouth is just inches from her ear. "In case you haven't noticed, you're the spitting image of Blue Branson."

She lunges at me, but I'm faster and dance out of reach. Before she can make contact, the detective is on his feet, moving between us. The corrections officer darts across the room and presses Weaver back into the chair.

I go through the door without looking back.

I find Tomasetti in the hall, waiting for me. "How did it go?" he asks.

"She confessed. To everything." I'm not ready to talk about it; I need a few minutes to regroup and dislodge the unsettling sense of ugliness that clings to me.

"You're shaking."

I'm not very good at sharing my emotions, especially when they're dark. It takes me a moment before I can look at him. "She married her half brother. They lived together as husband and wife for years."

"That's about as twisted as it gets."

More than anything in that moment, I want to go to him, put my arms around him because I need to be held. Instead, because we're in a public place surrounded by our peers, I touch his hand. "Tomasetti, I'm glad you're here. I don't know what I'd do without you."

"I'm not going anywhere," he tells me.

We start toward the elevator. "Any word on Pickles?" I ask.

"Glock sent a text ten minutes ago. He's out of surgery. Prognosis is good. Spleen didn't make it."

I choke out a laugh, release the breath I didn't realize I was holding. "Will you take me to the hospital?"

"You bet."

The elevator doors slide open.

We ride to the ground floor in silence and start toward the exit. We've just reached the Tahoe when Tomasetti takes my hand, stopping me, and turns me to face him. "What about us, Kate?" he asks. "Are we going to get our happy ending?"

I look into his eyes, wishing I were a good enough communicator to put everything I'm feeling at this moment into words. "I think that depends on us."

His gaze searches mine. "You were right when you told me I've been holding back. I haven't been able to let them go. Nancy and the girls. All this time, I've been looking back instead of forward. I'm sorry for that."

"They'll always be in your heart."

He nods. "I want you to know, I choose you. Not them. Not the past. You."

The words make me unbearably happy. "You know, Tomasetti, there might just be hope for us yet."

"I'm counting on it," he says.

Raising my hands, I set my palms on either side of his face and pull his mouth to mine. "Me, too," I whisper. "Me, too."

Read on for an excerpt from the next book
by Linda Castillo

AFTER THE STORM

Coming soon in hardcover from St. Martin's Press

CHAPTER 1

I was eight-years old when I learned there were consequences for associating with the *English*. Consequences that were invariably negative and imposed by well-meaning Amish parents bent on upholding the rules set forth by our Anabaptist forefathers nearly three hundred years ago. In my case, this particular life lesson transpired at the horse auction near Millersburg and involved a twelve-year-old English boy and the Appaloosa gelding he was trying to sell. Add me to the mix and it was a dangerous concoction that ended with me taking a fall and my father's realization that I saw the concept of rules in a completely different light—and I possessed an inherent inability to follow them.

I never forgot the lesson I learned that day or how much it hurt my eight-year-old heart which, even at that tender age, was already raging against the unfairness of the *Ordnung* and all of those who would judge me for my transgressions. But the lessons of my formative years didn't keep me from breaking the same rules time and time again, defying even the most fundamental of Amish tenets. By the time I entered my teens, just about everyone had realized I couldn't conform and, worse, I didn't fit in, both of which are required of a member of the Amish community.

Now, at the age of thirty-three, I can't quite reconcile myself to the fact that I'm still trying to please those who will never approve and failing as miserably as I did when I was an inept and insecure fifteen-year-old girl.

"Stop worrying."

I'm sitting in the passenger seat of John Tomasetti's Tahoe, not sure if I'm impressed by his perceptivity or annoyed because my state of mind is so apparent. We've been living together at his farm for seven months now and while we've had some tumultuous moments, I have to admit it's been the happiest and most satisfying time of my life.

Tomasetti, a former detective with the Cleveland Division of Police, is an agent with the Ohio Bureau of Criminal Identification and Investigation. Like me, he has a troubled past and more than his share of secrets, some I suspect I'm not yet privy to. But we have an unspoken agreement that we won't let our pasts dictate our happiness or how we live our lives. Honestly, he's the best thing that's ever happened to me and I like to think the sentiment runs both ways.

"What makes you think I'm worried?" I tell him, putting forth a little attitude.

"You're fidgeting."

"I'm fidgeting because I'm nervous," I say. "There's a difference."

He glances at me, scowling, but his eyes are appreciative as he runs them over me. "You look nice."

I hide my smile by looking out the window. "If you're trying to make me feel better, it's working."

Good humor plays at the corner of his mouth. "It's not like you to change clothes four times."

"Hard to dress for an Amish dinner."

"Especially when you used to be Amish, apparently."

"Maybe I should have made an excuse." I glance out the window at the horizon. "Weatherman said it's going to rain."

"It's not like you to chicken out."

"Unless it's my brother."

"Kate, he invited you. He wants you there." He reaches over, sets his hand on my thigh, just above my knee and squeezes. I wonder if he has any idea how reassuring the gesture is. "Be yourself and let the chips fall."

I don't point out that being myself is exactly the thing that got me excommunicated from my Amish brethren in the first place.

He makes the turn into the long gravel lane of my brother, Jacob's, farm. The place originally belonged to my parents, but was handed down to him, the eldest male child, when they passed away. I mentally brace as the small apple orchard on my right comes into view. The memories aren't far behind and I find myself looking down the rows of trees, almost expecting to see the three Amish kids sent to pick apples for pies. Jacob, Sarah and I had been inseparable back then, and instead of picking apples, we ended up playing hide and seek until it was too dark to see. As was usually the case, I was the instigator. Kate, the *druvvel-machah. The troublemaker.* Or so my *datt* said. The one and only time I confessed to influencing my siblings, he punished me by taking away my favorite chore: bottle feeding the three-week old orphan goat I'd named Sammy. I'd cajoled and argued and begged. I was rewarded by being sent to bed with no supper and a stomach ache from eating too many green apples.

The house is plain and white with a big front porch and tall windows that seem to glare at me as we veer right. The maple tree I helped my *datt* plant when I was twelve is mature and shades the hostas that grow alongside the house. In the side yard, I catch sight of two picnic tables with mismatched tablecloths flapping in the breeze.

I take in the old chicken house ahead and the big barn to my left and it strikes me how much of my past is rooted in this place. And how much of it is gone forever. When you're Amish, there are no photos. There are no corny albums or school pictures or embarrassing videos. My parents have long since passed which means everything that happened here, both good and bad, exists only in my memory and the memories of my siblings. Maybe that's why I can't stay away. No matter how many times my brother hurts me, I always come back, like a puppy that's been kicked but knows no other place to be, no other comfort.

I want to share this part of my past with Tomasetti. I want him to stand in the shade of the maple tree while I tell him about the day *datt* and I planted it. How proud I'd been when the buds came that first spring. I want to walk the fields with him and show him the fallen log that I took our old plow horse over when I was thirteen years old. I want to show him the pond where I caught my first bass. The same pond that saw Jacob and I duke it out over a hockey game.

He might have been older and bigger, but he didn't fight dirty; not when it came to me, anyway. I, on the other hand, was born with the killer instinct he lacked, and he was usually the one who walked away with a black eye or busted lip. He never ratted on me, but I'll never forget the way he looked at me all those times when he lied to our parents to protect me and was then punished for it. And I never said a word.

Tomasetti parks in the gravel area behind the house and shuts down the engine. The buggy that belongs to my sister, Sarah, and my brother-in-law William, is parked outside the barn. As I get out of the Tahoe, I see my sister in law, Irene, come through the back door with a bread basket in one hand, a plastic pitcher in the other.

She spots me and smiles. *"Nau is awwer bsil zert,* Katie Burkholder!" *Now it's about time!*

I greet her in Pennsylvania Dutch. *"Guder nammidaag."* *Good afternoon.*

"Mir hen Englischer bsuch ghadde!" she calls out. *We have non Amish visitors!*

The screen door slams. I glance toward the house to see my sister, Sarah, coming down the porch steps juggling a platter of fried chicken and a heaping bowl of green beans. She wears a blue dress with an apron, a *kapp* with the ties hanging down her back, and nondescript black sneakers. "Hi, Katie!" she says with a little too much enthusiasm. *"The men are inside. Sie scheie sich vun haddi arewat."* *They shrink from hard work.*

Irene sets the pitcher and basket on the picnic table then spreads her hands at the small of her back and stretches. She's wearing clothes much like my sister's. Blue dress that's slightly darker. Apron and *kapp*. A pair of battered sneakers. *"Alle daag rumhersitze mach tem faul,"* she says, referring to the men. *Sitting all day makes one lazy.*

"Sell is nix as baeffzes." That's nothing but tri-fling talk.

At the sound of my brother's voice, I glance toward the house to see him and my brother-in-law, William, standing on the porch. Both men are wearing dark trousers with white shirts, suspenders and straw summer hats. Jacob's beard reaches midway to his waist and is shot with more gray than brown. William's beard is red and sparse. Both men's eyes flick from me to Tomasetti and then back to me, as if waiting for some explanation for his presence. It doesn't elude me that neither man offers to help with the food.

"Katie." Jacob nods at me as he takes the steps from the porch. *"Wie geth's alleweil?"* How goes it now?

"This is John Tomasetti," I blurt to no one in particular.

Next to me, Tomasetti strides forward and extends his hand to my brother. "It's a pleasure to finally meet you, Jacob," he says easily.

While the Amish excel at letting you know you are an outsider—which is usually done for some redemptive purpose, not cruelty—they can also be kind and welcoming and warm. I'm pleased to see all of those things in my brother's eyes when he takes Tomasetti's hand. "It's good to meet you, too, John Tomasetti."

"Kate's told me a lot about you," Tomasetti says.

William chuckles as he extends his hand. *"Es waarken maulvoll gat."* There's nothing good about that.

A giggle escapes Sarah. "Welcome, John. I hope you're hungry."

"I am."

I make eye contact with Tomasetti. He winks and some of the tension between my shoulder blades unravels.

Neither woman offers her hand for a shake. Instead they exchange nods when I make the introductions.

When the silence goes on for a beat too long, I turn my attention to my sister. "Can I help with something?"

"Setz der disch." Set the table. Sarah glances at Tomasetti and motions toward the picnic table. *"Sitz dich anna un bleib e weil."* Sit yourself there and stay awhile. "There's lemonade and I'm about to bring out some iced tea."

Tomasetti strolls to the table and looks appreciatively at the banquet spread out before him. "You sure you trust me with all this food?"

Jacob chortles.

"There's more than enough for everyone," Irene says.

William pats his belly. "Even me?"

A gust of wind snaps the tablecloths and Jacob glances toward the western horizon. "If we're going to beat the storm, we'd best eat soon."

Irene shivers at the sight of the lightning and dark clouds. *"Wann der Hund dich off der buckle legt, gebt's rene."* When the dog lies on his back, there will be rain.

While Tomasetti and the Amish men pour lemonade and talk about the storms forecast for later, I follow the women into the kitchen. I'd been nervous about accepting today's invitation from my brother because I didn't know what to expect. I had no idea how they would respond to me and Tomasetti or the fact that we're living together with no plans to get married. To my relief, no one has mentioned any of those things and another knot of tension loosens.

The kitchen is hot despite the breeze whipping in through the window above the sink. Sarah and I spend a few minutes gathering paper plates, plastic utensils, and sampling the potato salad while Irene pulls a dozen or so steaming ears of corn from the dutch oven atop the stove and stacks them on a platter. We make small talk and I'm taken aback at how quickly the rhythm of Amish life comes back. I ask about my niece and nephews and I learn the kids walked to the pasture to show my little niece, who's just over a year old now, the pond, and I can't help but remember when that same pond was a fixture in my own life. I'd learned to swim in that pond, never minding the mud or the moss or the smell of fish that always seemed to permeate the water. Back then, I was an Olympian swimmer; I had no concept of swimming pools or chlorine or diving boards. I'd been content to swim in water the color of tea, sun myself on the dilapidated dock, treat myself to mud baths, and dream about all the things I was going to do with my life.

Brandishing a pitcher of iced tea and a basket of hot rolls, I follow the two women outside to the picnic tables. Out of the corner of my eye I see that Jacob has pulled out his pipe to smoke, a habit that's frowned upon by some of the more conservative Amish. But then that's Jacob for you. He's also one of the few to use a motorized tractor instead of draft horses. In keeping with the *Ordnung*, he only uses steel wheels sans rubber tires. A few of the elders complain but so far no one has done anything about it.

Within minutes we're sitting at a picnic table, a feast of fried chicken and vegetables from the garden spread out on the blue and white checked tablecloth.

At the table next to us, my niece and nephews load fried chicken and green beans onto their plates. I glance over at Tomasetti and he grins at me, giving me an I-told-you-everything-would-be-fine look, and in that moment I'm content.

"Wann der Disch voll is, well mir bede." If the tables are full, let us pray. Jacob gives the signal for the before-meal prayer. Heads are bowed. Next to us, the children's table goes silent. And Jacob's voice rings out. *"O Herr Gott, himmlischer Vater, Segne uns und Diese Diene Gaben, die wir von Deiner milden Gute Zu uns nehmen warden, Speise und tranke auch unsere Seelen zum ewigen Leben, und mach uns theilhaftig Deines himmllischen Tisches durch Jesus Christum. Amen."*

Oh Lord God, heavenly Father, bless us and these thy gifts, which we shall accept from thy tender goodness. Give us food and drink also for our souls unto life eternal, and make us partakers of thy heavenly table through Jesus Christ. Amen.

Upon finishing, he looks around and as if by unspoken agreement, everyone begins reaching for platters and filling their plates.

"The kids have grown so much since I saw them last," I say as I spoon green beans onto my plate.

"It seems like yesterday that Little Hannah was a newborn," my sister says with a sigh. "They grow up so fast."

Jacob slathers homemade butter onto an ear of corn. "Elam drove the tractor last week."

Sarah rolls her eyes. "And almost drove it into the creek!"

"Like father like son," William mutters.

Irene pours a second glass of tea. "Katie, do you and John have any plans for children?"

I can tell by the way the pitcher pauses mid-pour that she realizes instantly her faux pas. Her eyes flick to mine. I see a silent apology, then she quickly looks away and sets the pitcher on the table. "There's tea if anyone's thirsty."

"Maybe they should get married first," Jacob says.

"I love weddings." Sarah shakes pepper onto an ear of corn.

"Any plans for one, Katie?" Jacob asks.

In the interminable silence that follows, the tension builds, as if it were a living thing, growing and filling up space. I'm not sure how to respond. The one thing I do know is that no matter what I say, I'll be judged harshly for it.

"Let's just say we're a work in progress." I smile, but it feels dishonest on my lips because I know now that this Pandora's Box has been opened, it's fair game.

"Work?" Jacob slathers apple butter onto a roll. "I don't think getting married is too much work."

"For a man, anyway," Irene says.

"A man'll work harder to stay out of the house." William doesn't look up from his plate. "If he's smart."

"I think Kate's placing the emphasis on the 'in progress' part." Tomasetti grins at Irene. "Pass the corn, please."

"In the eyes of the Lord, the two of you are living in sin," Jacob says.

I turn my attention to my brother. "In the eyes of some of the *Amisch*, too, evidently."

He nods, but his expression is earnest. "I don't understand why two people would want to live like that."

Embarrassment and, for an instant, the familiar

old shame creeps up on me, but I don't let it take hold. "Jacob, this isn't the time or place to discuss this."

"Are you afraid God will hear?" he asks. "Are you afraid He will disapprove?"

Tomasetti helps himself to an ear of corn, sets down his fork and turns his attention to my brother. "If you have something on your mind, Jacob, I think you should just put it out there."

"Marriage is a sacred thing." He holds Tomasetti's gaze, thoughtful. "I don't understand why you choose to live the way you do. If a man and woman choose to live together, they should be married."

All eyes fall on Tomasetti. He meets their stares head on and holds them, unflinching and unapologetic. "With all due respect, that's between Kate and me. That's the best answer I can give you and I hope you and the rest of the family will respect it."

My brother looks away in deference. But I know that while he'll tolerate our point of view for now, he'll never agree with it—or give his blessing. "All right then."

I look around the table. Everyone is staring down at their plates, concentrating a little too intently on their food. Across from me, Irene scoots her husband's plate closer to him. "Maybe you should eat your food instead of partaking in idle talk like an old woman."

Sarah coughs into her hand, but doesn't quite cover her laugh. "There's date pudding for dessert."

"That's my favorite." Irene smiles at her sister in law. "Right after snitz pie."

"I haven't had snitz pie since Big Joe Beiler married Edna Miller," William says through a mouthful of chicken.

I barely hear the exchange over the low thrum of

my temper. Don't get me wrong; I love my brother and sister. Growing up, they were my best friends and sometimes, my partners in crime. There were many things I loved about being Amish: Being part of a tight-knit community. Growing up with the knowledge that I was loved not only by my family, but by my brethren. But this afternoon I'm reminded of two things I detested: narrow-mindedness and intolerance.

As if reading my mind, Tomasetti sets his hand on my arm and squeezes. "Let it go," he says quietly.

I'm relieved when my cell phone vibrates against my hip. "I've got to take this," I say, pulling out my phone and getting to my feet.

I walk a few yards away from the picnic tables and answer with my usual, "Burkholder."

"Sorry to bother you on your afternoon off, Chief. Just wondering if you've been following the weather."

It's Rupert Maddox, but everyone calls him "Glock" because he has a peculiar fondness for his sidearm. A war vet with two tours in Afghanistan under his belt, he's my most solid officer and the first African American to grace the Painters Mill PD.

"Actually, I'm not," I say. "What's up?"

"Weather Service just issued a tornado warning for Knox and Richland Counties," he tells me. "We got some serious shit on the way. It just touched down north of Fredericktown."

Thoughts of my family evaporate and I press the phone more tightly against my ear. "Casualties?" I ask. "Damage?"

"SHP says it's a war zone. There's a tornado on the ground and headed this way, moving fast. Fifteen minutes and we're going to be under the gun."

"Call the mayor. Tell him to get the sirens going."

"Roger that."

But I know that while the tornado sirens are an effective warning for people living in town and will give them time to get into their basements or storm shelters, Holmes County is mostly rural. The majority of people live too far away to hear the sirens. To make matters worse, the Amish don't have TVs or radios and have no way of knowing there's a dangerous storm on the way.

"Call dispatch and tell Lois I want everyone on standby. If things look dicey at the station, she needs to take cover down in the jail."

"Got it."

"Glock, do you and LaShonda have a basement?"

"Got it covered, Chief. I've got a weather radio down there. And a Wii for the kids."

"Good." I look over at the picnic table to see Tomasetti standing, his head cocked, looking at me intently. "Look, I'm at my brother's farm and we're about nine miles east of town. Can you give me a hand and help me get the word out?"

"I'll take the west side and go door to door. Sheriff's got some deputies out, too."

"Thanks. Do me a favor and stay safe, will you?"

"You, too."

I hit End and stride back to the table. "There's a tornado on the ground west of here and heading this way."